W9-ANM-023

WYATT'S REVENGE

WYATT'S REVENGE

A Matt Royal Mystery

H. Terrell Griffin

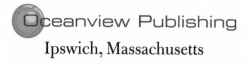

Oceanview Publishing

Ipswich, Massachusetts

ISBN: 978-1-933515-53-3

Published in the United States of America by Oceanview Publishing,
Ipswich, Massachusetts
www.oceanviewpub.com

2 4 6 8 10 9 7 5 3 1

PRINTED IN THE UNITED STATES OF AMERICA

For David W. Kendall, Jr.

My Friend

And if you wrong us shall we not revenge?

— William Shakespeare

ACKNOWLEDGMENTS

Writing, like life, moves at lightning speed. Or at least the deadlines loom ever closer and the novelist's need to put pen to paper or fingers to keyboard, becomes ever larger. I have the good fortune to share this journey with friends who spur me on, help me when I'm stuck, serve as my sounding boards for plot and character development, and generally stroke my rather large ego.

Peggy Kendall, Debbie Schroeder, and Jean Griffin provide me with ideas, editing, and ego-crushing comments when I get to thinking I'm better than I am. Maryglenn McCombs, Oceanview Publishing's wonderful and talented publicist, works her magic and charms reviewers and critics into thinking I am the real thing, whatever that is.

The gang at Oceanview Publishing could not be more accommodating, helpful, and supportive. Patricia and Bob Gussin, writers themselves, have thrown their lives into making Oceanview an outstanding publisher, and in the process, have supported writers, myself included, who might not have otherwise had a voice. It is the hard work of the Oceanview people, led by President Susan Greger that ignites the creative fires of the storytellers. They make it possible for our tales to be told.

My two best buddies, John Allred of Houston and the late Miles Leavitt of Longboat Key, have lent me their personas and allowed me to tinker with their personalities while I fashioned characters who bear some resemblance to their reality. They were amused at their transformation from real life to fiction and never waivered in their supoort of my efforts at writing. For their friendship, I will be forever grateful.

The people of Longboat Key, that paradise off the coast of Southwest Florida, bring me more pleasure than I can describe. They have been unfailingly supportive, lent their names to some of my characters, allowed me to use their stories, and, most importantly, have been my friends.

I am nothing without my family. My wife, Jean, has been my boon companion for most of my life and understands me better than I do myself. Yet she still loves me, or at least tells me that on a regular basis. I think she's serious. Our sons, Greg, Mike, and Chris and our daughter-in-law, Judy, give us love, and that is a treasure beyond reckoning. Our grandchildren, Kyle and Sarah, give us so much joy that they probably ought to be outlawed, or at least taxed.

Thank you, my friends and family. Thank you.

WYATT'S REVENGE

CHAPTER ONE

Laurence Wyatt was executed on a bright Sunday morning in late October when high white clouds drifted across the beach and out to the horizon where they kissed the azure water of the Gulf of Mexico. An on-shore breeze ruffled the fronds of the palm trees that bordered the sand and the smell of the sea wafted on the currents of air that drifted lazily over a tableau of death. The morning quiet was pierced by the raucous cries of gulls diving for their breakfast.

The executioner used a large-caliber pistol, a .45 perhaps, and shot Wyatt behind the left ear. The steel-jacketed slug tore though his brain, searing gray matter, disrupting synapses, destroying the connections that make us human. The bullet exited his face, taking his right eye and most of the zygomatic arch with it, splattering the balcony railing with the remains of one of the finest brains in America. By the time the bullet exited Wyatt's face, he was dead.

The murderer put another bullet into the dead man, shooting him in the back of the neck. Why? Insurance? Malice? Or just because the killer was a mean son of a bitch who gave no more thought to killing a fine and gentle man than he would to stomping a roach.

The second bullet didn't matter. Wyatt was already dead, and the shooter had sealed his own death warrant when he sent the first slug into my friend's brain. The killer was dead meat from that moment on. He didn't know it, but I did. I would hunt him down and kill him and make sure he knew why he was dying. I owed that to Wyatt.

When Wyatt died, I was jogging on the beach, enjoying the view that was probably Wyatt's last glimpse of life. If I had thought about it, and I didn't,

I would have guessed that Wyatt was looking at the sea, sitting on his balcony, reading the paper, and drinking the strong coffee he fancied. He did that every morning.

I would have been wrong. Wyatt was looking out to sea when he was shot, and the paper was spread on his lap. But there was no coffee cup. We knew what his last view was because of the blood splatter on the balcony rail. What we didn't know was whether Wyatt saw it coming, or if the shooter snuck up behind him and took the shot. Shots.

The news of Wyatt's death came to me as such news often does, in the person of a police officer. I was sitting on my sunporch overlooking Sarasota Bay when the knock came. It wasn't ominous in any way; just a routine rap on the front door of my condo. A friend coming for a visit perhaps, or the maintenance manager checking up on something.

I looked at my watch. Ten o'clock. I opened the door to find my fishing buddy, Bill Lester, standing at the threshold. He was wearing boat shoes, chinos, and a blue golf shirt with a Longboat Key, Florida police chief's badge embroidered on the pocket. He was not a tall man, about five eight, his dark hair cut short, a small belly beginning to protrude over his belt, a neatly trimmed mustache gracing his upper lip. He carried no weapon that I could see. On the surface he was not a prepossessing figure, but he had a presence that transcended his stature. I think it was because of the no-nonsense way he approached life, like a man who knew at any given minute what the next one would bring. He exuded confidence the way aging drunks exude the stench of old booze. It rose off his body, giving him a demeanor that put people at ease. They knew they had found the man in charge, and they were comforted by the discovery.

Not today. Bill's face was a little gray, his eyes moist, his hair uncombed. His body language screamed that bad news was coming.

"What is it, Bill?" I asked.

"Laurence Wyatt's dead."

"How?"

"Shot to death on his balcony."

We were still standing at the door. I felt as if I'd been kicked in the stomach. "Come on in. What happened?"

The chief went to my kitchen, pulled a mug from a cabinet and poured himself a cup of coffee. An act of familiarity bred between friends. We moved into the living room, and he told me what he'd found on Wyatt's balcony.

"His ex-wife found him. Called us," he said.

"Donna."

"Yeah."

"How's she holding up?"

"Not good. But she's tough. My detective had a few more questions for her, and Logan Hamilton was on his way to pick her up. I wanted to tell you personally. I know how close you guys were."

"Yeah. For a long time. Was it a robbery?"

"Doesn't look like it. Donna said his laptop is missing, but that's all. There was cash in a money clip on his dresser and a wallet with several credit cards. I don't think some moke would kill for a laptop and leave the cash and cards."

"You're probably right. Maybe the computer will turn up."

"Tell me about him, Matt. I didn't know Laurence well."

"Nobody called him Laurence. He never liked his first name and all his friends called him Wyatt. I was a nineteen-year-old second lieutenant at the tail end of Vietnam. My first tour. Wyatt was a thirty-two-year-old major on his third. He taught me how to be a soldier and a leader. Mostly, he taught me about honor. And he showed me how to be a man."

"Was he Special Forces, too?"

"Yeah. We both wore the Green Beret. But Wyatt was special, Bill. A West Pointer who didn't have to keep volunteering for combat. He just felt that he owed it to the men. He always said that he'd been given an opportunity to be a leader, and that meant that he owed the army some leadership. That's what he did. He led."

"You guys stayed close."

"When I got out of the army and started college, Wyatt was completing his Ph.D. in history on the same campus. When he finished grad school, he went to the University of Central Florida in Orlando to teach. When I was finishing law school, he introduced me to a partner in a big Orlando firm who hired me. When I got married, he was my best man, and when I got divorced, he talked me out of the bottle of bourbon I'd crawled into, and sent me packing to Longboat Key. He was only thirteen years older than me, but he was like the father I never knew. I loved him."

"Could there be somebody from his past after him?"

"I doubt it," I said. "Wyatt was a warrior who became a scholar. And he put the warrior stuff behind him. He'd been a fierce soldier, and he became a gentle professor. I can't think of anyone who'd want to kill him."

"We'll find the guy who did this, Matt. I promise you that. We'll get him."

I was alone in my condo. Bill had left after assuring me again that he'd do everything in his power to bring Wyatt's killer to justice. I knew a little about justice. I'd been a trial lawyer for a long time. I'd represented guilty men and convinced juries that they should acquit. I knew that good lawyers sometimes got bad people off. I didn't want that to happen to the animal who had killed my friend. I wanted him dead.

We Americans have an aversion to the death penalty. Polls show time after time that we condone the ultimate punishment, but when it comes right down to it, we're squeamish about imposing it. Most murderers are not caught. Those who are caught can usually plea bargain themselves into lighter sentences. Even when a jury finds a murderer guilty as charged, the good citizens sitting in the box often recommend life imprisonment.

Rarely, but sometimes, the death penalty is ordered. Then the lawyers get involved further, and the appeals take up the next twenty or thirty years. The victim's loved ones die of old age, and the animal who killed lives on, sitting on death row, three squares a day, a warm bed, air conditioning in the summer, and always a television set. And when the execution is finally carried out, if it ever is, no one remembers the crime or the victim, except the survivors.

The law is the only thing that keeps the animals at bay. It provides a patina of civilization that results in a modicum of safety. We are not allowed to seek personal revenge. We let the law do it for us. I believed in that law. But I also believed in revenge, and what I could not tell my friend Bill Lester, was that I would take my revenge on the bastard who killed the best man I'd ever known.

My buddy Logan Hamilton showed up and sat quietly, drinking coffee and letting me talk. I told him more about Wyatt and about the war than I'd ever told anybody. I let my grief at Wyatt's death roll out in waves that washed over Logan, sitting there, being a friend, because he knew I needed one. I raged at the cretin who would kill a good man in cold blood, and I vowed revenge. Finally, I ran out of words, and I too sat quietly, staring at the bay, musing at the colors cast by the autumn sun, knowing Wyatt would never again enjoy such a scene.

"Matt," Logan said after some time had passed, "you'll be okay."

And I knew he was right. Pretty soon, time would begin to erode the sharp angles of my grief, round it out, soften it, and I would tuck it away back in the corner of my mind where all the other dead soldiers live. Life would go on, but it wouldn't be as sweet as when Wyatt was part of it. His leaving would tear a hole in the heart of our island community, one that would never be completely filled. Stories would be told in the island bars of a good man with a quirky sense of humor who took care of his friends, gave generously of his money, and sometimes drank too much Scotch. We would talk of him with affection and laugh at his antics, and soon the stories would grow larger than life. I would live and remember, and over time the grief would dissipate like the fog of an early morning.

CHAPTER TWO

My name is Matthew Royal. I'd been a trial lawyer for a long time, so long that the profession turned into a business without my noticing it. When I finally figured it out, that money had become more important than the client's cause, I quit and moved to Longboat Key, Florida.

I live on an island that is a quarter-mile wide and ten miles long. It floats serenely off the southwest coast of Florida, south of Tampa Bay, about halfway down the peninsula. The key is separated from the mainland by Sarasota Bay, and you have to cross a bridge, drive across another island, and cross another bridge to find the real world. I liked it that way. It provided a sense of isolation.

I am also a trained killer. Or, at least, that's what I had once been. When I was seventeen, I joined the army. I went through basic training, advanced infantry training, jump school, Infantry Officer Candidate School, Ranger School, and Special Forces training. By the age of nineteen, I was ready to lead men in combat and kill our nation's enemies. I did some of that in Southeast Asia, and then I left it behind me. College and law school recivilized me, and I moved to Orlando to practice law. Over the years my wife tired of my lack of attention to her, divorced me, and moved to Atlanta. I stayed in Orlando until I realized that the law had lost its nobility, and I said to hell with it.

I challenge middle age every day, work to keep the golden years at bay, retain my boyish charm, and not lose sight of the fact that I am getting older. I'm not a gym rat, but I do work out. I run regularly on the beach and keep myself in reasonably good shape. I stand six feet tall and weigh the same 180 pounds I did when I got out of the army. I have a head full of dark hair, eyes that are brown and not my best feature, a nose that once experienced a fistful of grief and is a little off-center. My dentist keeps my teeth in good shape and I'm told that I have a nice smile. I don't think of myself as handsome, but I tend to grow on people.

I was young for retirement, but I had enough money to live modestly for the rest of my life. I found that I enjoyed fishing and drinking beer with my friends, jogging on the beach, and tumbling the occasional pretty girl. Not a bad life. And then some asshole slips in and puts out the lights of a good man who enjoyed the same things I did. I couldn't let that pass.

Dawn on Wednesday morning. A cool breeze was blowing out of the north, ruffling the surface of the Gulf. The sun was suspended over the mainland, having just cleared the Earth's curvature; hanging there like it had all the time in the world before it had to start its climb into the heavens.

My boat was anchored in Longboat Pass, just seaward of the bridge. The tide was going out, and the stern had wheeled around, now facing the open Gulf. Five other boats were rafted to mine, their anchors buried in the soft bottom, the tide straining their lines.

I put a CD into the stereo in the dash. The sound of Bob Dylan's "Like a Rolling Stone" drifted over the water. The twenty people in the rafted boats stood quietly facing astern, their heads bowed, some in tears.

As the last notes of the song faded away, I spoke in a voice loud enough to be heard on all the boats. "He was a good man, and I loved him." That said it all.

I tipped the small metal urn over the stern, and the ashes of Laurence Wyatt drifted on the breeze, settled onto the surface of his beloved Gulf of Mexico, and floated seaward with the outgoing tide. I heard a sob from Sam Lastinger's boat, rafted next to mine. Logan was standing there, tears coursing down his cheeks. He looked up at me, smiling sadly. "Let's go home," he said.

We spent the day mourning Wyatt in our way. On Longboat Key, that meant that we drank too much, told funny stories about the departed, and mused on the vagaries of life. We all wondered who would be the next to go. On our island, so filled with elderly people, death is a constant reality. We accept it, mourn our lost friends, and move on. It is only when one is taken violently and without warning that we become the shocked survivors.

We'd seen Wyatt off according to the instructions he'd left with Donna. Cremation, ashes drifting on an ebbing tide, Dylan singing "Like a Rolling Stone," and then revelry.

Wyatt's friends, who managed the Hilton on the island, opened the upstairs bar for the mourners, a going away party that befitted a man the islanders loved. Wyatt enjoyed a party, loved the gathering of his friends, the laughter, the stories told again and again. Every year at Thanksgiving and Christmas, he would feed many of the snowbirds who were far from home and family. Twenty people or more would crowd into his condo for the festivities. They always left sated with food and good cheer. On several occasions, Wyatt had put together what he called memorial parties for friends who had died. He would have wanted the same, and the islanders were out in force to see him off.

Cracker Dix was there, dressed in his usual — cargo shorts, Hawaiian shirt, and flip-flops. He's an expatriate Englishman who has lived on the island for years. He came over to me, sipping from a can of beer. "Can I talk to you for a moment?" he said, and beckoned me into a corner.

"Matt, do you know Leah, the deaf girl who cooks at the restaurant where I work?"

"Sure."

"She reads lips, you know, and she saw something the other day that didn't make any sense to her."

"What?" I asked.

"She'd come out of the kitchen and was standing just inside the dining room when she saw a man say, 'Wyatt's a dead man.' She didn't think anything about it until the next day when she heard about his murder."

I made a "come on" gesture with my hand. Cracker tended to drift off subject after too many beers.

"Leah said there were two men at a table eating dinner. One had his back to her, and the other one was facing her. That was all of the conversation she saw. She just didn't think anything about it. She sees parts of conversations all the time."

"Did she recognize the man?" I asked.

"No, but she got his name. After she heard about Wyatt, she went to the credit card receipts and got his name and credit card number. I wrote them down for you."

I looked at the scrap of napkin he handed me. It had a name, Michael Rupert, and a long string of numbers. "Does this mean anything to you?" I asked.

"No," said Cracker, "I never heard the name. The numbers are his credit card number."

"Thanks, Cracker. Have you said anything about this to anybody else?"

"No. I figured you might want to deal with this yourself. I told Leah not to mention it to anybody either."

Chief Bill Lester joined us late in the morning, coming to pay his respects, and bring me up to date on the investigation. "The autopsy results came in last night. No surprises. He was killed by the gunshot behind the ear. The crime scene investigators didn't find the slug that killed him. It's probably buried in the sand on the beach. Wyatt was sitting in his chair on the balcony when he was shot. They found the slug fired into the back of his neck under his chair. It had gone through his neck, taking out part of his chin, and then through his left thigh. The techs think Wyatt slumped forward when he was killed, and the second bullet was fired in a downward direction. It was pretty much spent by the time it went through his body twice, and it just bounced around on the floor."

"What was it?"

"The bullet?"

I nodded.

"Forty-five caliber."

"Can you match it to any other murders?"

"Not from around here. We'll run it through the federal database, but I don't have high hopes for that. The killer picked up his brass before he left, so we don't have that to work with. If we see another slug from the same gun, we can match it, but that's a very long shot."

"What about time of death?

"The medical examiner thinks he'd been dead about two hours when Donna found him. Puts it at about seven."

"There're security cameras in the elevators," I said. "Did you check them?"

"Yes. We think we've got a pretty good shot of the killer coming up the number two elevator at six fifty-five. Unfortunately, he had his head down, and he was wearing a ball cap. His face is completely shielded."

"Anything else?"

"No sign of breaking and entering. Either Wyatt didn't have his front door locked, or someone had a key. Nothing was missing from his condo except his laptop. No signs of struggle. No fingerprints; at least none that don't belong to people who had a reason to be there, friends and visitors. We're beginning to think it was a professional hit."

"On Wyatt?" I said. "That makes no sense. Who'd want to kill Wyatt?"

"I don't know, Matt. I'm just following the evidence."

CHAPTER THREE

Debbie was where she always was on an early evening, behind the bar at Moore's Stone Crab Restaurant on the north end of Longboat Key. She had been at the memorial, but left in mid-afternoon for work. She was a blonde forty-something refugee from Ohio winters and had been tending bar on the island for more than twenty years. Some years before, she had taken some computer courses and became a world-class hacker. Not many people knew that, and she liked it that way. However, she was a good friend, and I knew I could count on her to help. Particularly, since it would help solve Wyatt's murder.

The bar was horseshoe shaped and the plate glass windows gave a twelve-mile view down the bay to the city of Sarasota. There were docks and piers fronting the restaurant, and they were often crowded with boats bringing customers for the generous portions of seafood offered by the establishment. I arrived just before five to an empty bar. Debbie pulled a cold Miller Lite from the cooler and put it on a coaster in front of me. I cocked my head in a questioning manner, and she said, "Okay Royal. I'll get you a damn glass."

She came back with a frosted glass. "Sorry I had to leave early today," she said.

"The party was winding down. I don't think anybody's at the Hilton but Cracker, and he's drinking at the outside bar."

I hadn't been in for a couple of weeks, and we talked quietly, catching up on the island gossip. Occasionally, a waitress came to the back service bar, and Debbie would excuse herself to fill the order. The TVs were all tuned to ESPN, and highlights of Sunday's NFL games were being played and replayed.

"Deb," I said, "do you think you could hack into a credit card company's main server?"

"I can. The question is, will I?"

"If I asked nicely?"

"Okay. What do you need?"

I handed her a piece of paper with the credit card number and Michael Rupert's name. "I think this guy may have had something to do with Wyatt's death. Will you see what you can find out about him?"

"What's his connection?"

"I don't know. He may have been the trigger man."

"Where'd you get his credit card number?"

"I can't say, Deb. I promised absolute confidentiality to the person who gave it to me."

"No problem, Matt. If I thought I couldn't count on your discretion, I sure wouldn't go around hacking computers for you."

"You're a sweetheart."

"And Wyatt was my friend, too."

A couple I didn't know came into the bar and effusively greeted Debbie. It was the time of the year when the snowbirds were starting to return, and they would stop in to see old friends at the places they frequented while on the key. I waved at Deb and walked out into the gathering twilight.

I was on the dock in front of my condo just before noon the next day, washing my boat and sweating in the heat. My cell phone rang. It was Debbie.

"Matt, this guy is a ghost. That credit card is the only thing he has in his name. The bills are sent to a post office box in Fern Park, Florida, wherever the hell that is. The only other Michael Ruperts I found are way too old or still just boys. This has to be your guy, but there's nothing else about him anywhere."

"I'm not surprised. It was a long shot, but at least we know where the bills go. He's probably using an alias and has a fake driver's license and the credit card to use when he's traveling."

"You want me to keep looking?"

"No, thanks. I'll see what I can turn up with this information."

She hung up, and I went back to the business of scrubbing the boat's hull. Who was Rupert? The fact that he didn't seem to exist made me think that he might be a contract killer. But who would be interested enough in Wyatt's death to pay someone to kill him? And who was the man at Cracker's restaurant with Rupert the night before the murder? I'd have to find Rupert and backtrack to whoever ordered Wyatt killed.

CHAPTER FOUR

Logan Hamilton was my friend. He and I had come to the island at about the same time, and we discovered a mutual enjoyment of the watering holes on the key and the people who frequented them. Logan had worked in the financial services industry, retired early, and was enjoying life in the sun. He was originally from a small town outside of Boston. He'd come to Florida as a college student, and then was a soldier in Vietnam, first as an infantryman, and after flight school, as a helicopter pilot. He traveled the world in his business, never really settling down and never marrying. He was a gentle and kind man who quietly supported every charitable endeavor in our little world.

I found Logan at Tiny's, a small bar on the north end of the key. It took up a corner adjacent to the Village, the oldest inhabited part of the island, home to people who could never afford the condos on the gilded south end. He was sitting on his usual stool, a baseball cap covering his balding head. He was wearing a golf shirt, shorts, and running shoes without socks, his usual attire. Logan stood about five feet eight and had put on a little weight over the past couple of years. His graying hair was fighting a losing battle with baldness. A Scotch and water sat on the bar in front of him.

I took the stool next to Logan. "Hey, buddy."

He turned toward me and lifted his glass. "How're you doing, Matt?"

"Fine. I need to talk to you about something I heard yesterday."

"What's up?"

I looked around to make sure no one else was within earshot. "I think I know who killed Wyatt. I'm going after him."

"Whoa. Hold on a minute. Turn it over to the cops, Matt. They know how to handle these things."

"Won't work. I doubt they could get enough evidence to arrest him, much less convict."

"How do you know you've got the right guy?"

I knew that Logan would keep his mouth shut, so I told him what I'd learned from Debbie and Cracker. "It's not much evidence for the cops to go on. No prosecutor is going to take a case this thin into court. I'm not going to let this guy walk."

"Bill Lester says he thinks it was a professional hit."

"If that's the case, the shooter knows who hired him. I'll work up the chain."

"Matt, listen to yourself. You're a retired lawyer who hangs out on the beach. This guy's probably a professional. You could be getting in way over your head."

I was in good shape. I pointed out that I ran every day and worked out occasionally with a martial arts instructor, honing the skills the army had taught me long ago. I could take pretty good care of myself in a fight and knew how to use a gun. "I used to be a professional myself," I said. "I can handle this."

"Need some help?"

Logan had made his argument for sanity. It hadn't taken, and he was ready to do whatever it took to help out. That was vintage Hamilton. A friend.

We'd been in a couple of scrapes during the past year; more than one would think could happen on a small island resting in the sun of Southwest Florida. Logan always backed me up without question. It was his nature.

"Not yet," I said. "Let me take the first step and see what I find out. I'll let you know what happens."

"You ready for a beer?"

We sat for an hour or so. I told Logan my plans, such as they were. I wanted him to know where I'd gone in case I didn't come back. It was getting near evening, and the working people from the Village were stopping in for their after-work drink. Each one stopped to shake my hand and offer condolences on Wyatt's death. It was the island way.

CHAPTER FIVE

Fern Park is a small unincorporated village that straddles U.S. Highway 17-92 on the north side of Orlando. Convenience stores, shopping centers, car washes, grocery stores, topless joints, and a large sheriff's substation border the road. This was once a town, but when it went bankrupt in one of Florida's semiregular boom or bust periods, the city fathers decided to unincorporate the town and let the creditors stew.

The Fern Park post office occupied a small building on a side road directly behind a large carwash and small strip shopping center. I parked my rental car and went inside. I was looking for box 158. It was one of the small ones, with a glass in the door front. I saw three envelopes resting there, taking up most of the space. I couldn't read the addresses on the envelopes, and I knew that the postal employees wouldn't tell me to whom the box was assigned. I'd just have to wait to see if anyone came to pick up the mail. I hoped Mr. Rupert expected the letters and would be along to collect them. Not much of a plan, but I didn't have anything else to work with.

On the first Friday in November, the weather was still warm, the humidity high. Autumn in this part of Florida arrives when the air becomes drier and the temperature drops to a more bearable level. It was a little late in coming this year, but a cold front was predicted.

I took a seat on the bench at the bus stop in front of the post office. The schedule posted there told me that a bus came by at the top of the hour. That would give me about forty-five minutes. I could see box 158 from the bench, and I wouldn't raise anybody's suspicions by waiting for the bus.

A bus came and stopped. Two passengers got off and walked toward the shopping center. I waved the driver on, and sat through the cloud of diesel exhaust belching from the vehicle as it pulled away.

Another hour went by, and another bus stopped, this time going in the opposite direction. Same driver. I waved him on and sucked up more fumes. I'd brought a book and a bottle of water to the bench. I sipped and read, enjoying James Born's latest mystery. I glanced up every minute or so to see if anything was going on at the box. It was nearing noon, and I was sweating like a pig. My water bottle was empty, and I was getting hungry. Another bus stopped, moved on.

I was idly watching a young woman wearing shorts and a halter top entering the post office. Nice body, long legs, blonde hair to her shoulders, a little butt twitch as she walked. My kind of girl. Then again, I'm not all that choosy.

I was suddenly hit with the revelation that she was standing in front of box 158. My heart kicked up a notch. I got off the bench, and strolled toward the plate glass window that took up the front of the building. I couldn't see which box she was using, but as she moved away, I saw that box 158 was empty. The blonde had three envelopes in her hand as she walked to an ancient Toyota parked in the space next to my rental.

She pulled out of the parking lot, the old car spewing black smoke from the exhaust. I eased up to the road and let her get about a block ahead of me. I followed. She was traveling east and after about four blocks turned right and in another block turned into an older looking apartment complex. She made a couple of turns on the interior roads and parked in front of a one-story building housing four apartments. I pulled into a space twenty feet away. She went to one of the doors, knocked, handed the mail to the man who answered, and walked back toward her car.

I walked over to meet her and showed her a badge that identified me as an honorary officer of the Longboat Key Police Department. Bill Lester had given it to me along with a nice certificate when I'd donated five hundred bucks to a police charity. It looked real enough if one didn't examine it too closely, and I didn't give her a good look.

"I'm Detective Charles McFarland," I said. "I'd like to ask you a couple of questions if you have a minute." I gave her a big smile, the one that I was sure had melted the hearts of tougher women than she.

"Sure."

I gestured toward the apartment. "Is that Michael Rupert's place?"

"Is he in trouble?"

"No. Just routine."

"That's the name he told me, and that's the name on the mail."

"You don't know him?"

"No. I clean for him once a week and check his mail every day. He pays me in cash, and I don't ask questions."

"Ever see any other people with him?"

"No. You sure he's not in trouble?"

"Not yet. Thanks for your time."

She shrugged, got into the Toyota, and left in a cloud of exhaust.

CHAPTER SIX

I walked to the door, pulling a pair of latex gloves out of my pocket. I took the .38 out of another pocket, attached a silencer to the barrel. I knocked. The same man answered. He was about five feet eight and thin, with ropes of muscles binding his torso. His short-cropped blond hair was wet and matted to his scalp. He was shirtless and barefoot, wearing only gym shorts with an elastic waistband. He was sweating in the humid air, droplets coursing down his hairless chest. He looked at my pistol and, showing no surprise, turned and walked back into the room, gesturing for me to follow.

The living room was sparsely furnished, holding only a sofa, a large TV, and a set of barbells complete with a bench. The man had apparently been working out when I knocked.

He sat on the sofa. "Who the hell are you?" he asked.

"A friend of Laurence Wyatt's."

There was no change in his expression. "How did you find me?"

"That's not important. You don't seem too concerned that a friend of the man you murdered is standing in your living room pointing a gun at you."

"Ah. You're Matt Royal. I spent some time on Longboat Key, scoping the place out. I heard about you. Saw you at Mar Vista with Wyatt one day. You're a lawyer, an upstanding citizen. People like you don't kill in cold blood."

"You're pretty sure of yourself."

"I know your type. You'll turn me into the law, but there's no evidence connecting me to the murder of your friend, and if you were wired, my security devices would have let me know the minute you walked in the door. You'll never prove anything."

"Why did you kill him?"

"Because somebody paid me ten thousand dollars to do it."

"Who?"

"Even if I knew, I wouldn't tell you." He smirked, but it was more of a leer, a mocking face telling me I had nothing. "You know about client privilege, right?"

I shot him in his right ankle, the pistol making a small noise that could not be heard beyond the room we were in. Rupert recoiled in searing pain, a look of horror on his face. His brain was starting to comprehend that he may have been wrong about me, that maybe he was in big trouble.

"Rupert," I said, "I don't give a shit about you. You can live or die, and it won't make a fiddler's damn to me. I want the man who ordered Wyatt's death. You give him to me and you might survive today with nothing worse than a limp."

"I don't know who it was," he said through clenched teeth.

I aimed the gun at his other ankle. "You're going to have a hard time ever walking again with two shattered ankles."

"No. Listen." Genuine fear now edged his words, a tremor in his voice, a pleading look in his eyes. The carnivore trapped by a bigger, meaner, hungrier animal, one with no mercy in his soul, one who had pushed into the hidden lair without warning. "You've got to believe me. I don't know the man. Everything was handled by a middleman that I deal with all the time."

"Who's the middleman?"

"If he finds out I told you, I'm a dead man."

I raised the gun, pointing at his head. "You're a dead man if you don't tell me. Your choice."

He was in terrible pain, his facial features puckered. His shattered ankle was bleeding all over the carpet. His breath caught, something like a sob passed his lips.

"Okay," he said. "His name is Max Banchori. From Miami."

"Is that the man you had dinner with the night before the murder?"

A look of surprise skittered across his face. "No. That was just a local contact."

"What's his name?"

"I don't know."

I raised the gun again.

"No," Rupert said. "If I knew, don't you think I'd tell you? I've given you Banchori, and he's going to kill me if he finds out."

I believed him. He was too scared and in too much pain to hide anything else. "Did you take Wyatt's laptop?"

"Yes."

"Where is it?"

"I sent it to Banchori. He told me that was the only thing I was supposed to take out of the apartment."

"Why?"

"I don't know. Honestly."

"Give me Banchori's address."

"I don't know it. Honest. We always dealt by phone. I've never met the man.

"I've got to know something, Rupert. Did Wyatt know he was about to die?"

"Yes."

"Tell me about it."

"I came in through his front door. I knew he never locked it. He was on his balcony reading the paper. He heard me just before I got to him. I put the gun to the back of his head. He knew it was over. He said, 'Who sent you?' I told him it wasn't important. His last words were 'Then fuck you and the horse you rode in on.'"

It was a cold recitation of facts, no emotion from Rupert at all. He could have been talking about a TV show. I'd never been so close to pure evil. They're a type, these sorry bastards who roam our world and hide in our midst. They're sociopaths who have no empathy for others. They can't feel any of the emotions that normal people have, and so they don't understand them. They're good at playacting, at pretending to have feelings, so they're able to survive in a society that should fear them.

Rupert was a study in fear, his right hand clasping his ruined ankle, his left stuffed between the cushions of the sofa, his face a rictus of pain, teeth clenched, lips pressed tightly. The man seemed to have one real emotion, though. Fear of his own death. I put the gun to his head, the working end of the silencer boring into his forehead. "No, don't do it," he said, sobbing. "I've told you everything I know."

I wanted this cretin dead. My finger tightened on the trigger. A tiny bit of pressure more, and I'd send a bullet through his brain. I stood over the trembling man, gathering my feelings. Nothing. What the hell was wrong with me? I was about to kill a man in cold blood, and I felt nothing.

Was I like Rupert? I hoped not, but at that moment I wasn't sure. I'd killed men in combat and in firefights that had nothing to do with war. But that was always in the heat of battle, when the blood was running hot with the knowledge that it was them or me. Those situations called for one of us to die, and I'd rather it be the other guy than me. But here, I was about to shoot a helpless man in the head, deprive him of life, send a bullet into his brain, and push him into eternity.

The fact that he was less than an animal didn't change the reality that I was about to murder a human being. For the first time in my life. Where was the remorse, the regret? Maybe it'd come later. But I was afraid that it wouldn't. That I was about to cross the boundary that separates good people from the truly evil. I wondered if I could find my way back. What if I couldn't?

I'd promised myself that I'd take revenge on Wyatt's killers, but I couldn't do this. Rupert was right. I couldn't kill in cold blood. I'd have to let the law take its course. For good or bad. I released the pressure on the trigger and pulled the gun away from his forehead.

At that moment, Rupert jerked his left hand out from between the cushions. He was holding something, raising the hand to me, a threatening gesture. I pulled the trigger, sending a bullet into his simian brain, killing him instantly. The force of the slug pushed his head against the back of the sofa, his left hand unclenching and dropping the object of my fear into his lap.

I was stunned at the almost instantaneous events. I'd been distracted by his fear and hadn't paid attention to his left hand. Then, in a flash, a hand coming up, my finger squeezing a trigger, the end of a life. I looked at the object in his lap. A Kel-Tec P-32, a small .32-caliber semiautomatic pistol often carried as a concealed weapon. Now I knew why he'd sat on the sofa, seemingly so unconcerned about my holding a gun on him.

I sat on the weight bench, staring at the body of a man who deserved to die, trying to make some sense of it. I had made myself judge, jury, and executioner. Sure, I'd killed him in self-defense, but I had come into his home with a murderous intent. There's no jury in America that wouldn't convict me of first-degree murder. I could turn myself in and face the consequences, but I couldn't contemplate life in prison. I was a lawyer, a man who believed in the dignity of every person, who knew in his gut that he'd just committed a crime that he could never rationalize. I'd have to work on that. I had just moved outside the law for the first time in my life, and I felt cold in that bitter wilderness.

I moved into Rupert's bedroom. There was a double bed, unmade, the sheets tangled. A bedside table held a reading lamp and a semiautomatic pistol. I left it where it was. Across the room was a dresser with six drawers and a table on which rested a desktop computer and monitor. I ransacked the drawers, finding nothing but underwear and tee shirts and a wad of cash, fifty-dollar bills still in the bank wrappers, stuffed in a plastic bag from Publix. I put the money in the bag, unplugged the computer from its peripherals and left, taking the bag and the machine with me. Maybe Debbie could retrieve something from the hard drive. Hopefully, the cops who investigated would think it was a robbery. I'd let them figure out why the thief hadn't taken the gun.

I was a little concerned about the blonde having seen me, but I didn't think she'd be of much help to law enforcement. She hadn't gotten a good enough look at the badge to see that it was from Longboat Key, and the rental car was a nondescript Chevrolet. I'd smeared mud over most of the license plate number, so that it was unreadable. If a cop stopped me because of the obscured tag, I'd simply wipe it off and be on my way. Orlando was the largest car rental market in the world, and every day over one hundred thousand cars were rented out by the various agencies. I'd rented mine from the Sarasota airport. It would be just another anonymous vehicle, and nearly impossible to locate in the swirling mass of metal that rode the streets of the metropolitan area.

CHAPTER SEVEN

The death of a friend impales you with a barbed javelin of despair. The loss is so exquisite, the pain so acute, that you are numbed for a time. You walk into a place, a bar perhaps, or a restaurant where you've always found your friend sitting, drinking, eating, laughing, and he's not there. His absence, and the permanence of it, strikes you in the heart. It's a momentary feeling of inexplicable grief, an emotion not unlike that of a lost love. But while the lost love may reappear some day, the dead are gone forever. You feel helpless and a little lost.

I was driving back to Longboat Key, I-4 stretching out in front of me, an unkind sky looming in the distance. Lightning flashes streaked the dark clouds, a storm brewing. I'd be in it soon. The sky matched my mood, dark and somber.

Wyatt was on my mind, but so was Michael Rupert. The emotions that had abandoned me when I was standing over Rupert deciding whether to kill him were coming now, welling up in my mind like a tempest; regret, remorse, dismay. I was glad of that. It meant that I was still human. I'd slain a monster, an egregious accumulation of protoplasm who had killed randomly for money, without a thought of the consequences. He would have killed again and again, and by taking him out, maybe I'd saved the lives of future victims. Or maybe I had only ensured that a different killer would be hired to do the work of those who made the decisions to erase a person from this life. Maybe all I had done was taste the bitter bile of revenge.

Still, I was surprised that I had it in me to kill in cold blood. And that's pretty much what I'd done. If I hadn't been so intent on revenge, I wouldn't have gone to that apartment and put Rupert in my gun sights.

But the bastards who took Wyatt's life did not deserve to live. Maybe it wasn't in my province to make that decision, but I had made it, and I would carry out the punishment. When it was over, if I survived, I'd deal with the part of me that I didn't like, that didn't fit with my perceptions of myself. I hoped the killing was over, that I could make a case that would interest a prosecutor. But if not, I would do what I had to do. Maybe.

My windows were down. The air was heavy, the smell of rain drifting into the rental car. Droplets began to hit the windshield. I rolled up the windows and turned on the wipers. Bigger and bigger blobs came down, and soon streaks of water were running off the windows. Lightning flashed all around me, the thunder following close behind. Cars slowed, some pulling off the highway to wait out the storm. I kept going, plowing through the water that was beginning to accumulate on the road.

A semi passed me, throwing up sheets of dirty water, obscuring my view. I slowed more, concentrating on my driving. The rain slackened, slowed, the drops tapering off into nothing. The storm was moving on, and the traffic was picking up speed.

It was dusk now, and the cars and trucks had turned on their lights. I found the ramp onto I-75 and headed south for home. Rupert's ghost was riding with me, the storm a harbinger of the nightmares to come, the scene of his death playing over and over in my head.

I drove on into the night, knowing that others would die before I was finished, wondering who they were, and what reason they could have had for ordering the death of a gentle professor named Wyatt. My soul was as dark as the road, and I could see no light there, only the shadows of the dead.

CHAPTER EIGHT

The storm of the night before was part of a cold front pushing down from Canada. Saturday dawned bright with a cerulean sky devoid of even a wisp of cloud. This early in the year, the fronts don't drop the temperature so much as they cleanse the air of humidity. I rode my bicycle to the Blue Dolphin café for breakfast with Logan. Walkers, joggers, and cyclists crowded the sidewalk, waving and nodding at passersby, everyone enjoying the mood brought about by our first autumn day.

Except me. I hadn't slept much. My dreams were dark with dread and images of dead men; Wyatt and Rupert and soldiers I'd lost in fetid jungles. I twisted and turned in the bed and soaked the sheets with the sweat of the damned. I'd awake to the horror of what I'd done, the murder of a man who needed killing, but a man nevertheless. I'd drop off to sleep again, only to be met by Stygian images of men who no longer were in this world. Finally, I got up, made coffee, and watched the sun rise over the bay.

Logan was sitting in a booth sipping tomato juice and reading the morning paper. "You look like shit," he said.

"Good morning to you, too."

"I'm serious. You look like shit."

"That's the way I feel."

I ordered coffee and a Belgian waffle. Logan asked for eggs fried over hard and hash browns.

"How did it go yesterday?" he asked.

I told him. I told him every gory detail. I told him that I'd planned to murder a man in cold blood, and I told him of my decision not to kill the monster. I told him that I'd shot in self-defense and that I'd thought I'd feel good about it. I told him that I felt lousy, but at the same time, was glad that the man who'd killed my friend was dead. I told him that I was afraid I'd crossed a line, some sort of a border that kept the depraved and the sane separated. I told him that I was filled with remorse and elation, with apprehension and confidence, and with a burning desire to kill those who were responsible for Wyatt's death. And I told him I wasn't sure I had it in me to exact the justice that Wyatt deserved. "I'm going to Miami to see Banchori."

"I'll go with you," Logan said simply.

"Not this time, my friend. I need to do this alone. Stay here, and if I need you, I'll call."

CHAPTER NINE

I went home and counted the money from Rupert's stash. There were eight stacks of currency, each containing twenty-five one-hundred dollar bills. Exactly twenty thousand dollars. Rupert said he'd been paid ten grand to kill Wyatt. Where had the extra ten thousand come from? Too late to ask Rupert. I shredded the bank bands and put the cash into a manila envelope. I addressed it to the Longboat Key Library. I put the shredded bands, my .38-caliber pistol and silencer in the plastic bag I'd brought from Rupert's apartment. The computer was still in the trunk of the rental car parked in my condo lot.

I called Debbie. "I've got a computer I'd like you to look at. See if you can find anything in the hard drive."

"Whose is it?"

"Don't ask."

"Does this have anything to do with the information I gave you on Thursday?"

"Yes."

"What did you do about Mr. Rupert?"

"Don't ask."

"Geez, Royal. You're pretty damned secretive."

"It's my nature."

"Right. Everybody knows you can't keep a secret."

"This one needs to be kept, Deb. My life depends on it."

"No sweat, Matt. You know you can count on me."

"I know."

"Come on over."

"See you in a few minutes," I said, and hung up.

I left the computer with Debbie, and on the way back, I dropped the money at the post office. The library wouldn't know who their benefactor was, but they'd be pleased. You can buy a lot of books for twenty grand.

My boat, a 28-foot Grady-White walkaround, was moored at the dock in front of my condo. I took the bag with the gun and shredded bank bands, boarded the boat, and loosed the lines. I chugged out of the marina, motoring north on the Intracoastal and out Longboat Pass. I headed straight out to sea, and when I could no longer see land, I heaved the bag with the pistol overboard. No ballistics expert would ever tie my gun to Rupert's murder.

I came back to my condo, washed down the boat, and drove my Explorer to a gun shop in East Bradenton. I bought another .38, filled out the forms and left. I'd have to wait three days to actually get the gun. It's called a cooling off period, but it doesn't make a lot of sense to me. If somebody is pissed enough to want to shoot someone, I don't think three days is going to make a lot of difference. I told the clerk I'd be back Tuesday to pick up my pistol.

I drove back to Longboat Key, and spent the evening at the outside bar at the Hilton. The place was crowded with locals enjoying the cooler weather. More of the snowbirds were drifting back, and a few were sipping their drinks and catching up on the island gossip. A quiet night on a small island of serenity in an ever more dangerous world.

On Sunday, Logan and I and our buddies K-Dawg and Goldie went fishing. We took my boat out to an artificial reef three miles off Anna Maria Island and drank beer and let lines dangle in the water. We didn't catch any fish, but we joked and laughed, told a few lies and enjoyed the day. The dark cloud hanging over me was gradually dissipating.

On Monday morning I called Debbie to ask if she'd found anything on Rupert's computer.

"He's a pedophile. The bastard has all kinds of pictures of children in sexual poses. There're also some pictures of a grown man having sex with very small children. Both boys and girls."

"Anything else?"

"Isn't that enough? The sonovabitch ought to be shot."

"You're probably right. What else?"

"Nothing much. I think he used his computer as a picture album. He visited a lot of child porn sites and downloaded a lot of images. There're a few e-mails, but they mostly have to do with his getting more pictures."

"An address book, bank information, personal information, anything like that?"

"Nada. Just a lot of disgusting pictures."

"Describe the man in the pictures to me."

She gave me a description that could fit Rupert.

"Who did he communicate with by e-mail?"

"Mostly some guy in New York named Chardone. They were sending pictures back and forth."

"Thanks, Deb. You can toss the computer or keep it. Mr. Rupert won't be needing it anymore."

"If that means what I think, I'd say good."

"Doesn't mean a thing. Talk to you soon."

I checked the online version of Central Florida's daily newspaper, the *Orlando Sentinel*. There was nothing on the murder of Michael Rupert. I spent the rest of the day on my own computer, searching out anything I could find on Max Banchori. It wasn't much.

On Tuesday morning, I finished my coffee and donut breakfast and checked the online *Orlando Sentinel* once more. There it was. The cleaning lady, whose name was Tammy something or other, had found the body on Monday when she came in to clean. There was no identification on the body or in the apartment, but Tammy told the police that the man's name was Rupert. The mystery deepened when the detectives found that the apartment was leased to a New York City policeman named Rudy Chardone. Fingerprints confirmed the dead man's identity as the New York City police officer. The lead detective was quoted as being puzzled. There were no suspects, but with a dead cop the heat would be intense.

I called Debbie. "Is there anyway to identify the person who owned the hard drive I gave you last week?"

"Oh, yeah. His name was all over it. Those e-mails will tie Rupert to it without question."

"What about the other guy?"

"Chardone? Sure. Do you know who he is?"

"I think so. Get the hard drive out of the computer. I'll pick it up in an hour or so."

"I'll do it right now."

CHAPTER TEN

Miami is overwhelming. The city seems to breathe to a Latin beat. Spanish and English languages reside side by side, neither one dominant, but the bilingual residents have an advantage. Creole is making a dent, and the Haitian immigrants are becoming a force in the essentially Cuban political landscape. The beaches are sandy and topless, perhaps the only place in America where nudity is legally condoned. An international city acting like what it is; a vibrant, multilingual, multicultural mecca. I loved the place.

But often there is a dark side to beauty, and Miami's splendor was tempered by criminal shadows. Crime was endemic in Miami. There were as many ethnic gangs as there were ethnic communities. Contrary to many of our politicians' beliefs, the Hispanics are not monolithic. The Cubans, Puerto Ricans, Guatemalans, Mexicans, Hondurans, Venezuelans, Peruvians, and others have all spawned their own subcultures, replete with gangs and crime as well as good works and concerned citizens. The Haitians compete with African-Americans, the Cubans with the Puerto Ricans, and the Anglos with everyone else.

I had to insinuate myself into this melting pot of criminality, because Max Banchori was a player there. Not big-time, but not on the fringes either. My research told me that Banchori had been active in the Miami crime scene for more than fifty years. He was in his seventies now and had assumed a position as an elder statesman. He'd been arrested a number of times, but never convicted. His crimes ranged from numbers to drugs to prostitution and one murder charge. Nothing ever stuck.

I drove into the city late on Tuesday. I'd stopped in Bradenton to pick up my new .38 and turned south on I-75. I followed Alligator Alley across the Glades, the long rays of the sun reaching from behind me, bathing the water and saw grass in vibrant colors. I was still in the rental car from the Sarasota airport. I wanted to keep a low profile, because I was about to kill another man, and I'd just as soon nobody found out.

I stopped at the first mailbox I came to. I had the hard drive in an envelope along with a typed note that simply said, "Check the .45 against IBIS." The priority mail package was addressed to the lead detective at the Seminole County Sheriff's Department, which had jurisdiction in Fern Park. I dropped it in the box. I'd wiped the hard drive with a paper towel to clear it of any fingerprints, and had been careful not to touch the envelope with my bare hands.

IBIS is the acronym for "Integrated Ballistics Identification System," a database maintained by the federal government. Police agencies are able to input the ballistics information on a bullet and can then match it to other shootings.

Chardone had the perfect cover for his murderous enterprise; a New York City police officer. I knew that the heat was turned up anytime a cop was killed, but I thought the fire might go out of the investigation if local law enforcement determined that the dead man was a contract killer and a child sexual predator. I was sure that IBIS would turn up other murders committed by Chardone.

I knew a Miami-Dade detective named Carl Merritt. We'd worked together the year before on a case involving a friend of mine. I called him as I drove into downtown Miami.

"Matt," said Carl. "Good to hear from you. How are things on the west coast?"

"Almost as good as South Florida. You doing okay?"

"Sure am. But I've got the feeling you're calling for a reason other than passing the time of day."

"I am. Do you know anything about a man named Max Banchori?"

"Piece of shit. A lot of cops have spent their careers trying to nail that bastard. We got nothing."

"What can you tell me about him?"

"He's been a major player in this area for fifty years or so. He's semi-retired now, but we think he's involved in contract killings."

"How so?"

"I can't give you all the details. A lot of this is stuff we pick up from informants, but can't prove. It falls into an area of classified information that we accumulate, and hope one day it'll lead us to a conviction."

"Tell me what you can."

"Banchori seems to work as some sort of a broker. People contract with him to put a hit on somebody, and Banchori farms it out to a franchisee. Old Max sets the fee and then pays the shooter a part of it. It's pretty clean, and it gives the shooter another layer of insulation."

"If I wanted to talk to Banchori, how would I go about it?"

"You wouldn't Matt. He's a dangerous man. Stay the hell away from him."

"Can't do that, Carl. I've got to see him."

"What's this about?"

"Unfortunately, there're also things I can't tell you. I'm working on a case and you know how lawyer confidentiality works. But I need to talk to him." I hated lying to a good man, but Carl knew I was a lawyer. I'd been trying a murder case when we'd met before, and to be fair, I was sort of working on a case now.

"There's a bar over on the beach that's controlled by one of the crime syndicates. It's called The Hunt Club. Word on the street is that if you want to see Banchori, you talk to a bartender named Mickey. He sets up the meetings."

"Thanks, Carl. Stay well."

"Be careful, Matt. Be very careful." He hung up.

CHAPTER ELEVEN

If bad guys controlled The Hunt Club, I was sure there'd be a surveillance system. They'd want a record of who came calling. I didn't want my face on a videotape that the police, or friends of Banchori's, would surely look at after the coldhearted bastard went to the great beyond.

I stopped at a convenience store that still had a pay phone hanging on its front wall. I was in a poor section of Miami, and I guessed that not many people had cell phones. Either that, or the drug dealers used the pay phone so they couldn't be tracked by their cell phones.

The phone book was in tatters, pages and parts of pages torn out. If somebody needed a phone number, they just took the page. No sense in writing it down. Luckily, the Yellow Pages were for the most part intact. I found what I was looking for in Coconut Grove, an upscale neighborhood south of downtown. I also wrote down the address for The Hunt Club.

The costume shop was located on a small street off Grand Avenue in the Grove. It catered to the actors and makeup artists who worked the theaters in the area. I found a parking place and went into the shop. As I opened the door, I heard a tinkling sound. It was an old-fashioned bell suspended above the entrance. The door brushed against a lever causing the bell to sound. There were makeup kits, wigs, and fake mustaches and eyebrows arranged in a glass case that was set against one wall, each with a price tag. A price list was tacked to the wall over the counter. The prices charged made the place seem very professional indeed.

An elderly man came through the curtained doorway from what I assumed was a workroom. "Can I help you?"

"Yes. I'm looking for a mustache. I need one that looks real and matches my hair color."

"Come into the light." He motioned me over to the counter where an overhead fixture provided illumination. He looked closely at my head and disappeared into the back. He reappeared in moments carrying a tray of mustaches.

"Here," he said, "these are made of real human hair." He pulled one from its perch in the tray and held it up to my head. He nodded. "This one will do nicely."

"Can you put it on for me? I've never done this, and I want to surprise some old friends."

"Sure. Come on back."

We went into his back room, and he had me sit before a dresser with a mirror that had lighted bulbs all along its periphery. He placed the fake mustache on my lip and asked me to hold it. It was the right color and full enough to cover my entire upper lip. I looked at myself in the mirror and thought it made me look dashing. "That's good," I said.

"Okay. Let's put some spirit gum on your lip to hold the mustache." He squeezed the adhesive out of a tube onto a cotton swab and gently rubbed it onto my lip. He stood back to look at his handiwork. "We need to let that set for a minute," he said.

In a few moments he took the mustache and held it firmly against my lip. He stepped back, and I saw a different man staring at me in the mirror. It wasn't much of a change, but it was enough that it might throw off any hunters looking for me.

The old man gave me a tube of spirit gum remover and handwrote a bill. I paid in cash and left the shop. I stopped at a sporting goods store and bought a pair of mirrored sunglasses, the kind aviators wear, a Miami Dolphin ball cap, an extra large green and white Dolphin windbreaker, a belt four sizes too large for me, and a souvenir Dolphin throw pillow.

I drove across the bridge onto Miami Beach just as the sun was winking out on the western horizon. A large yacht, its superstructure ablaze in lights, was moving under the bridge, pointed south toward Lower Biscayne Bay. A cruise ship was putting out to sea from Government Cut. The buildings of South Beach were coming alive with lights, bringing a sense of gaiety and the promise of a night of revelry in the clubs that lined the streets.

I found a parking place on the street about two blocks from The Hunt Club. I used the new belt to strap the pillow to my waist and put the windbreaker on over it. I was wearing jeans, the legs pulled over cowboy boots I'd brought along for this purpose. The high heels added about two inches to my height. I put on the sunglasses and ball cap, pulled the brim low over my eyes, and walked toward the bar. It was dusk, but half the people I saw were still wearing shades. I caught a reflected glimpse of my-self in a store window that had not yet been lighted. I looked like an over-weight Dolphin fan out on the town. I sure didn't look like Matt Royal of Longboat Key.

The bar was not large, but it spilled out onto the sidewalk, its tables and chairs full of the beautiful people. Waiters in tuxedos rushed about filling drink orders. Large sliding glass doors were open to the interior.

I wound my way through the closely packed tables and reached the bar. A crush of people stood two or three deep, loudly ordering drinks from the three bartenders, two of whom were young women. The male bartender worked his way to the end of the bar near where I was standing. He wore black pants, a formal pleated shirt with a wingtip collar and French cuffs, a black bow tie, a cummerbund, and large gold cufflinks. He was about forty years old, six feet tall, and wiry. His head was shaved bald. He had a name tag pinned to his shirt that said, "Mickey."

I held up a twenty-dollar bill and waved him over. He leaned across the bar. "Can I help you?" he asked.

I handed him the bill. "I need to see Max Banchori."

"Who?"

"Tell him it's business. Tell him I'm a friend of Rudy Chardone's."

"Tell who?"

"Bring me a Miller Lite. I'm going to find a table and drink the beer. If Mr. Banchori wants to do business, point me out to him."

"I have no idea what you're talking about. I'll get you the beer."

He brought me a cold long-neck bottle, and I handed him another twenty, waving off any change. I found a table being vacated by a man in a thousand-dollar suit and a woman in a halter top and hip-hugger shorts. I sat and sipped my beer.

I was just about finished when a man wearing designer jeans and a designer tee shirt took a seat at my table. He was large and muscled, a body builder who regularly worked out with weights. He was wearing flip-flops, probably also designer, although I didn't look that closely. He had a fruity looking drink in his hand, some sort of rum concoction, I thought.

"Why do you want to see Mr. Banchori?"

"Business."

"What kind of business?"

"The kind he does."

"Be more specific."

"Do you know Rudy Chardone?"

"No."

"Michael Rupert?"

"No."

"They're in the kind of business I need to talk to Mr. Banchori about."

"What's your name?"

"Wally Shirra."

"Like the astronaut?"

"He's my uncle."

"Right."

"I still need to speak with Mr. Banchori."

"Stay here," he said, and got up and walked outside, pulling a cell phone from his pocket.

He was back in five minutes. "Come with me," he said, and I followed him out the door.

CHAPTER TWELVE

The man was walking at a fast pace down the sidewalk, dodging the diners who were seated haphazardly at outdoor tables that spewed out of the restaurants and bars along Ocean Drive. I hurried to catch up.

"Where're we going?" I asked, as I came up beside him.

"Mr. Banchori keeps a suite in a hotel in the next block. We'll see him there."

We crossed a street and moved to the middle of the block. One of the old hotels, done up in the art deco style of the 1930s, crowded the sidewalk. The place had been restored some years before, but must have recently had another facelift. It shined in the night air. We walked up two steps and entered the double doors.

The lobby was small, a registration desk taking up one corner of the room. The art deco theme dominated the area. The furniture, fixtures, floor tile, and drapes were right out of the 1930s. I followed my guide to the back of the lobby and waited while he summoned an elevator. We rode to the top floor, walked down a hall, and entered the suite. More art deco.

An elderly white-haired man rose from the sofa. He was wearing a gray suit, complete with vest, white shirt, a red foulard tie, and oxblood tasseled loafers. He was smoking a cigarette, and ashes had fallen onto the front of his vest. He held a clear drink in his left hand, gin probably, over ice. He had a long face, wrinkled beyond his years, and his blue eyes were bloodshot. His nose was large and sported three moles.

He walked toward me, hand outstretched. I stuck my hand out and felt someone grab me from behind. He pulled my arms back, his arms locked into mine. It was like being handcuffed behind your back, except the muscled arms of my guide were holding me above the elbows. The old man came forward, raised his hand, and slapped me across the face. He backhanded me and then slapped me again. My aviator shades and hat flew off and hit the floor.

Banchori put his face close to mine. I could smell the cigarettes and booze. "Who the hell are you?" he shouted.

"Do you always treat your customers like this?" I asked.

"Chardone is dead. Chardone was Rupert. Some asshole killed him. Took out one of my best men. He was shot in the ankle before he died. Somebody tortured him. He would've given me up. You come a few days later. You trying to kill me, asshole?"

"No. Chardone was my friend."

"Where did he live?"

"New York."

"Where, asshole?"

"I don't know. I never went to his house."

He slapped me again. Spittle flew out of my mouth, and I could taste the metallic hint of blood. My jaw was on fire. Then he backhanded me again. And again. This wasn't going well.

"Stop," I said. "I'm telling you the truth. I want somebody eliminated."

"Why come to me?"

"Because Chardone said you get things like this done."

"Do you think I'm stupid? Chardone would have taken the kill himself. He didn't need me in on the deal. That's the way we worked. He was a freelancer. He would never have sent you to me."

He had me. I stared stupidly at him. I hadn't thought about that. I'd assumed Chardone always worked for Banchori.

The old man slapped me again. "Who the hell are you?"

I spat in his face. Blood and saliva hit his cheek and ran down toward his shirt collar. He pulled a handkerchief out of his back pocket and wiped his face. He hit me again with the back of his hand.

"You pig," he said. "You'll regret that. Dennis, take this asshole out and kill him. Slowly."

CHAPTER THIRTEEN

I let my knees go, dropping like a sack of potatoes. Dennis came down with me, his arms still hooked through mine. I was almost in a squatting position, still moving downward. I lifted my left foot as high as I could from that awkward position and brought my boot heel down onto his bare foot with all the force I could muster. At the same time, I pushed up with all my leg power, and threw my head up and back, catching Dennis in the face. All this took a short second.

Dennis screamed and let go of me. By then I was back on my feet. I swung around to my left, bringing my elbow up and catching him high on the cheek. I felt the bone under his eye shatter. He was falling backward when I brought my right boot-clad foot into his nuts. He was done.

I turned to Banchori, grabbed him by the tie, and slapped his face. I backhanded him and slapped him again. "No more," he cried, fear and pain and humiliation tingeing his words.

"I thought you liked this slapping stuff," I said, drawing my hand back again.

"No, please. I'm sorry I hit you. I'm an old man."

I let him slide back onto the sofa, and reached into my pocket for my .38. Dennis was lying on the floor, moaning, and locked into a fetal position. I pointed the gun at the old man.

"Who paid you to have Laurence Wyatt killed?"

"I don't know."

I raised my hand to hit him again.

"Don't," he said, his voice tight, little more than a whisper.

"I ought to kill you."

"Don't hit me again. I don't know anything." He was pleading. The bastard could dish it out, but he didn't like being on the receiving end.

"You hired Chardone." It was a statement.

"Yes. He took care of things for me in Central and Northern Florida."

"How long?"

"He's worked with me for ten years or so."

"You've got about two minutes to tell me everything you know about Wyatt's murder."

"I'm telling the truth. I don't know who hired me."

"I'm about to plug you in the ankle, you piece of shit. Just like I did Rupert, or Chardone, or whatever you call him."

"No. Honestly. I don't know. It was all done by e-mail. A man I never saw again brought the cash."

I sensed Dennis stirring. I turned. He was coming off the floor, a crazed look on his face. He stood, weaving, blood dripping from his face. I pointed the gun at him. "Don't do it, Dennis," I said. "You don't want to die for this used up old bastard."

Dennis screamed. "Dad."

He came at me. I didn't have a silencer, and I knew the report of the pistol would be heard in the hallway. I stepped back and to the side, and chopped him in the neck with the side of my hand. He went down, holding his throat, gurgling. He was struggling for breath, his face turning blue. I'd hit something vital in his neck.

The old man ran to Dennis. It was too late. Dennis died. The old man cradled him in his arms. "You killed my only son." He was sobbing, tears running down his cheeks, a look of infinite sadness suffusing his face. "My only son. How am I going to tell his mother?"

"Maybe," I said, "the same way other fathers told their wives about the sons you killed." I was all out of sympathy for this animal. I put the muzzle of the gun to his head. "I can save you the trouble. I'll just kill you here."

"No."

"Who paid you to kill Wyatt?"

"I only heard one name."

"What?"

"Robert Brasillach."

"Spell it."

He did.

"Who's that?" I asked.

"He's the young man who came with the money."

"Who did he work for?"

"I don't know. We talked for a little while, but he was pretty drunk when he got here. He told me he came from Odessa."

"The city in Ukraine?"

"I think so. He had a foreign accent."

"Anything else?"

"He said he was rolling up ratlines when he got here. I think he was a sailor maybe."

"Why?"

"Because ratlines are what they call the steps on the rope ladders attached to the shrouds on sailboats."

I pointed the gun at him again. "You're holding out on me."

"No. I promise. I've told you everything I know."

I cocked the pistol, stepped forward and put the muzzle to his temple. Suddenly, he grabbed his chest, threw his head back, vomited, and died. Damn. The man had suffered a heart attack. That saved me from having to shoot him.

CHAPTER FOURTEEN

I stood there for a moment, looking down at the bodies. I was calm. The blood lust had come unbidden, taking over with such suddenness and with such overwhelming force that I was carried along, like a leaf in a raging current of anger. And then it was gone. Just as suddenly. I, Matt Royal, good guy, had just scared an old man to death. A mean, nasty piece of crap who had been responsible for more grief than I could imagine, but an old man, nevertheless.

The spirit gum had done its job. The mustache was still firmly attached to my lip. I hadn't touched anything, so my fingerprints wouldn't be in the room when the cops came. A careful search would probably turn up my DNA in the spit that had been knocked out of my mouth by the old man, but my DNA was not on file anywhere, and the only way I could be tied to the room was if I were arrested and the cops were trying to pin the deaths on me.

I picked up the hat and glasses, put them on, and left the suite, walking purposefully toward the elevator. I was sure there were security cameras somewhere, and I didn't want to look like the furtive Longboat Key lawyer that I was.

I went through the lobby, looking straight ahead, and out the door. I worked my way back to the rental Chevy and threw the windbreaker, pillow, and belt into the backseat. I exchanged the cowboy boots for running shoes. I sat in the car and used the spirit gum remover to get the mustache off my face. I drove south to 5th Street, headed west on the MacArthur Causeway to I-95, and drove north.

I left the Interstate in Hollywood, and rode through town looking for supermarkets that were still open. Every supermarket has a Dumpster outside, and they are emptied daily, usually the first thing in the morning before the store opens. I dropped each item of the disguise in a different Dumpster, and went back to I-95. I found a Holiday Inn Express and checked in, paying cash.

I didn't sleep well. I kept wondering if I would have shot Banchori if he hadn't had the heart attack. I'd wanted him dead, but I was still feeling the effects of killing Chardone. They weren't pleasant. I was a little more concerned about Dennis. I didn't know if he had been involved in his father's business, but he certainly knew about it. But I'd killed Dennis in self-defense. In fact, I hadn't meant to kill him at all. Just an unlucky, for him, blow to the neck. I'd probably crushed his larynx and caused him to choke to death. I could live with that.

I didn't understand a man like Banchori. He dealt in death like sane people deal in widgets. Bought and sold. No thought of the life he was taking. Yet, he was genuinely devastated by the death of his son. Could he not make the connection? Not understand that other people would love and grieve just as he did? Or, did he just not care?

I drifted off to sleep, and was awakened by the chime of my cell phone. I opened my eyes. Sunlight was drifting in under the drapes that covered the windows. I looked at my watch. Nine a.m. I rolled over and answered. It was Carl Merritt.

"Did you see Banchori last night?"

"No. I haven't gotten out of Sarasota yet." Another lie to a friend. "I'm headed your way today."

"I called you at home and got your answering machine."

"I'm not at home, Carl," I said pointedly. "I'm with a friend."

"Oh. Sorry. Well, you can save yourself a trip."

"Why?"

"Banchori died last night."

"Died?"

"Yeah. It looks like a heart attack, but we won't know for sure until the medical examiner gets finished. His scumbag son was in the room with him, and it looks like somebody beat him to death."

"I'll be damned."

"No great loss. The son was a stone-cold killer. He worked South Florida for the old man, but we could never get the proof to arrest him."

"Well, Banchori probably wouldn't have been much help anyway."

"Matt. Tell me why you wanted to see the guy."

"I wish I could, Carl. I can tell you it has to do with a civil case. It involved an investment that Banchori made. Nothing criminal. I just wanted to get his take on how my client handled the investment. I'd heard Banchori was a bad guy, and I couldn't find him the usual way, so I called you."

"Okay, Matt. Good talking to you." He hung up.

I got out of bed, showered, shaved, and drove back across the peninsula to Longboat Key.

CHAPTER FIFTEEN

Logan and I were on his balcony eating Chinese food. The sun had dropped into the Gulf of Mexico and a quarter moon was rising over the bay. The night was quiet. Now and then we heard the cry of a seabird that nested on the mangrove islands dotting the near edge of the bay.

I'd arrived at my condo a little after noon that day. I'd dropped the Chevy at the Sarasota-Bradenton airport and grabbed a taxi to the key. I spent some time in the afternoon searching the Internet for a sailor named Robert Brasillach. I called Logan, and he asked me over to share the huge amount of Chinese food he'd bought on St. Armand's Circle. We ate and sipped our beer as I told him what I'd learned and about my visit to Miami.

"So this killer named Rupert was really a New York City cop named Rudy Chardone?" he asked.

"Yeah. And a pervert."

"How could he get away with being a cop and a killer and a kiddy pornographer?"

"When you think about it, it's the perfect cover. Cop by day, killer by night. He was Banchori's Central Florida franchisee, I guess. The Fern Park apartment is probably his branch office. It was a place for him to go to ground when he was working in the area.

Logan chewed thoughtfully for a moment. "Who is Robert Brasillach?"

"I don't know. I Googled him, but the name only pops up as a French writer who collaborated with the Nazis and was executed by deGaulle at the end of World War II."

"Could it be his son?"

"I doubt it. I can't find any mention of Brasillach having children, and even if he had, the kid would be in his fifties now. Banchori said the guy who brought the money was a young man. And he wasn't French. Banchori said he was from Odessa. Probably Ukrainian, or maybe Russian."

"If he came in on a sailboat, he might not have been here legally."

"I thought of that. It doesn't really matter. There's no way for me to track anybody coming into the country. Besides, he may live here permanently. I'm afraid I've hit a brick wall."

"There's got to be a reason why somebody would kill Wyatt. A professional killer doesn't just take someone out by mistake. Plus, when you talked to him, Chardone knew you were Wyatt's friend. He hit the right target. But why?"

"That's what doesn't make sense. Maybe we're missing something. I'm going to go back through Wyatt's condo. See if there's anything the police missed."

"Not to change the subject, but I had a date last night," Logan said.

"A date?"

"Well, more than a date."

"A sleepover?"

"Yeah."

"Do I know the lucky lady?"

"Marie Phillips." He smiled smugly.

"You old dog. The widow Phillips. I'm impressed."

Marie Phillips was in her thirties, the widow of a man killed in a car wreck. She lived in a large condo on the south end of the key. When we'd met her, she was the administrative assistant to a man who later died as a result of some drug business gone bad. Marie, who had an MBA from the University of Florida, was not aware of the ugly side of her boss's business. She was cleared of any wrongdoing and now worked in administration at the Sarasota Memorial Hospital. I ran into her occasionally around the island.

"We've dated a few times," Logan said. "I didn't want to say anything, because I kept thinking she'd break it off. She didn't. Last night was the clincher. I think we're a couple." He grinned some more.

"Good for you both." I was happy for Logan. He'd been without a steady girlfriend for a long while. He'd date now and then, but he never found anybody he wanted to spend a lot of time with. Maybe things were looking up.

We spent the rest of the evening sitting on the balcony, talking quietly about absent friends, some who had died and others who had moved off the island. Wyatt came up occasionally, and we'd tell a funny story and worry some more with the problem of who ordered him killed, and why.

The wind shifted to the east, and the sound of music and laughter floated across the bay. Far out on the dark water, the brightly lit dinner cruise boat from the Seafood Shack was making its way north, headed back to the restaurant, full of sated diners enjoying their after-dinner drinks. It was a quiet night on the key, an autumn evening marked by good conversation with one of my two best friends.

We switched to good whiskey, Logan to Scotch and I to bourbon, sipping it neat, the evening winding down. Our lives were about to change drastically, but we didn't know it, couldn't have guessed it, and couldn't have altered the course of events if we had known.

CHAPTER SIXTEEN

My morning ritual is not complicated, but I'm kind of obsessive about it. I get up, turn on the coffee maker, pick up the daily newspaper from near the front door, and then sit on my sunporch overlooking the bay. I sip my coffee, read my paper, and enjoy the sunrise. It was no different on Thursday, the week after Wyatt's funeral.

My phone rang. I looked at my watch. Seven a.m. It was Wyatt's ex-wife Donna, a lawyer in Orlando. She'd spent the night of Wyatt's funeral in Logan's guest room, and left for Orlando the next morning, telling me that she would be out of pocket for a few days. Said she was going off somewhere to grieve.

"Hope I'm not calling too early," she said.

"Not at all, Counselor. How're you doing?"

"I'm fine. I've been in Atlanta with some friends. Trying to come to grips with Wyatt's death."

"Is it working?"

"Better than I would have thought. But, that's not why I'm calling. I just got into my office and in all the mail that's piled up while I've been gone, there was a package from Wyatt."

"What is it?"

"It's a data CD with notes on a project he was working on. He put a handwritten memo in it telling me that it was his only copy and that I should take good care of it, because he'd erased the data on his hard drive."

"What's the project?" I said.

"What I could retrieve is pretty bizarre. There were several files, but they were all corrupted somehow, except one. I'd like you to look at it and see what you think."

"Can you e-mail it to me?"

"It's on its way," she said, and hung up.

I finished my coffee and the newspaper, did the crossword puzzle, and took a shower. I put on clean clothes and fired up my computer. There was an e-mail from Donna with an attachment. I opened it and read the following:

> *Dick LaPlante*
> *Rene LaPlante*
> *Richard de Fresne*
> *Professor Paul Sauer-UF*
> *Klaus Blattner*
> *ICRC*
> *Organisation de ehemaligen SS-Angehörigen*
> *CBS – Zurich*
> *Alois Hudal*
> *Ratlines*
> *Genoa*
> *Buenos Aires*
> *Karlo Petranovic*
> *Augustin Barrere*
> *Klarsfeld, Beate & Serge*
> *Vichy*

I didn't recognize anything on the list except the name Dick La-Plante. I'd read about him in the newspapers. He was the richest man in Florida, and lived in the largest house on Casey Key, a nearby island known for its wealthy people and large homes. He was middle aged and had been married three or four times to trophy wives. It seemed that when a wife reached her mid-thirties, he dumped her and acquired another younger version. All the exes lived in lavish homes in the Sarasota area and appeared regularly in the society pages of the local newspapers.

LaPlante owned citrus groves, cattle ranches, citrus processing plants, and a fleet of cargo ships based at the Port of Tampa. He supported various politicians and wielded a lot of power in both Tallahassee and Washington.

I called Gwen Mooney. She had been the society editor of our island

weekly newspaper for so many years that she knew every socially prominent person in Southwest Florida, and everything about them.

"Do you know Dick LaPlante?" I asked.

"Sure."

"What can you tell me about him?"

"He's an asshole."

"That's all?"

"That about sums it up."

"Okay. Why do you think he's an asshole?"

"He marries and discards wives like most of us do old socks. Never
kept one long enough to have children. He's got more money than God,
and got it all from his old man. He always shows up at the charity events
during season, but he gives a whole lot less than he should. He sucks up
to politicians and gives them lots of money. I hear rumblings that if
Senator McKinley is elected president, LaPlante will be offered a cabinet
position. That's enough to make me vote for the senator's opponent, whoever that is. He's a leech. If his father hadn't hired good managers for the
businesses, Dick would have run them into the ground by now."

"What was his dad's name?"

"His name is René. He's still alive. Lives in one wing of that mansion
Dick built down on Casey Key. He's probably in his nineties now, but
sharp as a tack. I interviewed him a couple of years ago."

"So he's the one who made all the money."

"I'm not sure he made it. He's of French-Canadian heritage, but was
born in Vermont. His parents died when he was a boy, and he doesn't like
to talk about his childhood. His parents had a lot of real old money. They
came from two of the richest families in Canada. Rene was an American
Army officer in the Pacific during World War II, and he came to this area
shortly after the war was over. Married a local girl and settled down. He
had a lot of money and invested in lots of thing. He gave a bunch to
Jewish causes."

"Is he Jewish?"

"I guess. His wife's father was a rabbi in Sarasota."

"Why have I never heard of René?"

"He lived a quiet life. Didn't seek any publicity. His wife died while

Dick was in college, and when Dick graduated, he came back to the area and took over the family business. Dick loves the limelight, but he's an asshole."

"You mentioned that. Is there any chance Dick will make it to the cabinet?"

"The election is still two years off, but I hear a lot about McKinley. He comes from a wealthy family that can probably finance a campaign out of their own pockets. Only child, never did much but run for Congress and then the Senate. Married, but no children. Still in his forties."

I read her the other names on the list, but she didn't know any of them. I thanked her for her help, and hung up.

I called Donna, catching her at her office. "Did any of the names on that list mean anything to you?" I asked.

"No. I recognized the name 'Vichy' but I don't know if he meant the water or the town in France."

"What about Professor Sauer? Do you know him?"

"No. I'd guess he was a colleague of Wyatt's. Probably another history professor."

"Okay. I wish we had the rest of the files. Any chance of recovering the data from the disc?"

"I'm taking it to an expert this afternoon, but I'm not optimistic. Usually, when that stuff is corrupted, it's gone."

"Stay in touch, Donna. Don't be a stranger on Longboat."

"Bye, Matt."

I Googled Sauer, and found that he was a history professor at the University of Florida in Gainesville. I called the number of the history department, and a young-sounding woman answered. I identified myself and asked to speak to Professor Sauer.

"Ah, okay. May I say what this is in reference to?"

"It's personal."

"Hold, please."

I listened to the tinny sound of Beethoven on the local PBS station. Then a man with a deep voice picked up and said, "This is Doctor Spencer King. I'm head of the department. May I help you?"

"I'm trying to get in touch with Professor Sauer."

"Are you a friend of his?"

"Yes." I lied, but what was this all about? You'd think I was trying to talk to the governor.

"I'm sorry to tell you that Dr. Sauer has passed away."

"When?"

"A week ago Sunday."

The same day that Wyatt died.

"What happened?" I asked.

"He was working late in his office here at the department, and some-body shot him dead."

"A robbery?"

"The police don't think so. The only thing taken was the hard drive from Dr. Sauer's computer. Didn't even take the monitor or keyboard. Just ripped the drive out of the CPU."

"Did they catch the guy?"

"No, the police say they have no suspects."

"I'm sorry to hear that. May I ask if Dr. Sauer concentrated on any particular historical era?"

"I thought you were a friend of his."

"More of an acquaintance, really. We had a mutual friend. Dr. Laurence Wyatt."

"Sure. Down at UCF. I heard he died."

"Yes. I was calling to make sure that Dr. Sauer knew about Wyatt's death."

"ETO, W.W. two." King said.

"What?"

"Sauer's expertise was in the European Theater of Operations dur-ing World War II."

"Did he have anything to do with the Nazis?"

"If you mean did he study them, the answer is yes. He'd made a sub-specialty out of the study of particular Nazis, and what happened to them after the war."

"Thank you for your time," I said, and hung up.

Chardone would have had plenty of time to kill Wyatt and drive the three hours to Gainesville, have a leisurely lunch, do a little coed watching, and kill Sauer. I thought I knew where Chardone got the extra ten grand I found in his apartment.

CHAPTER SEVENTEEN

It was time to talk to Bill Lester. I called him at the police department and arranged to meet him for lunch at the Mar Vista, a restaurant clinging to the shore in the Village on the north end of the key. I asked Logan to join us. He was my sounding board, and I wanted him to hear as much as he could firsthand.

When I walked out of my condo, I was surprised at the coolness in the air. It wasn't so much cool as it was dry. The humidity had finally abandoned us a week or two later than usual. I decided to ride my bicycle the two miles to the restaurant.

The amiable hostess directed me to a table under the trees near the water and handed me a menu. I told her whom I was waiting for, and she said she'd send them over as soon as they arrived. I watched a commercial fishing boat chug south on the Intracoastal, a plume of black smoke emitting from the exhaust pipe that ran up the side of the pilothouse. A small tug pushing a barge with a construction crane on its deck passed slowly, heading north. The sun was high, the air cool under the trees. A fall day in Southwest Florida is hard to beat.

Logan and Bill arrived and pulled up chairs. The waitress brought us iced tea. We chatted about the fishing, or lack thereof, the stone crabs that had just come into season, and gossiped a bit about our friends on the key. Bill told us that some benefactor had anonymously mailed the library twenty thousand dollars in cash. "Some of our people have more money than sense," he said. "There're a lot of sticky fingers between the mail box and the library."

When we ran out of small talk, I said, "Bill, a University of Florida professor named Paul Sauer was killed on the same day as Wyatt; shot to death in his office. He was a historian, and his name was on some papers Wyatt left. I'm wondering if there's a connection. Can you check with Gainesville PD?"

"I got some interesting calls just this morning," Lester said. "A New York City cop was shot to death over near Orlando last week. The Seminole County detectives working the case found a .45 in his apartment, and when they ran the ballistics through the national data bank, they found our entry and one from the murder at UF. It looks like the gun killed both Wyatt and the professor in Gainesville."

"What was a New York cop doing with the murder weapon?" Logan asked.

"That's very interesting. The dead guy's name was Michael Rupert. There were credit card receipts in the apartment and a post office box in Rupert's name. When the detectives checked with the credit card company, they found charges at a restaurant here on the key for the night before Wyatt's murder, and another from a barbeque joint in Gainesville the day of the murder there. Then, somebody anonymously sends the lead detective a computer hard drive with pictures showing Rupert and the New York cop, a guy named Rudy Chardone, having sex with young children. The pictures were e-mailed back and forth from Rupert's computer to Chardone's in New York, but the funny thing is that the pictures of Chardone and Rupert were of the same person. NYPD confirmed that it was Chardone. Apparently, he wanted the pictures on both his computer at home and the one in Florida. The guy was a pervert, and the working theory is that he was moonlighting as a hit man."

"So, you think he killed Wyatt?" I said.

"It looks that way."

"Why? Does anybody have any ideas as to why?"

"Sorry, Matt. That seems to be a dead end."

"Do they know who killed the hit man?"

"No," said Lester, "but the cleaning lady told the detectives that a man had been asking about Rupert the day he was killed. Described the guy as nondescript, but he may have been a cop. He showed her a badge."

I was not at all flattered by the description, but I liked the idea that Tammy couldn't really identify me. "Why would a cop kill him?"

"Maybe because Chardone was a bad cop, or maybe his killer wasn't a cop at all. Used a .38. You've got a .38, don't you Matt?"

"Yep. A brand-new one."

"I thought you'd had one for a number of years."

"I did, but I lost it in that fracas down in the keys a couple of months ago. Was anything taken from Sauer's office? Was it a robbery gone bad?"

"The only thing missing was the hard drive from his computer."

"Just like at Wyatt's."

"Yeah."

We finished our lunch, and the chief went back to work. Logan and I sat and enjoyed the weather and ordered a beer.

"I didn't like that question about your .38," said Logan.

"Neither did I. I've got to be very careful here. Bill Lester's a good friend, but he's also a cop. I hate being on the wrong side."

Cracker Dix came over and asked if the information he'd given me turned out to be any good. I told him to have a seat.

"Cracker," I said, "Logan knows what you did about the credit card information from that guy Rupert, and we both appreciate it. Unfortunately, it was a dead end. Either the deaf girl misunderstood Rupert or he was talking about some other Wyatt. He turned out to be an accountant from Jacksonville."

I didn't like lying to Cracker. He was a good friend who'd helped me out in the past, but I didn't want that kind of gossip going around the island. Ours is like many small towns. Secrets are hard to keep, and I wouldn't want anybody to ever tie me to Rupert/Chardone or to his death. Particularly after the question about the pistol from Chief Lester.

After Cracker left, I showed Logan a copy of the list from Wyatt's disc. "Does any of this mean anything to you?" I asked.

He took a moment to peruse it. "Not really. I know who Dick La-Plante is, or at least who the papers say he is. I used to look for his picture in the society pages just to see what was falling out of the dress of the woman he was with."

"You're a pervert yourself."

"I know. I like it that way."

"How's Marie?"

"I talked to her this morning. She misses me. We're going to dinner tonight. I think I'm smitten."

"Smitten?"

"Yeah, smitten."

"Is that like being in heat?"

"Exactly like it. Only those of us who are more highly evolved prefer 'smitten' to 'horny.'"

"Whatever. Let's have another beer." And that's what we did.

CHAPTER EIGHTEEN

I threw my bike into the back of Logan's convertible, and we drove south toward my condo. Traffic was picking up, and I saw two car carriers along the side of Gulf of Mexico Drive. They were bringing the snowbirds' cars down while the owners came by plane. Pretty soon, traffic would be heavy. Our island swells from about 2,500 people in the summer to 25,000 in the winter. It's a trial, but the cold weather in the North brings a lot of old friends back to paradise.

Logan said, "I don't get the connection between Sauer and Wyatt. You got any ideas?"

"None. Donna didn't know him, and I never heard of him, so he and Wyatt probably weren't real friendly. Maybe just colleagues."

"But why would the same person kill Sauer and Wyatt, and on the same day?"

"I'm guessing that the timing of both murders was so that one victim wouldn't find out about the other and go to the police with whatever he knew. But who knows?"

"These guys were both history professors," said Logan. "Maybe the names on that list have some historical significance. Why don't you call Austin Dwyer? He might recognize something."

Austin Dwyer was a retired history professor at a small college in Connecticut. Logan and I had met him in the Florida Keys earlier in the year and formed a friendship. If he didn't know who the people on the list were, he might be able to tell us the name of somebody who would.

"Good idea, Logan. I often underestimate you."

I e-mailed Austin, attaching the list, and asked him to see if any of it made sense to him. I gave him my cell phone number and asked him to call. Minutes later, I got an automatic response telling me that Austin would be away until Friday and that he would respond then.

I searched the Internet for the names on the list, but what little information I found made no sense to me. I'd have to wait to hear from Austin.

I was at loose ends. I paced my living room trying to put the puzzle together. The pieces didn't fit. None of the information I had so far fit together in any coherent pattern.

I gave up and turned to more mundane things. My Explorer had been hard to start the past couple of days. The starter would drag and almost die before catching. I probably needed a new battery. It was also time for an oil change and a brake job. I called the shop I used on Cortez Road and made an appointment for the work. The manager said he'd have one of his men pick the car up the next morning.

I needed to clear my head. A jog on the beach, a shower, and a nap finished off my afternoon, and I drove down to the Hilton. There is always a gathering of locals on Thursday evening at the outside bar. Logan was on the mainland having dinner with Marie, and I needed a little company.

Billy Brugger, the long-time bartender, poured me a Miller Lite, shook my hand, and said, "I understand you've been asking around about Dick LaPlante."

"Are there no secrets on this island?"

"Nope."

"Where did you hear that?"

"Dora Walters over at the paper told me you had an interest in LaPlante. Said Gwen Mooney told her you were asking about him."

"Not so much an interest as curiosity. His name showed up on a list I found in Wyatt's stuff, and I wondered what the connection was."

"I know the guy. He's an asshole."

"There seems to be a consensus on that."

"He's been in here a couple of times. Always with a different woman. He treats the staff like they were his personal servants, and he doesn't tip worth a damn. When the manager asked him to be nice, he threatened to buy the hotel and fire us all. A real asshole."

"Anything else?"

"He speaks French. Last time he was here, he was talking to his date in French. A couple of our regular snowbirds from Quebec were here and said he was fluent."

"His dad's French-Canadian."

"But the snowbirds said he was speaking with a Parisian accent."

CHAPTER NINETEEN

I was up early on Friday morning, sitting on the sunporch with my coffee and newspaper. Low dark clouds hung over the bay. The wind was blowing from the north, hard enough to kick up whitecaps on the gray water. A sailboat was motoring south, its sails furled, a lone helmsman wearing bright yellow wet gear hunkered over the wheel. Not a pleasant day for boating.

I went to answer the knock on the front door. It was a young man, mid-twenties maybe, wearing jeans and a work shirt with the name of the auto shop sewn over the right breast pocket. His name, Jimmy, was above the left pocket. I gave him my car keys and went back to my paper.

The morning quiet was ruptured by an explosion. My first thought was incoming artillery, but then I realized where I was. Home, not a war zone. My second thought was that a boat in the marina had exploded. But the noise had come from the parking lot. I ran to my front door, which overlooked the lot. The first thing I saw was the smoldering remains of my Explorer.

The car parked next to mine, a Buick with Alabama plates, was burning, flames eating the interior, the paint cracking and peeling, glass blown out. I knew it belonged to an Episcopal priest named Ben Alford. He and his wife, Lynn, were visiting from Wetpumpka and were supposed to leave that morning for home. I saw an airline ticket in their future. Father Ben would not be pleased.

My neighbors were coming out of their apartments, some still in pajamas. They milled about on the walkway, talking, worrying, wondering whose car it was that blew up. I'd backed into a guest parking space away from the building the night before, because I wanted the mechanic to have easy access to the car in case he had to jump-start it. Had I been in my regular place, we'd have lost part of the building. Pieces of the car were strewn across the lot. I saw no sign of Jimmy and knew he was dead, blown to bits by an explosion powerful enough to destroy an SUV.

I hadn't really known Jimmy, but I'd seen him around the shop when I took my car in for service. He was always polite, and I was vaguely aware that he had a wife and a child. He should not have died on a drab morning in an empty parking lot. And his death was my fault; not directly, but a result of my obsession with Wyatt's killers. I would have to live with that, but how would I explain to his son or daughter that Daddy had been killed because I was seeking vengeance?

The death of a man I hardly knew brought the same exquisite pain that I had associated with Wyatt's death. Now I had another reason to get the bastards who killed Wyatt. That reason's name was Jimmy.

I heard sirens in the distance, getting louder as they got closer. Moments later, two fire trucks and an ambulance wheeled into the parking lot, a police cruiser behind them. I took the elevator to the ground floor and walked over to the cop who was standing alone, watching the firefighters, a confused look on his face. I knew him.

"Steve," I said as I approached, "that was my car. There was a young guy from the auto shop over on Cortez driving it. You've probably got a murder scene here."

"Shit. I'd better call the chief."

I left him while he made calls on his cell phone. The firefighters had doused the car with water and were now packing up their equipment. One was stringing crime-scene tape about the remains of the Explorer. "Is this your car?"

"Was," I said. "There's probably a body in there. Young guy from the auto shop."

"I know. I saw parts of him. I've called the fire marshal and my chief. They'll want to talk to you."

I gave him my name and apartment number and went back upstairs to my coffee. I was shaken. The bomb was obviously meant for me. Why?

And who? Had somebody figured out my role in Chardone's death and taken revenge? I didn't see how that could be. I'd covered my tracks very well.

I knew Chief Bill Lester would arrive soon. I put another pot of coffee on and went back to the walkway that ran in front of my condo. I stood at the rail and watched the police and fire personnel. They mostly just stood around, talking quietly. Many of my neighbors had moved into the parking lot and were standing in clumps, talking and watching the activity. In a few minutes, I saw Bill Lester pull up in his unmarked car. He talked briefly to his officer and then started toward the building. He saw me and waved.

He got off the elevator and shook my hand. "You okay, Matt?"

"Yeah. I guess. Somebody meant that bomb for me."

"Without a doubt. Let's go inside and talk."

"Fresh coffee's brewing."

"Good. I need it."

We sat in my living room, drinking coffee and talking. "Who wants you dead?" asked Bill.

"I don't know of anybody." I was telling the truth.

"I've called in Manatee County. They'll handle the murder investigation and the state will look into the arson angle."

Longboat Key is about ten miles long and divided in the middle by the county line. The northern half is part of Manatee County, and the southern end lies in Sarasota County. The Longboat Key Police Department was very professional, and that was one of the reasons crime was an anomaly on our island. When the rare major crime did occur, the county sheriff was called in to investigate. The deputies worked for the sheriff, but reported to Bill Lester.

"Is this connected to Wyatt's death?" he asked.

"Bill, I've got no idea. Maybe it was mistaken identity."

"I don't think so. You own the only Explorer in this complex. Anybody smart enough to put that bomb together isn't stupid enough to make that kind of mistake."

"You're probably right. But I can't think of any reason anyone would want to kill me."

"Alcohol, Tobacco, and Firearms is coming in to look at the mess. Maybe they'll find some sort of signature. Bombers tend to use the same technique, and the ATF boys can usually find a connection between bombings. We'll see what turns up. In the meantime, you need to be careful."

CHAPTER TWENTY

I was responsible for young Jimmy's death. Not directly, but I must have gotten too close to somebody, and now they were trying to kill me. They'd gotten Jimmy instead. The army called it collateral damage, but that wouldn't be much comfort to the young man's family. He was still dead.

I called Logan's cell phone.

"Somebody just tried to blow me up."

"What?"

"Somebody put a bomb in my car last night."

"Are you all right?"

"Yeah, but the kid from the auto repair shop was killed."

"Shit. I'm on my way."

"Where are you?"

"At Marie's."

"Stay there. I'm fine."

"She's about to leave for work. I'll be at your place in ten minutes."

I could always count on Logan. He'd have been on his way to me even if Marie were still naked in bed begging him to stay.

My phone rang just as I hung up. It was Austin Dwyer.

"Matt, that's strange company you're hanging around with."

"What do you mean?"

"Most of the people on the list you sent me are Nazis. Or at least, they were. They're all dead now. The Klarsfelds are still alive. They're French Nazi hunters. They've spent most of their lives bringing old Nazis to justice."

"Nazis?"

"Yes. As in Germany, Third Reich, all that."

"Shit." I told him about the list, Wyatt's and Sauer's murders, and that the only thing the killer had taken out of Wyatt's apartment was his laptop. I also told him that Sauer's hard drive was missing from his computer. "I thought the list might be a lead to who killed them and why."

"There is an interesting coincidence to the names on the list. Most of the people were involved in the ratlines."

"Ratlines? Isn't that something on a sailboat?"

"I think so, but in this case it's a reference to escape routes the Nazis used to get out of Europe after the war. Are you familiar with ODESSA?"

"The city?"

"No, the *Organisation de ehemaligen SS-Angehörigen,* which translates as the Association of Former SS Officers."

"Yeah. They were part of the effort to get their people out of Europe."

"Right. But, they weren't as big a deal as some people believe. Actually, there were a number of ratlines. Some were run out of Italy by priests. One of the names on that list was an Argentinean bishop who was involved in getting Nazis out of Europe and into Argentina. Several of the names on the list were Croatian priests who had moved to Italy and were involved in getting the members of the Ustashi, the Croatian Nazis, to South America."

"What in the world does that have to do with a couple of history professors getting wacked?"

"Maybe nothing. On the other hand, there're still people around who believe in that master race crap spewed by the Nazis. And some of the Nazis are still alive. Every now and then, one turns up in Argentina, or even in the U.S. France recently prosecuted one of their Nazis, and Italy tried one of theirs for war crimes a year or so ago."

"Do you think Wyatt was onto something dealing with old Nazis?"

"Could be," said Austin. "The ones who're still alive are pretty well hidden. Maybe Wyatt came across some information that would bring some of them out of the shadows."

"Sauer was a specialist in World War II and particularly the Nazis and what happened to them after the war."

"That may be your key, Matt. If Wyatt and Sauer were collaborating, it might have to do with those old Nazis. Did Wyatt concentrate on a particular historical period?"

"Pretty much on the diplomatic history of the period between the World Wars."

"Then between them, they'd be able to cover a lot of the history that impacts us today. Those were bad times."

"Where can I find out more about the people from that time?"

"There are archives in Germany that have detailed records of the people who were involved in the Nazi party and the death camps. They're pretty well indexed now, but you'd have to have a researcher who knew what he was doing to understand them. And, you're not likely to get into them unless you know some strings to pull. They're pretty much restricted to historians, and then only to a small group who study that period of time."

"Do you know anybody who could help?"

"Afraid not. The first hurdle is getting into the archives. And, don't forget, the records are all in German."

"Thanks, Austin. You've been a big help."

"I hope so. Let me know if you need anything else." He hung up.

Logan knocked on my door and came in. "I had to park out on the road and walk in. The parking lot's full of police and firefighters. I don't think your car's drivable." He smiled, taking some of the sting out of the morning's events. "You look like shit. Again."

"That kid Jimmy from the auto shop. I got him killed, Logan."

"No, you didn't. Some asshole was trying to kill you and got the kid instead."

"It was my fault."

"How do you figure that?"

"If I hadn't gotten involved in this thing, nobody would be trying to kill me."

"You don't know that. It might be somebody from your past."

"I don't think so, Logan. If it were, why would they wait until now to take their shot? Too much of a coincidence."

"And you never liked coincidences."

"I don't believe in them."

"You can't undo what's done."

"Ah, more New England wisdom. That doesn't help."

"Look, Matt. You've got to stop beating yourself up. Let's find the bomber and square things for Jimmy's murder."

"You're right. I'll call his family. Offer condolences. That's about all I can do."

I told him about my conversation with Austin. "If Chardone hadn't taken the computers, I wouldn't think there was a connection between the list and the murders. But there must be a link of some kind. Why else would Wyatt have sent the disc to Donna? Why would the killer take the computers? What was in there that he didn't want anybody else to know?"

"Too bad the other files Wyatt sent Donna were corrupted. They might have told us something."

"You can bet on it."

"What now?"

"I did a computer search of some of the names on the list. It didn't make sense to me at the time, because most of the ones I could find had to do with Nazis. I couldn't make any kind of connection, but after talking to Austin I think they may have all been involved in smuggling Nazis out of Europe."

"What's that got to do with Wyatt?"

"I have no idea."

"Where do we go from here?"

"I need to talk to someone who has access to the German archives from the war. Maybe there's some connection between Wyatt, Sauer and, the people on the list. I've got an old friend in Germany who may be able to help."

It was not yet mid-morning, mid-afternoon in Germany. I called the American Embassy in Berlin, and asked to speak to General Burke Winn, the military attaché. The operator told me that the general was not in the embassy, but that she would put me through to somebody who could help me.

"Marine detachment, Master Sergeant Tom Butner speaking, sir."

"My name is Matthew Royal," I said. "I'm trying to get hold of General Winn. I was told that you could help me."

"I'm sorry, sir, but the general is at the consulate in Frankfurt this week and next. You can probably reach him there on Monday. I know he's in meetings in Cologne today, but he's due back in Frankfurt on Monday."

"Thank you, Master Sergeant." I closed my phone.

I explained to Logan that Burke Winn and I had served together in Vietnam. He'd stayed in the army, and I knew that he was presently posted to Berlin as the military attaché. He'd been there for a couple of years, and I was pretty sure he'd have some contacts that could get me into Germany's World War II archives. Maybe I could pick up a trail there.

"I'm going to Germany," I said.

"When?"

"Burke's due back in the office on Monday. If I leave here Sunday afternoon, I'll be in Frankfurt the next morning."

"Do you think that'll do any good?"

"It can't do any harm."

CHAPTER TWENTY-ONE

When you travel by Delta Airlines, you always change in Atlanta. It's a rule etched in stone somewhere. My flight from Tampa to Atlanta was uneventful. I took the tram across Hartsfield-Jackson airport to the international terminal, did the customs thing, and boarded the 757 that would take me to Germany. It was late afternoon, and with the time change, the nine-hour flight would get me to Frankfurt a little before eight the next morning.

I settled into my business-class seat and was reviewing the safety placard when I sensed someone standing over me. I looked up into the blue eyes of a tall blonde flight attendant.

"Hey, soldier," she said, "looking for a good time in Frankfurt?"

"The only problem I can see with that is that you'd never be satisfied again with Russ.

She laughed. "I didn't know you were flying with us."

Patti Coit and her husband, Russ, lived in the Village on Longboat Key. He was a pilot, and both worked for Delta. They were old friends of mine, and it was just happenstance that I ended up on her flight.

"Just made the reservation yesterday. Kind of an unplanned trip. How's Russ?"

"He's fine. He's in the cockpit tonight."

"Does he know how to fly this thing?"

"Probably not, but these new planes are so automated a monkey can fly them. Russ's job is to keep the monkey happy."

I laughed. "Well, don't distract him."

"Russ or the monkey?"

"Neither."

"I haven't seen you since Wyatt's funeral. Are you holding up okay?"

"I'm fine, thanks."

"Are you taking a vacation?"

"No. I've got to see an old friend tomorrow afternoon in Frankfurt. Somebody tried to kill me yesterday, and I'm hoping my friend can help me unravel this mess."

"Tried to kill you? My God, Matt, what happened?"

I told her about the car bombing and that the police had no idea of who was responsible.

"I'm glad you're okay. Russ and I were in Hawaii until yesterday. We didn't even go home. Came straight to Atlanta to go back to work. Why would anyone want to kill you?"

"I'm beginning to wonder if it had something to do with Wyatt's death."

"What's the connection to Frankfurt?"

"An old army buddy is there, and I'm hoping he can put me in touch with some people who can get me into the World War II archives dealing with France under the German occupation."

"The Vichy Regime?"

"Yeah. Do you know anything about that period?"

"Some," she said, "but that's only because a friend from college did a doctoral dissertation on Vichy. She about drove me nuts talking about it. She works for the embassy in Paris, but she's in Frankfurt tomorrow. Russ and I are going to have lunch with her. Why don't you join us?"

I accepted the invitation, and Patti went about the cabin taking care of her passengers. My mind kept wandering back to Jimmy Griner, the kid who was killed in my blown-up car. He had a wife and a young son. I had talked to his wife and then I called his parents. I told them that it was my car Jimmy was in. I assured them that I didn't know who was responsible, but I was going to do my damndest to find out. I wanted to see some justice for their boy.

Nine hours is a long time to be cooped up in a plane, but I made the best of it. I dozed on and off during the trip, and at some point Russ came back and sat with me for a few minutes. I told him about the bomb and that

I was hoping to find out something in Germany. We chatted about our friends on the key, and in a few minutes I shooed him back to the cockpit. I was worried about him leaving the monkey alone.

Frankfurt is a large and bustling city, the commercial hub of the resurgent Germany. Its airport is one of the busiest in the world, but we cleared customs with a minimum of fuss. The blustery cold of November in central Germany hit us as we stepped out of the terminal. We grabbed a taxi to the small hotel where Delta put up its crews on layovers, across the street from the main train station.

I took an hour's nap, showered, shaved, and dressed in slacks, a long-sleeve shirt, and a heavy jacket. I met the Coits in the lobby, and we walked the three blocks to a small restaurant tucked between mid-rise office buildings.

We entered the vestibule, the steam heat hitting us with warm air. A woman stood with her back to us, talking to the hostess in German. She turned, a grin breaking out on her face, and stepped quickly to hug Patti and then Russ. She was beautiful; mid-thirties, five seven or so, dark hair framing her face and hanging to her shoulders, light makeup, slender with enough roundness to catch my interest. She wore a gray skirt, navy blue sweater, and low-heel pumps. A single gold chain hung from her neck, a small dolphin at the end nestled between her breasts. She took my breath away.

"Matt Royal," said Patti, "this is Jessica Connor. Jess knows everything there is to know about Vichy France."

"Well, almost everything," said Jess, and displayed a smile that made me fear that I was going to faint. I'm not kidding.

We were shown to a table, and Patti explained that I was a friend from home and why I was in Europe. "I told him you did your doctoral dissertation on the Vichy government. Matt," she said turning to me, "did I mention that Jess is fluent in both German and French?"

Jessica took a sip of her wine. "Why do you think your friend's murder had anything to do with a bunch of Fascists who've been dead for more than half a century?"

"Wyatt was a historian," I said, "and he was working on something that had to do with Vichy. He was in contact with another history professor at the University of Florida who was murdered the same day as Wyatt. The only thing we have concerning his research is a list of names."

I handed her a copy of the list. "I'm told that many of these people were involved in the Vichy government and others were Croatian Fascists. Some of them were priests and others were Argentines. Somehow, they all relate back to Vichy, and I think if I can put the lines together, I might be able to figure out why Wyatt was killed."

"What brings you to Frankfurt?"

"An old army buddy of mine is a general and is the military attaché to Germany. He's been working out of the consulate here for the past couple of weeks, and I'm hoping he can get me into the German archives dealing with Vichy."

"Maybe I can help," Jess said. "I don't have to be back in Paris until Monday."

"I'd really appreciate it, Jess."

"I'm staying at the Intercontinental. Call me after you've seen the general. We'll have dinner."

We finished our meal as Patti and Jessica reminisced about their college days. Russ rolled his eyes a couple of times, but otherwise seemed content to sit and listen to stories he'd heard dozens of times. I was content just to sit and watch Jess.

I asked the Coits to join Jess and me for dinner that night, but they had to be rested for the flight back to Atlanta the next day. They begged off and went back to the hotel. I put Jess in a taxi, and got another for myself. I gave the driver the address of the consulate on Giessner Strasse and sat back in the seat, visions of Jessica ruining my concentration on the scenery passing by.

CHAPTER TWENTY-TWO

I showed my passport to the Marine guard at the door of the Consulate and told him I was looking for the military attaché's office. He directed me down a hall and up some stairs. I found it easily enough. The door was open and I walked in.

A young man wearing a U.S. army uniform sat at a receptionist desk. The epaulets of his long-sleeve green shirt held a small brass insignia, indicating the rank of sergeant. The black plastic name tag over his right breast pocket bore his surname, Olenski. He was working at his computer, intent on the monitor screen.

I cleared my throat and got his attention. He looked up from the screen and said, "Can I help you, sir?"

"I hope so. I'm looking for a raggedy-assed corporal named Burke Winn."

He looked a little surprised and discomfited. "I'm sorry, sir. The military attaché is a brigadier general named Burke Winn. I never heard of a corporal by that name."

"Would you be kind enough to ask the general if he knows a raggedy-assed corporal named Burke Winn?"

"Sir, I don't think that would be appropriate."

"Son, I think you're going to get a major league ass chewing if I leave here without that question being asked."

"May I tell the general your name, sir?"

"Matthew Royal."

The sergeant picked up the phone and punched two buttons. "Sir," he said into the receiver, "there's a gentleman here inquiring as to whether you know, and I'm quoting sir, a raggedy-assed corporal named Burke Winn."

The sergeant was silent for a beat, then, "Says his name's Matthew Royal, sir." He pulled the phone from his ear, stared briefly at the receiver, a puzzled look on his face, and hung up.

The door to the inner office burst open, and out strode a man in army green, wearing his uniform tie and jacket with one silver star on each epaulet. The area above his left breast pocket held eight rows of ribbons, topped by the Combat Infantry Badge. Paratrooper wings were pinned to the pocket flap. He had a unit patch on his left sleeve that I didn't recognize, with a ranger tab over it. His right sleeve, the one on which a patch designating the unit with which he served in combat would appear, had the patch of the Army Special Forces, the storied Green Berets. He was about five foot ten and probably weighed two hundred pounds. It looked like all muscle. He had shaved his head completely bald, and I could see a fringe of a day's growth of stubble bordering the crown. He had a grin on his face.

"Matt, you old hound dog. God, it's good to see you."

He grabbed me in a bear hug, lifted me off my feet, set me down, and kissed me square on the cheek. "Sergeant," he asked, "do you know who this frigging civilian is?"

"No, sir."

"This is the former Lieutenant Matthew Royal, who had the honor of being my commanding officer when I was but a raggedy-assed corporal. He pulled that ass out of the fire on more than one occasion. I left the Nam, and the next week he got his ass shot off. Just couldn't do it without me."

"I didn't even want to try, Sergeant," I said, glancing at the young soldier.

The general turned serious. "Ski, this guy won the Distinguished Service Cross in his last firefight. You know what that is?"

"Yes, sir. The second highest award for valor the army gives."

"Right you are, Sergeant. And then he and a beat-up old major named Wyatt pulled some strings and got me into West Point. Without them, you'd no doubt be working for some candy ass who'd never seen a war. You owe this man, Ski."

"Yes, sir. I rightly do. As I understand it, sir, because of Mr. Royal, I get to work for a raggedy-ass corporal."

"Don't forget I'm a general and you're a sergeant, and generals are supposed to be shown respect by sergeants."

"Yes, sir," Olenski said, and winked at me.

Winn grabbed my arm and said, "Come on back, Matt. Let's do some catching up."

I hadn't talked to Burke since he was at West Point. I went up for his graduation and commissioning. Wyatt was there, too, and we wet him down like a new officer deserved. Lots of booze and plenty of war stories. Then, I'd let him drift away, just as I'd done with most of the people from that period of my life. I've often wondered if it was because the war memories always involved dead soldiers — some of them my soldiers — the ones I couldn't save. And the fact that those memories were just too painful to relive.

Wyatt kept up with many of his soldiers, and I knew that he and Burke had maintained a correspondence over the years. Wyatt would always tell me when he'd heard from Burke. I knew he'd been promoted to brigadier general just a few months before. And I knew that Wyatt had kept Burke up to date on my life.

Burke's office was less impressive than I would have expected. There was room for a large executive desk and chair, a credenza, and two side chairs. A sofa took up one wall. As I sat in one of the side chairs, I saw on the credenza a framed picture of three soldiers in battle dress, holding M-16s. They were ragged and dirty, and very young, and I could tell by the way they held their bodies that they were exhausted.

Burke pointed at it. "Remember that?"

I peered more closely. It was a picture of Wyatt, Burke, and me. I remembered the day it was taken. We had just come out of the bush after a patrol that lasted several days and included a couple of firefights with North Vietnamese regulars. It was Burke's last day in the jungle. He was heading home that evening with orders to report to the United States Military Academy at West Point.

Burke picked up the photograph, a serious look on his face. "The day this picture was taken Wyatt told me that I'd be a general one day, and that I should always remember when I was but a raggedy-ass corporal. He said it'd make me a better officer. That picture has been with me at every step of the way."

"Wyatt's dead," I said.

Burke leaned back in his chair. He put his hand to his eyes and groaned quietly in anguish. "No. Not Wyatt. What happened?"

"Some sonovabitch shot him in the back of the head."

"Any idea who?"

"I know who. A rogue cop named Chardone. He won't be executing anybody else."

"You took care of it, L.T.?" he asked, using the nickname the troops had for fresh lieutenants.

"I did."

"Thank you. Do you know why he was killed?"

"No. That's the reason I'm here. I'm chasing a theory. If I'm right, I'll know why, and I'll know who ordered the hit."

"And then there will be justice."

"Yes. Legally if I can, and if not, jungle justice will be done. One way or the other, I'll take Wyatt's revenge on the bastards who killed him."

"What can I do, Matt?"

I told General Burke Winn everything that had happened from the moment Wyatt had been killed. I told him everything I had found out about the people I thought were behind his murder. And I told him that when I had the package all tied up neatly, payment would be exacted.

The general leaned over his desk, his face an impassive mask. "There's a man named Thomas Speer who lives in Dusseldorf. He works for the German federal government and is in charge of the SS archives that survived the bombings. When the federal government moved to Berlin, they left the archives in Bonn. It almost takes an act of Congress to get into the archives, but Speer is in charge, and he's an old friend of mine. I'll make a call and arrange for you to meet Speer. The bigger problem is that most of the documents are in German and the others are in French. You'll need a translator."

"I've got one."

"I'll call you after I talk to Speer. I've known him for years. He's married to an American named Kim, who was my wife's roommate at Catholic University."

We reminisced some, mostly about Wyatt, and I gave Burke my cell phone number. He had a diplomatic party that night and couldn't join Jessica and me for dinner.

I left the consulate and decided to walk a bit. It was a crisp fall day, the temperature hovering in the low fifties. I headed south on Giessener Strasse. I would walk until I got tired, and then find a taxi. I crossed Marbachweg and walked along a wooded area that bordered a large cemetery. As Giessner Strasse crossed Marbachweg, it became a four-lane thoroughfare, divided by a grassy median. The traffic was heavy in both directions, and the exhaust fumes of diesel busses tingled my nose. I heard a horn blowing behind me, a long, loud blast. I looked over my shoulder and saw a black Mercedes moving slowly in the outside lane, the one nearest the curb. A large truck had slowed behind the car, the frustrated driver laying on his air horn, gesturing angrily at the driver ahead of him. I saw a rifle barrel poke out of the open passenger window of the Mercedes, drawing a bead on me. I didn't think. I just dove headfirst into the shrubbery along the sidewalk, rolling further into the forest as I heard the crack of the slug rend the air above my head.

The sound of the accelerating car reached me as I rolled to a stop. I crawled to the edge of the bushes and peeked out. The car and the truck were gone. Traffic was flowing smoothly, the drivers unaware that murder stalked the road.

I brushed myself off and walked back to the corner, keeping the row of trees between the road and me. I hailed a taxi and had him drop me off at the main train station. I mingled with the crowd, trying to see if I was being followed. I couldn't spot a tail, but that didn't mean one wasn't there. I didn't think the shooting was random. Drive-by shootings were part of the American culture, not the German. Somebody knew I was in Frankfurt, and had followed me. That meant that they knew where I was staying.

I pulled out the key to my hotel room, found the phone number, and dialed it on my cell. I asked the concierge to go to my room and bring my bag to the reception desk. I hadn't yet unpacked, so there was nothing to do except retrieve the one suitcase. Somebody would pick it up later. I told him to put the charge for the day on my credit card.

I put in another call to Houston; to Jock Algren. Jock was my life-long friend, closer than a brother since we were in junior high school. He was an operative of our government's most secretive agency; part spy, part assassin when needed, and still on the job, although only part-time.

"Jock," I said, "I'm in Frankfurt, Germany. Long story. I need a weapon."

"What the hell's going on?"

"I'll fill you in later. But I'm trying to find out who killed Wyatt, and now somebody's trying to kill me. I need some protection. Can you help?"

"What do you want?"

"Probably a .38 snub-nosed. I need something small that will work close in."

"I can take care of it, but you know if you get caught in Europe with a gun, you'll go to jail."

"I know. It's a chance I'll have to take. I also need some cash. I don't trust my credit cards."

"Meet my man tomorrow at noon at the Dornbuscher Bierstube on Schifferstrasse. Cross the river on the pedestrian bridge called the Eisen-ersteg, turn right for a block and then left on Schifferstrasse. The Dorn-busher is in the third building on your left."

"How'll I know your man?"

"He'll know you." The phone went dead.

CHAPTER TWENTY-THREE

I was worried about my friends. If somebody wanted me badly enough, they might take a run at Patti, Russ, or Jessica. I called Russ and told him what had happened, and why I was concerned. He said that he and Patti were tired, and would eat in the hotel that evening. They'd take the crew bus to the airport the next morning, and be on their way back to Atlanta.

I called Jessica and filled her in. "I don't know how serious this is," I said, "but I don't think the shot taken at me was random. Somebody might try to use you to find me."

"I'll check out of here and come meet you."

"No. Pack your bags and leave them in the room. Walk out the door and get a cab. Make it look like you're going out for the evening. Have the cabbie bring you to the main train station. I'll meet you by the bank in the terminal. I'll make sure nobody's following you, and then we'll decide what to do from there. Give me your cell phone number."

I loitered around a kiosk that sold bratwurst and beer, sipping on a drink and nibbling the sausage. A side door leading out of the terminal was a few feet behind me. I had a clear view to the bank. I'd turned up the collar on my coat and was wearing a jaunty fedora I'd picked up in one of the shops. I'd pulled the brim of the hat low on my forehead. It was rush hour, people leaving the city for their homes in the suburbs. I was virtually invisible.

I saw Jessica when she entered the terminal and walked up to the bank entrance. She stood for a moment, looking around, puzzled that I wasn't there. I called her cell phone, watched her dig it out of her purse, answer it.

"Don't look around," I said. "I see you. I want you to just stand there for a minute or two and make sure you're alone. Hang up your phone and put it on vibrate. Put it in your pocket and when it goes off again, ignore it, but walk to your right toward the bratwurst stand. I'll have my eye on you all the way."

She stood quietly, hands in the pocket of her overcoat, as if waiting to meet someone. I gave it five minutes. The crowds swirled around her, but no one seemed to take notice of her. I dialed her number again, let it ring twice, and closed my phone. She turned and started toward me. As she got close, I raised my head and waved. She came toward me, smiling. A workingman carrying a lunch pail was behind her, head down, intent on his journey home. Jessica was about ten feet from me when the man reached out and grabbed her arm, pulling her toward the side door of the terminal. She jerked back, and the man dropped the lunch pail and grabbed her other arm, using his weight to propel her toward the door. She screamed, and the man said something in German. The people nearest Jessica shrugged, grimaced, and moved on.

Jessica's face was frozen in fear and pain. The man's grip on her arms was powerful. I could see his hands straining with the effort. They were coming toward me. I stood still, looking into my beer stein, trying to ignore the commotion. As they passed by, I swung the heavy glass stein into the back of the man's head. He dropped like a sack of potatoes. Jessica turned as he released her, her eyes locking onto me. She drew back her foot and released a sharp kick to the unconscious man's face, then looked at me, and said, "Are you ready?"

We hurried out the side door, leaving the thug on the terminal floor bleeding from the mouth. Several people near us were pointing and yelling for the police. We exited the terminal in a hurry, and I signaled for a taxi.

"What's going on, Matt?" she asked as the taxi sped away from the train station.

"I'm not sure. Somebody's trying to kill me, I think."

"Does it have to do with your friend's murder?"

"Probably. I can't think of any other reason for somebody in Germany to try to kill me."

"How'd they get onto me?"

"They must have followed me from the airport. Saw us having lunch and had somebody watching you. Probably Patti and Russ as well. When they missed me this afternoon near the consulate, they had you followed, thinking you'd lead them to me."

"And I did."

"My fault. I should have seen the guy following you. They're pretty good. I don't think he saw me. He probably thought you were meeting me, and when I didn't show up by the bank, he thought I'd gotten on to him. Decided to take you instead."

"Rotten bastard."

"What did he say when you screamed?"

"He said I was his wife and he was taking me home. Where're we going?"

"I don't know. We can't go back to either hotel. Let's find a restaurant, and I'll make a phone call and see about getting our bags."

The cabbie knew of a small neighborhood restaurant near downtown that served good food. We took his advice.

Once in the restaurant, I used my cell to call the consulate. I asked for Sergeant Olenski and was told that he'd left for the day. I assured the person on the other end of the line that it was extremely important that I talk to the sergeant, and asked her to call and ask Olenski to call me on my cell.

In a few minutes, my phone rang.

"Sergeant," I said, "I've got a problem and need some help."

"Whatever I can do, sir."

I told him about my afternoon and the fact that Jess and I'd left our bags at our hotels. He agreed to go to the hotels wearing civilian clothes and pick up the bags. He assured me that he'd be discreet. He suggested a small hotel on Eschenheimer Landstrasse that tourists never used. He'd reserve us a room using his name and leave our bags with the concierge. He'd tell the desk clerk that his friends would be in later. I thanked him, and hung up.

Jess didn't seem too upset by her ordeal. I was concerned about a delayed reaction and asked her how she was feeling.

"I'm fine, Matt. I didn't really have time to get scared before you conked him with that beer stein. I knew you were there, and Russ had told me enough about you that I knew you weren't going to let the bastard get out that door."

"You're a toughie."

"Yes, I am. My dad was a navy fighter pilot and a POW in Hanoi for a couple of years. He raised us tough."

"I think we'd better part ways," I said. "Get you back to Paris."

"No way. That sonovabitch put his hands on me. I want to find out who they are and get them all arrested."

"You took out a couple of that guy's teeth with that dropkick. Isn't that enough?"

"Not even close, Matt. Not even close."

"We'll talk about it in the morning."

"Nope. I'm in. You need a translator, and I need some answers."

I told her about Thomas Speer, and that I hoped he would help get us into the archives. Jess had heard his name, but had never met him.

The night wound down. The restaurant was emptying out, patrons, most of whom lived in the neighborhood, going out into the night, heading home to bed. The owner came over to ask if we needed anything else. Jess asked him to call us a taxi. In a few moments, the cab pulled up in front. I paid the check and we left.

The hotel was small, but comfortable. It was apparently used mostly by mid-level businessmen, the ones whose companies wouldn't pay the price for a room at the Intercontinental. The night clerk, a young man in his early twenties who spoke impeccable English, checked me in. I used a false name. The clerk asked for my passport. I whispered to him that I didn't have a passport with me and that I wasn't supposed to be with the woman who accompanied me. I winked. I told him, between a couple of men of the world, that I would think fifty euros might make up for the lack of a passport. The clerk beamed and held out his hand.

I paid from my dwindling cash reserves. I had no idea who was after me or what resources they had. If they had access to credit-card records, they could track me in real time. I knew that every morning the hotels gave the police a list of the foreigners who had spent the night. I didn't want my name on that list. Who knew who had access to it.

Jess and I retrieved our bags from the concierge and walked to the small elevator. I punched the button for the third floor. "Are we on the same floor?" she asked.

"Same room," I said, and explained my subterfuge. "Plus, I'll feel better about your safety if we're together. I'll sleep on the floor."

And that's what I did. Regrettably.

CHAPTER TWENTY-FOUR

The next day, a cold and blustery Tuesday, Jess and I were sitting at a table in the Dornbuscher Bierstube waiting for Jock's man. I'd gotten a call first thing in the morning from Burke Winn. Olenski had told him about my call the evening before, and he was worried.

"I'm all right, Burke," I'd said. "I've got a friend who works for the government, and he's seeing to it that I'm armed."

"Be careful, Matt. If you get caught with a gun in Germany, there's going to be very little I or anyone else at the embassy can do for you."

"I know, but I've got to have some protection. Did you get in touch with Speer?"

"Yes." Winn gave me a phone number. "He's waiting for your call. He'll get you into the archives, but he's not sure how much help that'll be. The records are indexed, but he said you have to know what you're looking for."

"Thanks. I'll give him a call when I get to Bonn."

Jess was sipping a hot cider and I was nursing a pilsner in a tall glass. She put the small mug on the table. "I've been thinking about that list of names. One of them jumped out at me, Robert Brasillach. During World War II, he was a leader of what might be called literary fascism. He was a writer and perhaps the best known Nazi collaborator during the Vichy years in France. He was editor in chief of an anti-Semitic weekly newspaper and was executed by the French after the war."

"The young man who brought the money to Banchori to pay for Wyatt's murder had the same name. He would have been too young to be Brasillach's son. Grandson maybe?"

"No. Brasillach didn't have any children. He was openly gay."

"It was some kind of twisted joke. Robert Brasillach, a dead man, from Odessa. Not the city, but the SS organization. Banchori just assumed that the drunken ramblings about ratlines had to do with a sailboat. What could he have meant when he said he was rolling up the ratlines?"

"I don't know. Maybe he was trying to protect some of the people involved in them after the war. Not many of them would be alive today."

"Did you recognize any of the other names?"

"Yes. Your information was pretty good about who most of these people were. I'll have to do some research on others. I'm not very knowledgeable about the postwar activities."

I looked up every time the door opened, but it was just another local coming in for lunch or a beer. The clock ticked past noon, and on around to twelve thirty. I was about to give up when the door opened and a wiry man about six feet tall walked in, carrying a black attaché case. He wore a black leather jacket, black designer tee shirt, black slacks, silk socks, and black Italian loafers. A Houston Astros baseball cap topped out his attire. It took me a second to realize that the man was Jock Algren.

I was too stunned to open my mouth. He looked at Jess, and said, "You can do better than this guy."

I was out of my chair, enveloped in a bear hug from my oldest friend. "Jock," I said, "this is Jessica Connor. Leave her alone. Jess, this is Jock Algren, a truly dangerous man."

She laughed. "I heard all about you last night, Jock. He said I wasn't supposed to tell you he slept on the floor. Something about his manhood, I think."

Jock laughed. "Such as it is."

"I hate to break up a good conversation, but what are you doing here, Jock?"

"It sounded as if you needed backup. I was able to get the last flight out of Houston. It was running late, so that's why I'm late."

"I'm glad you're here, but it's a long way to come."

"No sweat. What's going on?"

Jock had known Wyatt for a number of years and had flown to

Longboat Key for the funeral. He'd arrived on the morning of the memorial and left the same night. He was often a busy man, but he loved our key, and when he had time, he visited often.

I told him what I'd learned about Wyatt's death, leaving out the execution of Chardone. I'd tell him about that privately. I didn't want Jess to know that I was capable of such a thing. Hell, I didn't want myself to know I was capable of such a thing. I explained how I'd met Jess, my meeting with the general, the attempt on my life, and the aborted kidnapping of Jessica.

He looked perplexed. "What do you think you'll find in these archives?"

"I don't know, but I don't know where else to start. Wyatt and Sauer were working on something to do with that period of history, and somebody is dead set on burying whatever it was they'd discovered. Jess has a Ph.D. in history and did her dissertation on the Vichy government. She's fluent in German and French. I'm hoping she can find something in the records that makes sense."

"Not much of a plan, podner."

"You got that right."

"Mind if I tag along?"

"Not at all. I can always use a boy like you."

He punched me in the arm.

CHAPTER TWENTY-FIVE

We had a lunch of goulash soup and weisswurst, washed down with beer. I told Jock that I thought whoever was after me was using some sophisticated methods. "I'm afraid to use my credit cards in case they're tracking me that way."

"I've got a snub-nosed thirty-eight and five thousand in euros in the briefcase. If you need more cash, we can get it."

"I need to get to Bonn. There's a guy there who's willing to help. He works for the German government and is a curator at the archives."

"I've got a rental car," said Jock. "That's an easy trip."

I paid the check, and we walked out into the early afternoon. A cold wind was blowing across the river, and the air was tinged with the smell of snow. The sky was dark with low-hanging clouds. I pulled up the collar of my jacket and settled the hat more securely on my head. Jess sunk further into her heavy overcoat, a scarf pulled over her ears, hands in her pockets.

We walked down Schifferstrasse for a couple of blocks to where Jock had parked the rental in a curbside parking space. He was driving a midsize Mercedes, light gray in color. It would be virtually invisible in a country where thousands of gray Mercedes sedans plied the roads.

We left Frankfurt for the two-hour trip on the A-3 highway to Bonn, an ancient town on the Rhine River. Snow was hitting the windshield, the wipers working hard to clear it. The wind was up and the Mercedes was buffeted by the occasional gust. The car's heater chugged along, creating a cocoon of warmth as we traveled through the dismal afternoon.

I was in the back, Jess in the front. We were talking about our visit to the archives.

"What are you hoping to find?" asked Jess.

"I'm not sure. I'd like to know if there's a connection among the people on Wyatt's list," I said.

"That's a pretty tall order. There're likely to be a lot of documents dealing with each one of the people. And there won't be any information on the ratlines. At least from the postwar period. The records we'll be looking at stopped with the fall of Germany in the spring of 1945."

I hadn't really thought that through. Obviously, the records of the German Reich would have stopped when the Reich fell. "There were a lot of Germans who knew their country was in big trouble, especially after the allied invasion in June of 1944. Maybe there'll be some records about these people setting up escape routes."

"Probably. We'll just have to see."

"Tell me about Vichy," I said. "I know it was Germany's puppet government in France after the fall of Paris, but that's about it."

She sat quietly for a few moments, a look of concentration playing on her face. "You have to understand the times and the French psyche. Paris had fallen to Germany in the Franco-Prussian War in 1871, had come close to falling again in 1914 at the outset of World War I, and finally in June 1940, the Germans marched into the capital without firing a shot. The French had been shocked by the slaughter of the First World War, and in the 1930s many were afraid that the Communists were about to take power. The country was in turmoil. France was the center of European anti-Semitism and the Fascist organizations had more members than the Communists and Socialists combined."

She took a breath and paused for a minute. "Many of the leading French literary figures of the period were Fascists and virulent anti-Semites. Fascism promised a stable society ruled by men of vision and charisma. It was an easy trap to fall into.

"The Third Republic had been formed after the Franco-Prussian War. It grew out of an inability of the Monarchists to decide on who should be king. Since the Monarchists were a majority of the politicians, the republic never was entirely secure. In 1940, after the fall of Paris, the old Monarchist head of the military forces, General Weygand, was able to force Premier Reynaud to cede power to the hero of the Great War, Marshal Petain. Petain immediately put his own people into the cabinet and the government was dominated by the military. They decided to surrender. It was called an armistice, but the French agreed to surrender all Jews living in France to the Germans and to pay the occupation costs of the Germans.

"Petain moved the government to the city of Vichy. Under the terms of the surrender with Germany, this government controlled about two-fifths of France bordering on Spain. The Royalists had taken over the government, and many of the cabinet members were Fascists. They operated as a puppet for their German masters until the end of the war.

"Vichy even had its own secret police called the Milice, run by a Frenchman named Darnand who held the SS rank of Sturmbannfuehrer and took a personal oath of loyalty to Adolf Hitler. The Vichy government turned over as many as seven hundred fifty thousand Jews to the Germans. Most of those went straight to the death camps."

"That's not generally known, is it?"

"No. The French did their best to cover it up after the war. Most of the people involved in the government were allowed to go on with their lives as if nothing had happened. The Vichy bureaucrats became the functionaries of the postwar governments."

"Doesn't seem fair," I said.

We were quiet for awhile, the air close in the warm car, each of us lost in his own thoughts. I wondered what I'd gotten myself into.

Bonn, the birthplace of Beethoven, is graced with many eighteenth-century Baroque buildings, standing proudly among the modern structures that house the federal bureaucracy. For many years, beginning in 1949, Bonn was the capital of the Federal Republic of Germany, what we knew as West Germany. Some years after the reunification of West and East Germany, the government and parliament moved to Berlin, but most of the ministries remained in Bonn.

We found a small hotel and booked three rooms for the night. For an extra one hundred euros, the desk clerk was happy to put all three rooms in Jock's name. I called Herr Speer in Dusseldorf and arranged to meet him at his office at ten the next morning. He recommended a restaurant for dinner, but in my paranoia, I suggested that we find our own place. One never knows where danger lurks.

CHAPTER TWENTY-SIX

Speer was a large man, not tall, but strapping. He had a ruddy face and blond hair going to gray, a sharp nose, toothy smile. He was wearing a blue pinstripe suit, white shirt, and a paisley tie. Not all that fashionable. He greeted us in fluent English, and nodded as I introduced myself, Jock, and Jess. I emphasized Jess's title, *Frau Doktor*, because in Germany that seems to be very important. He asked his secretary to bring us all coffee.

His office was small as befitted a bureaucrat, but it was nicely appointed. His windows overlooked the Rhine, and an original oil painting of a hunt scene took up most of one wall. His desk was large, and with the exception of a computer monitor, was absolutely clean; not a scrap of paper, pencil, paper clip, or outbox on the surface. It filled the room, leaving only enough space for two side chairs and a small table. The table contained a picture of a pretty blonde woman and a young man.

He saw me looking at the photograph. "My wife Kim and our son," he said. "He's in college in the States. I'll get another chair." He left us for a minute and returned, rolling a desk chair into the office. He took his seat, a large leather executive chair, and made small talk while we waited for the coffee.

"My wife's from Pennsylvania," he said. "I'm used to Americans. I like them."

It sounded as if he were talking about some sort of pets that he tolerated for the benefit of his wife. I wasn't sure I was going to like him. I must have frowned.

"That came out wrong," he said, smiling. "What I meant was that I understand the American psyche, the need to get things done without a lot of beating around the bush. I'm that way myself, so I understand it. Tell me what I can do for you."

I smiled back. He was okay. "Did General Winn tell you why I am here?"

"No. He just asked me to help you. He's a good friend."

"Dr. Connor is a historian," I said, "and she's helping me do some research on some people who were involved in getting Nazis out of Germany after the war."

Speer nodded. "A lot of them stayed, you know. Even some of the really bad ones went right back into government and stayed there until they retired. It was only the worst of them that had to get out."

Jess shifted in her chair. "Herr Speer, we're not sure exactly who we're looking for. We have a list of names that may or may not be important. Tell me about how your files are indexed."

"First," Speer said, "you have to understand that I am only a repository for the documents that have been digitized so far. The actual documents are in archives spread all over the country, and a vast number of them have never been released or digitized. The copies on the computers are scanned from the originals, most of them handwritten, and not a few of them in Old German script. We do have an index of some seventeen million names, and if you can find the names, you should be able to go to the document. Here, I'll show you."

He turned the computer monitor around on the desk so that we could all see it. He pulled a wireless keyboard from a drawer, set it on the desktop, and stroked the keys. An image came up on the screen, some text in German that I couldn't read. He stroked again, and a list of names appeared in alphabetical order. After each name, there was a series of numbers punctuated with hyphens.

Speer pointed to one of the names on the screen. "The numbers tell us where to find the documents with this person's name on them." He gave us a short course in how to use the search engine, none of which I understood. Jessica nodded her head as if she understood everything he was saying. I hoped she did.

Jock had been sitting quietly, sipping his coffee, taking it all in. He hadn't said a word since he shook hands with Speer. "What if we wanted to see the original documents?" he asked, finally.

"You couldn't," said Speer. "They're too fragile to be handled. The government spent enormous amounts of money putting them all on computer disks so that no one would have to touch the originals."

"Makes sense," Jock said, and disappeared back into his coffee cup.

Speer stood up. "I'll get you to a room with a computer terminal. If you need anything, just dial zero on the phone and my secretary will come to you."

We were being dismissed. We trooped down the hall to a bare room with one computer terminal and several straight-back chairs. Speer said he had some things to attend to, and that he would send his secretary in with fresh coffee and notepads. He shook hands all around and left.

Jessica sat down in front of the computer. "This is going to take a while. Why don't you two go and find something to do. Come back at lunchtime."

Jock and I left the building and stepped out into the wet cold blowing off the Rhine. We found a coffee shop in the next block and went in. The space was small and warm, with heat blowing out of ceiling vents and a fireplace at one end of the room. The floors were aged hardwood partially covered by large Oriental rugs. Oil paintings depicting river scenes hung on dark paneled walls. Upholstered chairs and sofas were arranged about the room. The place appeared more like a gentlemen's club than a coffee shop.

A young blonde hostess dressed in a business suit and high heels escorted us to a sofa and took our order. A waiter appeared with our coffee and left. We sat quietly, sipping our drinks, savoring the strong blend.

The door opened and a man entered, hung his overcoat on a peg beside the door, and came directly to us. He was wearing a blue suit, white shirt, and solid blue tie. He had dark skin and black hair, a prominent nose. He sat in the chair facing the sofa. He scowled at us, and said in accented English, "What do you want?"

"Excuse me?" I said.

"What do you want? Why are you in Germany?"

"I'm afraid you have us mixed up with somebody else," I said.

"No, Mr. Royal, I know who you are."

"Then, maybe you'd better tell me who you are."

"That doesn't matter. I'm here to tell you that you should go home."

Jock leaned forward on the sofa, his elbows on his knees. "And why should we do that?"

"I don't know who you are, sir, or what business you have here, but Mr. Royal needs to, as you say, let sleeping dogs lie."

"If I knew what dogs you were talking about," I said, "I might take your advice."

"Old dogs," the man said, and got up to leave. He walked a few paces, stopped and turned. "If you don't leave now, Mr. Royal, you will die in Europe." He retrieved his topcoat and left the shop.

I looked at Jock. "That wasn't a German accent, was it?"

"No. It was Arabic."

CHAPTER TWENTY-SEVEN

"What have you gotten us into this time, podner?" Jock asked, as we walked back through the bleak day toward the archive building. "First we're chasing Nazis, and now we're being chased by Arabs. You must have kicked over somebody's hornet nest."

"You got me. I don't have any idea who that guy was, but even worse, how did he find us?"

"Good question. We've only used my credit cards, and those are untraceable. Different card and different identity for every charge. I don't think he had any idea who I was either. So, somehow, these guys are tracking you."

"Probably, but I can't imagine how. Or why, for that matter."

It was a little after noon as we entered the building. When we got to the room where we'd left Jess, she was working so intently on the computer that she didn't hear us come in. "Ready for lunch?" I asked.

She started, turned, a little distracted. "No. You guys go on. I'm not hungry, and this is fascinating stuff. I'll see you back at the hotel later."

Jock said, "Jess, call us when you're ready to leave. I don't think it's safe for you to be out alone."

"Why? Nobody knows we're in Bonn."

"We can't be sure of that. Let's play it safe, just in case."

"Okay, I'll call," she said, and turned back to the computer, dismissing us.

We went to a small café next to the hotel for lunch, and then told the desk clerk we would be checking out later that evening. If somebody was on to us, they probably knew where we were staying. If they knew we were leaving, maybe they would assume that they'd scared us off.

I went to my room and took a nap. At three, the room phone rang. It was Jess. "I'm ready."

"Did you find anything?"

"I'll tell you later."

"We'll be there in the car in a few minutes. We're checking out of the hotel today. Time to make a change. A moving target."

"Are you trying to scare me?"

"Yes. Somebody doesn't like us, and you need to be very careful."

"My bag is packed and in my room. If they'll let you in, get the bag and we won't have to go back to the hotel."

"Okay. Don't leave the building until you see us pull up. We'll be there in twenty minutes."

For another fifty euros the desk clerk let Jock into Jess's room to get her bag. We pulled up in front of the archives building, and I could see her through the glass door, standing and talking to a young man dressed in slacks and a dress shirt, no tie. Jock touched the horn to get her attention. She saw us, shook the young man's hand, and trotted to the car. She got into the backseat, and we drove away, headed for Koblenz.

Jock took a circuitous route through the back streets of Bonn. He was a professional and if anyone was following us, he'd figure it out. We eased onto the Adenauerallee southbound, which turned into highway nine, hugging the Rhine as we moved farther toward Koblenz.

We made the trip in a little over an hour, driving though a light dusting of snow. Jessica was excited about her research. Most of the names on the list were not in the archives, but she had found one, Richard de Fresne.

"De Fresne was a bad guy," she said, "a really bad guy. He was an officer in the Milice, the French secret police who worked with the Gestapo. He was responsible for transporting Jews from the south of France to the concentration camps. When the Allies invaded France, he moved to Germany and worked for the Gestapo in Frankfurt."

"What happened to him after the war?" I asked.

"There's no record of him. He just disappeared. The archives only went to the end of the war, but one of the assistant curators put me onto another Web site that tracked the French Nazis. De Fresne was one of those who just disappeared. There was speculation that he was killed in the bombing of Frankfurt near the end of the war, but no one knows for sure."

"Maybe he used one of the ratlines to get out of Europe."

"Could be. I also found a reference to another name on Wyatt's list, CBS in Zurich. I think that's the Confederated Bank Suisse. A lot of the Nazis used it to hide money during the war. Some of them weren't very secretive, and the Gestapo recorded their names on a list of accounts held at CBS. De Fresne was one of the names on the list."

"Was there an account number?" asked Jock.

"No. Some of the names had account numbers next to them, but not de Fresne's."

"Maybe the account's still in existence," I said.

Jessica shook her head. "I doubt it. The Swiss would have closed those accounts after this long and kept the money. Besides, with their secrecy laws, there's no way we're going to be able to find out anything about Swiss bank accounts."

Jock chuckled. "Don't be too sure about that."

Dusk comes early during the late fall in northern Europe. Traffic was building as we neared Koblenz. We'd chosen it because it was a sizable city, and three American tourists would not be that unusual. The snow was getting heavier, and I could hear the slush of the highway bounce off the undercarriage of the Mercedes. Jock drove steadily, concentrating on the darkening road.

Jock had the address of the local branch of the rental car company that owned the Mercedes we were driving. We stopped there and returned the car. Jock mentioned that we were going to take the train back to Frankfurt, and the clerk arranged for a courtesy bus to take us to the train station in the city center. Jock used a different passport and driver's license to rent another car at the kiosk in the terminal. He went to the tourist office and booked a suite at a nearby hotel, picked up another gray Mercedes, and drove off.

Jessica and I found a beer bar next to the station and waited for Jock to get settled in. He would check into the hotel with our bags and sneak us in later. We didn't want to register in our own names, and we didn't want to try to bribe another clerk. Whoever was looking for us didn't know who Jock was, and certainly wouldn't be on the lookout for his assumed names.

Jessica sipped her beer, and a small frown danced across her face. "I'm not much of a beer drinker. Matt, do you know who the Klarsfelds are?"

"They're on Wyatt's list."

"Yes. They're French Nazi hunters. They've been responsible for finding some of the worst of the French collaborators. They were just children during the war, but they've been relentless over the past few years. They do a lot of good. They have a foundation based in Paris that may be able to help us."

"Maybe Wyatt had some contact with them."

"It's worth a phone call."

"Will they tell you anything on the phone?"

"I think so. I know one of their researchers." Jessica looked at her watch. "It's too late to call today. I'll talk to them in the morning."

We sat quietly, Jess taking an occasional sip of her beer, making a face with each swallow.

I watched her wince for the third time in as many minutes. "You don't have to drink that, you know."

"Maybe I won't." She pushed the glass away and sat back in her chair.

"Guess I'll be sleeping on the floor again tonight."

She laughed. "If your plan was to ply me with beer and compromise my maidenly virtues, you screwed up. You should've tried whiskey."

"Does that work?"

She smiled. "Sometimes."

I was about to suggest another bar, one where they served whiskey, when my cell phone rang.

"There's a restaurant in the hotel," said Jock. "Walk two blocks down Bahnhoff Strasse, turn right on Rizza Strasse and the hotel is in the next block. I'll meet you in the restaurant."

•   •   •

Dinner was surprisingly good. The menu featured traditional German food; several kinds of schnitzels and wursts, pork, sauerkraut, sauerbraten, potato pancakes, and goulash. We drank a dry Rhine wine, made from grapes grown in nearby vineyards. I offered to buy Jessica some whiskey, but she declined, grinning at me.

The suite was two rooms and a parlor. Jock took the sofa in the living room. I could hear him snoring through the door to my room, and hoped Jessica didn't think it was me. That kind of noise would doom my chances of ever sharing a bed with her. Not that I thought my chances were that good anyway.

The next morning, Thursday, Jock and I went down to breakfast. Jessica ordered room service, telling us that she would call the Klarsfeld Foundation in Paris and see if they knew anything about de Fresne.

Over coffee and sweet rolls, Jock and I tried to figure out what to do next. There was no need to stay in Koblenz, and if Jessica didn't have any luck with Klarsfeld, I couldn't see much sense in staying in Germany.

"Maybe we've hit a dead end," I said.

"I'm not sure about that, Matt. Somebody wants you out of Europe. Maybe if you stick around and let them know you're here, they'll make another move, and we can figure out who they are."

"I'm not sure I like the feeling of being bait, but that may be our only option."

"If you go back to Florida, you're never going to find out who ordered the hit on Wyatt. And, whoever's after you may just follow you home."

"I hadn't thought about that. How do we let the bad guys know where I am?"

"If we could figure out how they found us in Bonn, we could use that connection."

"Maybe Speer blew the whistle on us," I said.

"That's possible, but why would he do that?"

"Who knows? Maybe he's one of the latter-day Nazis."

My cell phone beeped, letting me know that a text message had come in. I opened the phone. The message on the screen was short. "Go home or die."

I held the phone up so that Jock could see it. He smiled, a cold smile that didn't reach his eyes, the smile of the hunter in sight of his prey. "Does the message show a sender?"

"No."

"That's okay. They know your phone number, but they don't know where you are. Otherwise, they'd have sent somebody in person. It's scarier that way."

"Also more dangerous. They might think that we'd try to get to them through the guy who brings the message."

"They don't know who I am," said Jock, "and I doubt they know what you're capable of. They might not think we're much of a danger. Maybe Jess talked to somebody at the archives yesterday, or someone there knew what she was doing. It didn't have to be Speer."

We were interrupted by Jessica joining us. She signaled the waiter for coffee and took a seat. "You're not going to believe this," she said. "I found somebody who knew de Fresne."

CHAPTER TWENTY-EIGHT

"Klaus Blattner," Jessica said. "He's on Wyatt's list."

"Who is he?" I asked.

"He was part of a German underground group known as the Edel-weiss Pirates. They were mostly kids from working-class families who hated the Nazis. Blattner was a middle-class kid whose dad was a profes-sor at the Goethe University in Frankfurt. He'd been a member of the Hitler Youth, but became disenchanted with the Nazis. He joined the Pirates and became very active in the organization's anti-Nazi efforts. When the group started appearing on the Nazi radar, a large number of them were arrested and some were executed.

"Blattner escaped notice, probably because he wasn't part of the underclass that made up most of the membership, and because he'd used a false name when he joined. When the Pirates organization was rolled up, he enlisted in the Waffen-SS under his real name and was posted to France. He worked with the Milice, the Vichy government's secret police, and became a conduit to the French underground on what the Gestapo and Milice were doing. When the Allies invaded, the underground got him out of Vichy and hid him for the rest of the war."

"He's still alive?" I asked.

"Yes. He's an old man now, but he came back to Germany after the war and worked for the West German government in one of the minor bureaus. He's retired and lives in Fulda. I called him, and he's happy to see us. Today, if we can get there."

"Where the hell is Fulda?" asked Jock.

"About three hours from here," Jess said. "Over where the East German border used to be."

I stood up. "Give Blattner a call and tell him we'll be there early this afternoon."

We drove across central Germany. The weather was still bleak, and snow occasionally drifted onto the windshield. Jock was quiet, concentrating on his driving.

Jessica was in the front passenger seat, turned so that she could talk to me. "From what my friend at the Klarsfeld Foundation told me, I gather that Blattner has been a reliable source for them for years. He knew a lot about the inner workings of the Milice and its Gestapo masters."

"Had anybody at the foundation talked to Wyatt?"

"There's no indication of that. Sauer either. Maybe Wyatt got Blattner's name from some other research. Since the Klarsfelds were on his list, I'd guess he meant to talk to them."

"Maybe. Did Blattner say whether he'd talked to either Sauer or Wyatt?"

"I didn't ask him. Didn't want to scare him off."

"What did you tell him?"

"The truth. That I'm a historian specializing in the Vichy period in France and I wanted to talk to him."

"Not the whole truth."

"Well, not all of it. Try not to scare the old gent when we get there."

We drove for the better part of three hours, stopping once for lunch at a roadside restaurant. We pulled into the old cathedral town of Fulda in early afternoon. Fulda had once been a garrison town for American soldiers guarding the East German border. They were gone now, as was the border. Reunification had obviated the need for troops.

Blattner had given Jessica good directions to his home. He lived in an apartment house near the old town in the center of Fulda. We found a parking place a block away and walked back to his building. His apartment was on the ground floor.

The door was opened by a robust man with a shock of white hair. He was tall and appeared fit, not carrying any excess weight. He was wearing a checkered flannel shirt with brown slacks held up by suspenders, sturdy shoes. "Dr. Connor, I presume," he said. "Come on in and bring your friends." His English was almost accentless, and spoken with a fluidity that only comes with a lot of practice.

Jessica introduced Jock and me, using our real names. We followed Blattner through the foyer and into a small living room that contained a sofa, recliner, and large-screen TV. One wall was a solid bookcase, filled with titles in both English and German. As we sat down, an elegant woman, tall with perfectly coiffed white hair, entered the room. The men all stood, and Blattner introduced us to his wife. Frau Blattner offered us tea or coffee in passable English, and when we declined, she left us to what she called our reminiscences.

Blattner leaned back in his recliner, seeking a comfortable position. He looked at Jessica. "I'm guessing that your quest isn't entirely historical in nature."

Jessica returned the smile. "Not entirely. Have you lived in America? Your English is perfect and sounds American."

"No, I've never even visited the States. I worked here in Fulda as a German government liaison to the American military. I dealt with Americans every day, all day. It was a wonderful experience. I liked them all. Can you tell me why you're here?"

"Certainly," said Jess. "I am a historian by training and did my doctoral dissertation on the Vichy government. But I'm here to help Mr. Royal find out who killed his friend. Mr. Algren is helping also." She explained what happened to Wyatt, and what we'd discovered so far.

"Ah, Dr. Wyatt," Blattner said. "I had several long telephone conversations with him. He was particularly interested in the same man you are. Richard de Fresne. I'm sorry to hear that he's passed on."

I leaned forward on the sofa. "Can you see any connection between de Fresne and Dr. Wyatt's death?"

"No. Nobody's heard anything about de Fresne since the war ended. The French government tried to find him after the war, but lost the trail in Frankfurt. De Fresne was working for the Gestapo at their headquarters there. The city was flattened by Allied bombing near the end of the war, and it has been assumed that de Fresne was just another of the thousands of unidentified dead found in the rubble."

"What do you think?" I asked.

"I think he's still alive."

"Why?"

"De Fresne was in charge of transporting the Jews from southern France to the concentration camps. I worked in the same office with him, and when a transport order was about to be issued, I would get the names to the French underground. They couldn't save a lot of them, because that would have led the Germans to suspect a leak in their office. But, they did save some, and that's better than none."

"How did de Fresne decide who was going to be sent to the camps?" I asked.

"At first, he targeted the wealthiest of the Jews. He would make a deal with them. For a lot of money, he would keep their names off the lists. He collected millions in cash, artwork, silver settings, jewelry, real estate, and whatever else the Jews could scrape up. He left the ones who donated off the lists, and the word got around among the Jews that they could buy their lives from de Fresne. The loot poured in, and when he'd tapped them all out, and there were no rich Jews left, their names went on the transport lists. They all died in the camps, and de Fresne put his millions in a Swiss bank."

"How do you know all this?" asked Jock.

"It was common knowledge. De Fresne bragged openly about his growing wealth. He said that he'd been a poor kid and was going to finish the war rich. He thought the Jews deserved what they were getting, and he deserved their money."

"I didn't know the French were so complicit in the Holocaust," I said.

"Oh yeah. A lot of them were. De Fresne had grown up in North Africa. His father was a career military man, a sergeant I think, and his mother was American. She had worked as a maid and nanny for a rich American family living in Paris. That's where she met the sergeant. They got married and moved to Africa.

"When de Fresne was a teenager, his dad was killed in some sort of skirmish with the Arabs, and the kid was sent to Marseilles to live with a relative of the sergeant's. He never spoke of his mother, so I don't know what happened to her. He did well in school and was at the Sorbonne when the war broke out. Because of his mother, he was fluent in English and spoke with an American accent. He found work in the Quai d'Orsay, the French Foreign Ministry, and worked with the American Embassy in some capacity, maybe a translator for his bosses at the ministry.

"How did he end up in the Milice?" I asked.

"I'm not sure, but he was very vocal in his anti-Semitism. He'd been a member of a Fascist group in Paris before the war. He was running in a fast crowd; the Sorbonne, Diplomatic Service. Sergeant's kids didn't usually get into that part of French society. He once told me that if it hadn't been for the Jews, he could have gone further and faster. I think, though, it was his social status that held him back. Maybe the Milice took him because he wasn't afraid to get his hands dirty."

There was a knock at the front door. Blattner excused himself and went to open it. He came back, followed by the man who'd accosted Jock and me in the coffee shop in Bonn.

CHAPTER TWENTY-NINE

The man stopped at the doorway to the foyer and said something to Blattner in German. Blattner sat in the chair he'd vacated to answer the door. The Arab had a nine-millimeter pistol in his hand. He pointed it at me. "I told you to go home, Mr. Royal."

"We were just on our way," I said. "Why are you so interested in my going back to Florida?"

"That doesn't matter. What does matter is that you didn't listen. Now you'll pay a price."

I stared at him. "How did you find us?"

He laughed. "Ah, that's very simple my friend. We have a tap on Herr Blattner's phone."

A piece of the puzzle clunked into place. That's how they knew about Wyatt. But why did they care?

"Do you work for de Fresne?" I asked.

A puzzled look appeared on the Arab's face. "Who?"

"Richard de Fresne."

"I don't know anybody by that name."

"Then why are you so intent on killing me?" I said.

"I really don't know, Mr. Royal, and I don't care. My boss tells me where to go and what to do and I do it. I only know about the tap on Herr Blattner's phone because the boss chose to tell me about it."

"Do you know who I am?" asked Blattner.

"No, and I don't care. You have lived a long life, old man, so your death won't be a great loss." He snorted, a stab at laughter. "Except maybe to you."

He was still laughing when Jock shot him through the head. He

dropped like a stone, his gun falling to the floor. The Arab had been concentrating on Blattner and didn't see Jock ease his pistol out of the pocket
of his windbreaker. There was no reason for the man to think that either
of us would be armed. Germany had strict gun laws, so good people
weren't expected to carry weapons. Only the bad guys had them. Or so
they thought.

Jessica hadn't moved in the seconds since the shooting. She was
frozen, rooted to her seat on the sofa, her hands grasping her face. "My
God," she said, finally, "My God, Jock."

Frau Blattner hurried into the room, her hand going to her mouth
when she saw the body on the floor. "Klaus?" she whispered.

Blattner went to her, put his arm around her shoulders, made a
shushing sound. He looked at Jock. "What was that?" His voice was shaky.

"I'm not sure," said Jock, and explained where we had seen the man
before. "Have you had any problems with anybody, Herr Blattner?"

"No. Never. Does this have to do with de Fresne?"

"It must. I can't imagine any other reason this guy would be following us or that your phone would be tapped. Can you?"

"No, Mr. Algren, I can't. I must call the police."

"Please don't do that, Herr Blattner," I said. "I think you'll be a lot
safer if we can figure this out ourselves. The police will only complicate
things, and Jock will be in trouble for having a gun."

Blattner frowned. "Mr. Algren did break the law."

Jock shrugged. "And if I hadn't, we'd all be dead."

"We can't leave a dead man here," Jessica said, finally finding her
voice. "We have to call the police."

Jock pulled his cell phone out of his pocket, punched in a number,
and waited. Then, "I need a cleanup. In Fulda. As soon as possible." He
recited the Blattner address, and turned back to the group. "Somebody
will be here in a couple of hours. They have to come from Frankfurt."

Jessica stood up and walked to the window, trying not to look at the
corpse on the floor. "Jock, who are you? Matt said you worked for the
government. What part of the government?"

"The part that can get this mess cleaned up, Jess. That's about all I
can tell you."

"Why are these men looking for you?"

"I don't think they're after me. They're trying to scare Matt off for some reason. I'm just part of the scenery."

She pointed to the dead man. "He had an Arabic accent."

"Yes, I noticed."

"He said he'd told you to go home, Matt. What's that all about?"

I told her about the encounter in the coffee shop in Bonn.

"And you didn't think that was important enough to tell me about?"

"I didn't want to worry you."

Her voice rose. "Stop treating me like a child, damn it."

"Okay. I'm sorry. It was a bad call on my part."

"Do you know how he found you and Matt at the coffee shop?"

"No. Maybe Speer is involved with these guys some way."

"I don't think so. I told you about the assistant that was helping me. The young man who walked me out of the building."

"Yes."

"His name is Hassan. His parents were Moroccan immigrants."

"Damn," said Jock. "That's how they knew we were in Bonn. But why would they have Herr Blattner's phone tapped?"

Blattner cleared his throat. "I think I know. I sent an e-mail query to the archives in Bonn a couple of months ago. The Klarsfeld Foundation was trying to find out more about de Fresne. One of their investigators came to see me. I told him what I could, but it got me to thinking about how de Fresne may have gotten out of Europe. I e-mailed the archive and said that I was interested in anything they had on de Fresne. I got an e-mail back a couple of days later from an assistant curator named Hassan telling me that they had no records on de Fresne."

Jessica shook her head. "Obviously they do have the records, because I found them. They were right in the index. Certainly, anybody that works there would be able to find them."

Jock nodded. "Somebody's trying to protect de Fresne. I would have thought this guy was just hired help, but with Hassan at the archives, it makes me wonder if one of the Muslim terror groups is involved somehow."

"But why?" I asked. "What connection could there be between an ancient Nazi and a modern terror group?"

Jess spoke up. "A lot of the Muslims were pro-Nazi during the war. I think they were more anti-British than anything, but some of them fought for the Germans. Maybe there's a connection there."

"Possibly," I said, "but that's a long way back."

"Money may be the common thread," Jock said. "Herr Blattner, do you have an estimate as to how much money de Fresne extorted from the Jews?"

"He bragged that he had about twenty million dollars in Swiss francs in the bank."

"Holy shit," said Jock. "That would be a quarter of a billion dollars in today's money. Think if that had been invested wisely over the years. Just a half-assed investment would have turned that into billions of dollars by today. That kind of money would draw a lot of flies."

"Could he have really had that much?" I asked.

Jock held up his hands in a "who knows" gesture. "Even if he only had half or a quarter of that, it would be real big money."

"And he would have needed help in investing it," I said. "That much money being dropped into any economy is going to draw government interest."

"Maybe that's where the Arabs come in," said Jess. "Maybe they were de Fresne's investment bankers."

We moved into the kitchen to wait for Jock's cleaners. Frau Blattner was still upset, but we were all coming to terms with the fact that we'd come close to death on a dreary afternoon in a quaint German town.

Three men arrived in a van with a logo on the side written in German. Jess said it was a firm of carpet cleaners. Jock greeted the men with some sort of code word, and they went to work. They brought a carpet into the house, rolled the body into it and took it to the truck. Anyone on the street would have thought the men were delivering a clean rug and taking a dirty one back to their place of business. They took the Arab's gun with them and left, not saying another word to any of us.

"They'll fingerprint the body, run DNA, and everything else. If this guy is in the system in any country, they'll find him."

"What are we going to do about the Blattners?" I asked. "We can't leave them here now."

Jock turned to Herr Blattner. "Sir, if you'll go to Frankfurt with us, my government will put you up in a place where you'll be safe until we can get to the bottom of this."

The Blattners had a hushed conversation in German, and Blattner nodded at Jock. "We'll pack a few things and go with you."

CHAPTER THIRTY

The city lay in rubble. What had been home to half a million people and the financial center of Germany, was now a pile of bricks. Men and women clad in rags, some holding children's hands, picked through the debris, the master race no more. Corpses rotted in the anemic sun, the odor causing a gag reflex in the soldier wearing American battle fatigues. He stood a little over six feet tall, and the months in the field had made him lean and hard. His face was creased with fatigue, a chronic state for soldiers at war. He had dark brown eyes that squinted in the pale sun, and his nose was a little off center, as if broken in a long-ago fight. Wisps of brown hair escaped from the helmet perched on his head. He carried a pack on his back and tugged occasionally at the straps, settling it a little, easing the strain on his shoulders. The man picked his way carefully down the rubble-strewn street, rifle at the ready, locked and loaded. He was wary of snipers, even though there had been no reports of such. He didn't want to get shot dead this near to the end of the war.

The United States 5th Infantry Division had taken the city of Frankfurt the day before, March 28, 1945. There had been almost no resistance, and soldiers were already setting up headquarters in the I.G. Farben Building near downtown. It was one of the few structures still standing, the result of Eisenhower's order to the 8th Air Force not to bomb it.

The American was looking for 27 Linden Strasse, but he was disoriented by the destruction, not sure where the street was. He'd driven his jeep from the Hauptbahnhoff, the main train station, still mostly intact.

He'd gone northeast on Mainzer Landstrasse and turned onto Bocken-heimer Landstrasse. After a few blocks he came to an area so saturated with rubble that he had to walk. There were no street signs, and the destruction made it impossible to determine where the intersections lay.

The American hailed a man digging through the remains of what had probably once been his home. "Do you know where Linden Strasse is?" he asked in German.

"*Ja*," came the answer. The man pointed to the west and continued in German. "You go one more street that way. The cross street is Linden Strasse."

"*Danke.*"

The American trudged on until he came to what appeared to be the street he was looking for. It was hard to tell, because the ruins of buildings were spread haphazardly across the landscape. He picked his way carefully down the block, ignoring the people who were digging in the mess that had once been homes and businesses.

He stopped in what he thought to be the middle of the first block. There were no landmarks, just a sea of destruction. No one was near the place, no one picking through the debris. The American had the fleeting thought that he was standing on poisoned ground. The building he sought, if in fact this was the right building, was like the rest of the street, a pile of blocks and timber, tumbled inward as if a giant had stepped on it. He walked carefully over the debris, looking for some sign that he had reached his goal. There were bodies entwined in the rubble, and he had to cover his nose. A chill wind was blowing, kicking up little eddies of dust. He pulled up the collar of his field jacket, seeking warmth for the back of his neck. He removed his helmet, the steel pot with the gold leaf insignia of his rank, wiped his brow, stirring the dust that had collected there, and resettled the headgear. He took a swallow of tepid water from his canteen, put it back in its case hanging from his web belt.

He stood, surveying the remains of a once important city. There were no trees, no shrubs, no greenery of any kind, just the colorless debris that had once been homes and offices, stretching as far as he could see. No building stood to block his view, no structure to give substance or scale to the landscape. Just devastation. War, he thought, brought to an unsuspecting people by a maniac who cared nothing for their suffering. Nobody could ever imagine the horrors wrought when modern men decided to kill each other for the glory of their nations. You had to see it for yourself. And he'd seen more than he believed he could live with.

He turned to leave, afraid that his mission was a failure. He stepped on a brick in the rubble, turning it over. He saw the arm of a dead man, clad in black, the death's head insignia on the cuff indicating that he was an officer of the SS, the dreaded storm troopers of the Third Reich. The American looked more closely and saw the edge of a swastika flag peeking out of the rubble. He pulled at it, but it wouldn't budge. He kicked aside more rubble and as he neared the far edge of the flag, he realized it was attached by its grommets to a flagpole that had been sheared in the bombing. No other place in this part of town would fly the flag. He'd found what he was looking for.

The American moved through the area of what had once been a large building. Parts of the walls were still standing, but the building had been gutted. He came to what had been the back yard, an area that contained very little debris. The house had fallen in on itself, probably from a direct hit by a bomb or perhaps an artillery shell. A Mercedes sedan, its tires flat, its shiny paint pocked with shrapnel scars, sat alone at the end of a concrete driveway that emerged from the rubble.

He stood quietly, listening. He heard only the wind as it whipped about the broken building, making an eerie whistling sound, not unlike a low moan. Fitting, thought the American. It fit this place.

He walked some more, careful where he stepped, rifle held in a combat-ready position, finger on the trigger, safety off. He was nervous, edgy, ready to shoot anything that moved. He saw more bodies, some in civilian clothes, heaped in a mound near the back wall, most of which was still standing. He moved closer, saw that they'd all been shot in the back. Recently. There was no stench of decay, but it wouldn't be long in coming. Three men and six women, the females all naked, hands tied behind them. They'd been executed, their last vision of earth the partially destroyed wall they were facing when shot.

He'd seen it before, in North Africa, France, the Low Countries, and in the Fatherland itself. Civilians killed by the retreating Germans. People just taken out and shot. The American had become inured to death, to a cruelty that he would never have imagined before the war. More than anything, he wanted to go back to that life, the one before the war, the one where he was a respected professor of history in a small southern college, where he lived with a beautiful woman who wanted to give him children.

He'd like to erase the bitterness that had crept over him almost unnoticed as he moved about the battlefields, trying to discern the enemy's intentions. The bitterness that was sharpened by the letter from home, the one asking for a divorce, because his wife had fallen in love with another man, and she wanted to give him children. Surely, the American would understand, what with his absence of three years. Loneliness was depressing, and she knew her husband would not want her to be depressed. Surely, he could understand the reasonableness of her request for a divorce. Yes, he wanted that life back, but he understood about impossibilities.

That life was gone, another casualty of war. He'd kissed it good-bye the day he joined the Office of Strategic Services, the clandestine arm of the military. His fluency in German and his doctorate in history had attracted the recruiters from the OSS. They came to the campus and convinced him that he could contribute the most to the survival of the United States by becoming one of them. So he did. And now, he was brought to this place of execution, this wasteland in the heart of what had once been a nation of culture and refinement, this country that had slipped into a savagery undreamed of by even the most barbaric of historical figures.

The desolation of the city matched that of his soul. His war was over, but he knew that the stunted remnants of his spirit would remain, raging forever at some amorphous thing that transcended the understanding of sane men. And on this day, the American had come, like a vengeful wraith, intent on retribution and, with a little luck, great wealth.

He walked farther into the backyard. He noticed air vents set into the ground, short black stovepipe-like structures with steel mesh covering the openings. The slight hum of a generator emanated from the one closest to him. He moved about, finding more of the vents, each one emitting the quiet sound of working equipment. He went back toward the wall where the bodies lay and worked his way to the corner. He peered around the edge of the wall and saw what appeared to be an entrance to a basement, two doors on hinges lying almost flat on the ground. It was what he'd been looking for.

The American moved toward the doors, reached for the handle of one of them, and pulled it open, standing away as he did, the door between him and the opening. Nothing happened. No movement. He looked over the door and saw stairs descending into a dim space. There appeared to be some sort of anteroom at the bottom, and he could see artificial light splaying outward from the area.

He put one foot on the top step, his rifle pointed downward, his finger on the trigger. He moved cautiously, one step at a time. He stepped down and stopped, waiting for a noise or movement, rifle ready. Nothing. He moved down another step. He came to the bottom of the stairs and stopped again. He saw a large open room with bunks and a rifle rack, the weapons stacked.

A row of cells lined the right side of the room, their bars glinting in the artificial light of overhead fixtures. They were all empty. Stacks of shelves containing row after row of files lined the opposite wall. Four men in black uniforms sat at a table in the middle of the room, a plate of food in front of each of them.

The American stood quietly for a moment, unobserved. "Good afternoon, gentlemen," he said in English. The men jumped to their feet, hands in the air, looks of surprise on their faces. "Who's in charge?" asked the American, this time in German.

"I am," said a tall man with blond hair. His eyes were ice blue, unblinking above a dueling scar etched into his right cheek. His tunic was open, tie askew, white shirt open at the collar. "I will surrender my command to you, but I expect to be accorded the honors due my rank."

The American looked steadily at the commander, aware of each of the other men around the table. He was pointing his rifle at the group, the stock under his arm, finger on the trigger. "Are there others here?"

"*Nein*. We are the only four who survived the bombing. We've been waiting to surrender to an American officer."

"Who ordered the civilians upstairs shot?"

"I did," said the tall German. "They were enemies of the people. Jews."

The American pulled the trigger. The bullet caught the German commander in the chest, knocking him backward, a look of disbelief clouding his face as he died. The sound of the shot was loud in the confined space, and the other three men ducked instinctively.

"Stand up, you bastards," said the major in German, waving his rifle at them. The men complied, looks of fear darting over their faces. "I ought to shoot you all. Every goddamnned one of you."

"Sir," said one of the men, "we are soldiers. We have surrendered."

"You are murdering bastards who don't deserve to see another sunrise." The American pulled a photograph from the pocket of his fatigue pants and held it up so that he could look at it without taking his eyes off the men he held at gunpoint. "Which one of you is de Fresne?"

No one answered. The American looked at the picture again. He spoke rapidly in English. "I'm going to shoot each one of you, but I have orders to bring de Fresne back safely."

One of the men raised his hand, and spoke in American-accented English. "I am he," he said. "These idiots all know me by a German name. None of them speaks English."

"Step away," said the American.

De Fresne moved a few feet to his right. The remaining two men began to move too, having finally realized what was about to happen. The American shot each of them in rapid succession. He then handed his pistol to de Fresne and stepped back, his rifle trained on the Frenchman. "Shoot each of them in the head. I want to make sure they're dead. If you even think about pointing that pistol at me, you'll be as dead as they are."

De Fresne did as he was told, putting one bullet into the head of each man. He then turned the pistol around, holding it by its muzzle, and slid it across the floor to the American. The major picked up the pistol, pointed it at the Frenchman, and leaned his rifle against the wall.

"Take your clothes off," said the major. "Every stitch."

The Frenchman didn't question the order. He left his clothes in a pile and stood naked. The American removed his backpack and slid it across the floor to the Frenchman. "There's an American uniform in there. Put it on." De Fresne complied.

The major took a set of handcuffs from the side pocket of his pants, held them up. "Put your hands behind you and back up to me slowly."

De Fresne was nervous as he stood in the uniform of an American private, hands cuffed behind his back. "May I ask what we're doing?"

"Monsieur de Fresne, I know a lot about you. I know that you stole twenty million dollars from the Jews in southern France, and I know that it's in the Confederated Bank Suisse in Zurich. I want part of that money. I'm not greedy, so half will be about right."

"I don't know what you're talking about."

"Yes, you do. We can discuss it, or you can join your buddies over there."

"A quarter of the money."

"We're not negotiating, de Fresne. You have a choice. One-half or none. Dead men don't need money."

"Kill me and you won't get any of it."

"That's a chance I'm willing to take."

"Okay. How do we get to Switzerland?"

"We don't. I'm going to get you out of Europe, and we'll get the money transferred back to the States after the Germans surrender."

"How?"

"I'm OSS. I can do a lot of things without anybody asking questions. For now, you're a soldier in my custody. Keep your mouth shut unless you're asked a question. Nobody's going to look too closely at an American OSS major with a private for a prisoner."

The major holstered his pistol and picked up his rifle. He motioned to the steps and followed de Fresne out. The OSS would be here anytime now. This was the Gestapo headquarters for the Frankfurt region, and the army wanted the records stored there. If he met any of his colleagues on the way out, he had a story for them. He'd been planning this for weeks, and had left a trail of evidence concerning a private who was fraternizing with the Germans and selling them weapons. His people knew he was looking for the soldier and would think nothing of the fact that he'd found him.

They made it back to the jeep without running into Americans. Dusk was approaching, and the air had cooled further. The major unlocked one end of the cuffs and relocked it to the seat frame on the passenger side of the jeep. De Fresne had been quiet during the walk, treading carefully with his hands locked behind him, afraid of falling and not being able to catch himself. The American had walked a few paces behind him, his rifle in a ready position and trained on the Frenchman's back.

"Where to now?" asked de Fresne.

"Out of Germany."

"Not France, I hope."

"Holland."

"What's there?"

"Transportation Stateside."

"Then what?"

"You'll see."

"I'd like to know where I'm going."

"Shut the fuck up."

"Okay."

The American negotiated the ruined streets of Frankfurt and out into the country. Military Police checkpoints were situated every few miles on the main roads. At each stop, the major showed his credentials and explained that he had captured the prisoner in Frankfurt. No, the prisoner didn't have any ID. He'd lost it while on the run. The major had been after him for three months, and had finally caught up with him. He'd been selling information and weapons to the enemy. The private had been hiding in other military units while on the run. With the fluidity of the front, a lot of men were losing contact with their units and were attaching themselves to the first outfit they found. It wasn't unusual for a strange soldier to be with a unit for a few days and then disappear back to his old company.

They stopped overnight near the French border. "I'm going to turn you over to an MP outfit for the night. They'll feed you and give you a cot in a cell. I'll tell them you're not to be interrogated. Don't make small talk. You might get tripped up on some little thing that any American would know about and you don't. If anybody is persistent in trying to talk to you, tell them you are under orders from me to keep your mouth shut."

When the American picked de Fresne up the next morning, the Frenchman was frantic. "You told me we were going to Holland. I know where we are. The French border isn't ten kilometers from here."

"I didn't want to spook you. We're going to get on an American military train at Strasbourg. That will take us to Lyon. From there, we take another military train to Nice. The trains are moving troops. The French won't stop us, and even if they do, unless someone who knows you personally recognizes you, you'll just be another soldier in custody."

"Then what?"

"I'm putting you in a military prison."

"What?"

"Just until I can get you out of Europe. You'll be safe there. Nobody will know anything about you except that you're being held for the OSS."

"I don't like this."

"I don't think you'd like being turned over to the French either, but those are pretty much your options."

"Okay. How long do I have to stay in jail?"

"A month or two. The war is still going on. There's fighting in Italy, but when that settles down, I think I know how to get you out. As soon as I can get you to Rome, you'll be on your way to America."

"Rome is in American hands."

"Yes, but northern Italy isn't, and I haven't figured out a way to get you to Rome except by some sort of ground transportation. That means waiting until your German buddies are out of Italy."

"Can you guarantee that I won't be handed over to the French?"

"Yes. I can also guarantee that you will be handed over if you so much as hint to anyone that we have an arrangement. You'll be watched constantly, but you won't know by whom. You won't be allowed any visitors except me. If you try to escape, I'll know about it, and you'll be given to the French. Are we clear?"

"How did you arrange all this?"

"Planning. And I'm an OSS officer.

"You mentioned that."

CHAPTER THIRTY-ONE

"We're being followed," Jock said, when we were about an hour out of Fulda. "I didn't see him until we got on the autobahn. A white Audi."

"Can you tell how many are in the car?" I asked.

"At least two. I can't see into the backseat. Don't turn around."

"How long have they been with us?"

"I'm not sure. Probably since we left the Blattners' apartment. He's stayed right with me, about three or four car lengths behind."

Jessica was in the front passenger seat, and the Blattners and I were wedged into the back, with Frau Blattner in the middle, her husband's arm around her. I leaned forward. "What do you want to do?"

"Let's go on to Frankfurt. Maybe we can lose them there."

Jessica had turned in her seat, facing Jock. "And if we don't?"

"We'll kill them."

A scowl crossed Jess's face. "Great. Just great." She turned abruptly and stared out the window.

Jock looked at her, grinning. "Or we could let them kill us."

"We could go to the police," said Jessica.

"That's not an option right now," I said.

"Bullshit. It's always an option."

I put my hand on her shoulder. "Trust us on this one, Jess. Somebody wants us dead. Probably all of us, and until we can figure this out, we have to stay away from the cops."

She turned and stared coldly at me, not saying a word. She turned back to the window. I didn't think even a little whiskey would help this situation.

The berms of the highway were stacked several inches high with dirty snow and ice, but the roadway itself was clear. The occasional snow-covered village, a setting befitting a postcard, appeared at the edge of the superhighway. Trees with bare limbs flanked the road, framing fallow fields pocked with deposits of snow, giving the terrain a gaunt appearance.

Jock kept a steady speed in the Mercedes, the speedometer topping ninety miles per hour. Our pursuer stayed with us. There was quiet in the car, the only sound the swoosh of tires on wet pavement. The Blattners had said nothing, and Jessica had gone silent too. Traffic picked up as we neared Frankfurt, dusk falling on us.

Jock took an exit ramp at high speed, and pumped the brakes as we came to the intersection with the surface road. He made an abrupt turn to the right, throwing the Blattners against me. He showered down on the accelerator, gaining speed rapidly. He braked, snapped the car into a left turn, and then pulled into a parking lot in the middle of the block. He cut the lights and pulled into an empty parking space. I looked to my right and saw the Audi rush by.

Jock backed out of the parking space and pulled onto the street, following the Audi. We stayed several car lengths behind, our lights off for part of the way. The Audi slowed and pulled into a parking spot on the street. Jock made a right turn onto a side street, cut the lights and U-turned. He eased back up to the stop sign, looking to his right toward where the Audi was parked.

"He can't figure out what happened to us," Jock said.

The Audi pulled out into traffic with us following. We drove for several miles through residential streets and finally onto a four-lane thoroughfare. After about ten minutes, the Audi turned left onto another residential street. Jock pulled to the curb at the corner. We watched the brake lights of the Audi come on a half-block away. The car turned into a driveway and disappeared behind a house. Jock sat quietly for a few minutes, then opened his door. "I'll be right back."

He returned in a few minutes. "The house he pulled into is a mansion. I've got the address. Maybe we can find out who owns it and get a line on why they're after us. We can't do anything else tonight."

"Too bad," said Jessica. "Now you won't get to kill them."

Jock glanced at her. "Jess, I hate killing. I really do, but sometimes it's necessary. I'm sorry we got you into this. We'll make arrangements to get you back to Paris."

"You didn't get me into anything. I joined up to help Matt. I'll go back to Paris when we finish this."

"Are you sure, Jess?" I asked.

"Yes. De Fresne was responsible for a lot of deaths, and it looks like he might still be in business. I want him finished."

The deal had been struck. She was with us, even if reluctantly. I patted her on the arm. "Can I buy you a whiskey?"

CHAPTER THIRTY-TWO

Jessica laughed, loud guffaws gushing from her diaphragm. She couldn't stop. Her breathing came in gasps. Tears rolled down her cheeks. The others in the car started laughing too, not sure why, but caught up in the contagious hilarity. It was a release from the tension of the chase, of the killing of the Arab, and of the near-death experience in the Blattners' living room.

Jessica patted my hand, her laughter subsiding. "I think that's a good idea."

Jock was still chuckling. "What the hell is so funny?"

"We're alive, Jock," I said. "We're alive, and we're on our way to get some whiskey."

We drove to the Frankfurt suburb of Bad Vilbel. Jock negotiated the streets as if he knew the area well. We turned into the driveway of a house that might have been occupied by a middle class family, and drove around to the back. Jock turned off the engine.

"We're here. Herr and Frau Blattner, you'll be safe in this house. It's owned by my agency and is staffed with a maid and a bodyguard. I'll help you with your bags. Matt, you and Jess stay here. I won't be but a few minutes."

They unloaded the bags from the trunk of the Mercedes and disappeared into the house. They were expected. I turned to Jessica. "Are you really okay?"

"Yeah. I've never seen anybody shot before. That's all. It took the wind out of my sails. Who is Jock?"

"My best friend."

"Do all of your friends go around killing people?"

"Jock is different. He works for our government and does things that nobody wants to talk about. They're things that have to be done, people who have to be neutralized for the good of our nation."

"By neutralize, you mean kill people."

"Sometimes. When it's necessary. Like today. If Jock hadn't been willing to kill the Arab, we wouldn't be having this conversation. We'd be dead. People like Jock do what they do so that the rest of us can live like human beings."

"I know you're right, and I know we have to have people who do the dirty work. I've just never thought much about it, and I certainly never thought I'd be a part of it."

"It's a tough world, Jess. Somehow we've gotten caught up in a very dark side of it."

Jock came out of the house and leaned into the car. "We can stay here tonight. Tomorrow we'll try to figure out who's after us. Come on in."

We ate a quiet supper of lasagna and fresh Italian bread. The woman, who ran the house, did the cooking and cleaning and took care of the occasional guest, ate with us. A man carrying a sidearm in a holster at his hip stayed in the living room. He would be relieved in another hour by another armed man.

We went to our assigned rooms, Jessica across the hall from me. I took a shower and fell into bed exhausted. I dropped off into sleep, burrowing into the bed. Time passed, I wasn't sure how much. I was sleeping on my right side, blankets pulled to my chin. I awoke immediately when I heard the door to my room open. I lay perfectly still, trying not to vary my breathing, pretending to sleep. I opened my left eye to a slit, trying to see the intruder, ready to pounce. It was Jessica.

She slipped into bed beside me, facing me, and put her arm over my shoulder. She was shivering, and she was naked. "You didn't need whiskey after all," she said.

I held her, burying my face in that sweet part where her neck met her shoulder. She was still shivering slightly. I could feel the tremors gently shaking her body.

"Are you cold?" I asked.

"No. I'm scared. No, not scared, nervous. Maybe. I don't know what I am. I almost died today, and I saw a man killed. I've never seen anyone die before."

"It's okay. You're having a reaction to terrifying events. It happens to us all."

"I want you, Matt. Does that make me a slut?"

"No. I'm glad you're here. But the need for sex is sometimes part of the reaction to almost dying. I don't want you to do anything you're going to regret."

"I won't regret it."

"You might."

She laughed. "If I do, I won't tell you."

We made love, an intense, quick, urgent coupling. She was frantic in her need for an orgasm, and she wanted it immediately. She groaned when she came and held onto me for a long time, not moving, just lying there quietly. I started to say something, and she put her finger to my lips. "Not now," she whispered. "We'll talk later."

We made love again, this time at a more languid pace, taking our time, exploring, tasting, and finally bringing each other to vivid climaxes before sliding gently down that slope of post-coital torpor.

We drifted off to sleep wrapped in the warmth of each other. I dreamed of being chased by men in burnooses riding camels.

The chirp of my cell phone woke me. It was still dark outside, and my watch told me it was six in the morning. Jessica was gone. I opened the phone. It was Chief Bill Lester of the Longboat Key police.

"Matt, where are you? Never mind. I don't want to know. I've got some information on that bomb that took out your Explorer."

"Good morning, Bill. I'm in Germany. It must be midnight where you are."

"Yeah, but I've been waiting all evening to call. I knew you were somewhere in Europe, and I didn't want to wake you in the middle of the night. I got a report from ATF on my desk late this afternoon, and I thought you'd want to hear about it as soon as possible."

"What?"

"It's strange. The signature on the bomb belongs to some unknown bomber who's blown up several people in the last couple of years. All in Europe."

"Nothing else in the U.S.?"

"No. There were two bombings in Madrid, one in Paris, one in Naples, and one in Munich. A terrorist group that calls itself Allah's Revenge claimed responsibility."

"Tell me how the ATF knows this?"

"Each bomb maker has a unique signature. It has to do with how certain wires are cut or looped, the angle of switches, the material used to create the bombs, tool marks on metal parts that survive the blast. There is a worldwide database with all this information in it. The ATF boys are almost certain that the guy who made your bomb made those in Europe."

"But no others in the States."

"Not yet anyway."

"Thanks, Bill. How's the weather there?"

"Sunny and low seventies." He hung up.

Jessica, Jock, and I ate breakfast in the kitchen. The woman who ran the place put plates of eggs, sausages, and sweet rolls on the table and pointed out the coffee pot. She left us alone. I related my phone call from Lester. Jessica kept her head down, concentrating on her food. She looked up at me once, smiled, and reddened a little.

Jock grinned. "Did you guys sleep well?"

"Like a baby," I said.

He chuckled.

"What?" I said.

"Nothing." He tried to get serious, but kept grinning.

"What is wrong with you this morning?" I asked.

"Nothing. You just look a little tired. Like something kept you awake most of the night. What about you, Jess?"

She looked up from her eggs, smiling. "I have no regrets."

I laughed.

Jock swallowed a bite of sausage and changed the subject. "I talked to my office in Washington last night. A Saudi named Mohammed Allawi owns the house where we left our pursuers. He uses it when he's visiting Frankfurt. The CIA suspects him of having ties to Islamic terrorists, but they can't pin it down."

"That might explain the bombs in Europe, and the one in my car."

"Maybe. If this guy is hooked into the terrorists, he'd have access to bombs and the guys who make them."

"Why does Allawi have a house in Frankfurt?" I asked.

"He owns oil-drilling supply companies and banks all over the world. One of his banks is in Frankfurt, and he comes here for regular physicals. Bad heart. He had triple bypass surgery about three years ago. He was only in his early fifties; young for such a bad ticker. I guess it's easier to have a house here than stay in hotels."

Jessica looked up from her plate. "Could his bank have ties to the Confederated Bank Suisse?"

"De Fresne's bank," I said.

"I didn't think to ask," Jock said. "I'll check on it."

"Did you find out anything about the guy you killed?" I asked.

"Nothing on him in our system or anybody else's. He's a cipher."

He excused himself from the table and left the room. He was back in a few minutes. "No direct connection between the banks, but Allawi's father opened his first bank in Riyadh, Saudi Arabia, right after World War II and immediately established a corresponding relationship with CBS."

CHAPTER THIRTY-THREE

The sun baked the afternoon air, turning the cell into a furnace. No breeze blew through the barred window overlooking the courtyard of the mud fortress. But the sound of rifle fire did. Outside, against the mud wall that enclosed the dusty space, men were placed one at a time, hands bound behind their backs, hoods over their heads. A volley of shot would ring out, and then a detail of prisoners would appear to drag the body of the executed man out of view.

Abdul el-Gailani had made a mistake, the biggest of his life, and surely the last one. On the morrow he would join the men at the wall, and a life full of promise would be no more. He was a small man, standing only about five foot six, and he wore the flowing robes of the desert Arab. His beard was full and black, untrimmed. The area around his dark eyes was wrinkled from years of squinting into the sun. He was dirty and sunburned, the result of weeks of hiding in the merciless wasteland that was the Middle East.

El-Gailani paced his cell, trying to make his last day on earth one of reflection. It had only been ten years ago that his government had sent him to Paris to study finance. He was a nineteen-year-old boy, a Saudi whose family was close to the House of Saud, the royals. Some largesse flowed from that relationship, but not enough to make them rich. But he did have the benefit of good schooling in the English run academy in Riyadh, and he was handpicked by one of the princes to go to Paris for study.

He returned to the Saudi capital in 1939, just as war was enveloping

Europe. His prince embraced him and sent him to a bank in Damascus that was owned by the Saudi royal family. Although Syria was nominally an independent country, France had never ratified the treaty that would free Syria from French control. El-Gailani was not much bothered by this, as he had become a Francophile while living in Paris. He was convinced that French culture was superior to any in the world, and he was taken by the fact that France was an anti-Semitic country. He hated the Jews with the same intensity, and had once considered joining the Palestinians in their attempt to keep their land from Jewish hands.

After the fall of Paris in July 1940, Syria came under the control of Vichy France. When the Free French and British invaded and occupied Syria a year later, el-Gailani went underground. He became a guerrilla fighter, supporting the Syrian nationalists and the Germans. Finance was forgotten. He learned to blow up things and kill people, and he excelled at it, taking the nom de guerre of Rashid Ali.

In February of 1945, Syria, which had been recognized by the Allies as an independent republic, declared war on Germany and Japan. El-Gailani went farther underground, hiding from the authorities who had sentenced him to death in absentia. His war was over, and he wanted to go home to Saudi Arabia. He planned to resume his identity and seek the protection of his princely sponsor. The name el-Gailani did not appear on any list of subversives, only Rashid Ali. Once back in Saudi Arabia, it would be impossible to connect el-Gailani to the acts of Rashid.

But he had made a mistake. He was riding with a trucker whom he had met in a small town outside Damascus, heading for the Trans-Jordanian border. He'd agreed to pay the driver an exorbitant amount for the trip, but he was in a hurry to get out of Syria. His plan was to cross the neck of Jordanian land that separated Syria from Saudi Arabia, and then get in touch with his family in Riyadh. Somehow, they would be able to get him to the capital.

There was a roadblock at the border, manned by the Desert Patrol, an elite unit of the Trans-Jordanian army known as the Arab Legion. El-Gailani had not expected them on the Syrian side of the border, but he was not particularly concerned. He still had the documents that identified him by his real name and as a Saudi banker posted to Damascus. This wasn't the first roadblock they'd come to, and he'd had no trouble from the Syrians posted at the others.

They were ordered out of the truck, their papers scrutinized. There were three other trucks parked on the side of the road, each pointed toward the border. The soldier who held their papers motioned for them to follow him. "We will have to wait until our officer returns before we can let you go on. It shouldn't be long."

The soldier led them to a large Bedouin tent and motioned them inside. The space was plush, with carpets covering the sand floor and large pillows arranged for lounging. A samovar sat on a table in the center, teacups surrounding it. A dozen men were there, sipping tea, talking quietly.

One of the men looked up from the group. His beard covered only half of his face. The rest was scar tissue, the eye milky and without sight. The scars ran down his neck and into the filthy robe he wore. He'd been terribly burned.

The scarred man looked directly at el-Gailani and smiled crookedly. "Rashid, my old comrade, come join us."

"My name is Abdul el-Gailani. You have mistaken me for someone else."

"Nonsense, Rashid. Do you not remember the explosion that took part of my face? We were there together. It was fantastic."

"You are mistaken. I am a banker from Damascus."

The man's one eye held a glint of insanity, or maybe confusion. His smile disappeared. "You are Rashid Ali, a hero of the Resistance."

The soldier had been standing just inside the tent's entrance, listening to the exchange. He unslung his rifle and pointed it at el-Gailani. "You had better come with me."

El-Gailani turned. "The man is mad. You can see that. You've seen my papers. I am not this Rashid fellow."

"Come with me. My officer will sort this out."

The officer didn't sort things out. He simply put el-Gailani in the back of a truck, trussed like a goat, and sent him back to Kiswe. He'd been hauled before a court and given a cursory trial. It hadn't taken an hour. Three of his old comrades were in custody, and they identified him as

Rashid Ali. He was sentenced to death, the execution to be carried out in one week.

Yes, he'd made a fatal mistake. He should have walked across the desert as his ancestors had done for thousands of years. He should not have put himself in a position where soldiers could check his identity at roadblocks.

His week was about up. He'd watched many men die at the wall while he waited. Now it was almost his turn. Well, he'd go out with dignity.

Night comes quickly in the desert. One minute the sun is hanging low on the horizon and the next minute darkness falls. There were few lights in the compound where el-Gailani was being held, and the stars were bright against the night sky.

He heard the rattling of keys in the lock of his cell. Dinner was served. My last meal, he thought. He doubted they would waste food on him in the morning. He'd be dead before he got hungry.

The door opened and the jailer stepped back. A tall man in the uniform of the United States Army entered. He was wearing pinks and greens, the class A uniform of American officers, an olive green tunic and beige trousers. His brown shoes had been spit shined, but were now marred by grains of sand clinging to the gleaming leather surface. He wore the crossed rifles of the infantry on his lapels and the gold oak leaf of a major on his epaulets. He had a head of dark brown hair, and appeared to be about thirty years old, the same as el-Gailani. A bead of sweat escaped from the major's hairline as he removed his hat. He brushed at it with his free hand.

"It's hot as hell in here."

El-Gailani frowned. "Yes it is," he said in heavily accented English. "You get used to it."

"Maybe not as hot as where you're going tomorrow."

"You think I will go to hell?"

"I do. You murdered a lot of people."

"And you, Major. Are you going to hell for killing people?"

"Probably."

"That does not bother you?"

"Not especially. It can't be any worse than the past three years have been."

El-Gailani laughed. "Maybe you are right."

"I came to get you out of here."

"Why?"

"I have a proposition for you."

"What?"

"I can't discuss it here. I've got your release papers in my pocket."

"I cannot see any reason to stay."

"Put your hands behind you and turn around."

El-Gailani did as ordered. The American pulled a set of handcuffs from the pocket of his tunic and put them on the Arab's wrists, locking them down.

The major handed some papers to the jailer, who looked them over, and nodded. They walked out of the cell and exited the jail. The American handcuffed el-Gailani to the frame of the passenger's seat in a jeep, and they left the execution ground bound for Damascus.

CHAPTER THIRTY-FOUR

Jessica and I were clearing the table while Jock finished his coffee. "There has to be a connection," I said.

Jess put a stack of dishes in the sink. "What is a corresponding relationship between banks?"

I thought about it for a minute. "I think it depends on the banks, and how they put together an agreement. Basically, it's an agreement between banks where they help each other with liquidity management and short-term borrowing and investment needs. They may have an agreement that one bank will cash the other's checks, and take deposits of each other's customers."

"Sounds complicated."

"It's probably a lot more complicated than I know, but then I don't know much about it. It does seem a little odd that a start-up bank in Riyadh would have a corresponding relationship with an established Swiss bank. I don't see what would be in it for the Swiss."

"Saudi cash?"

"Well, maybe, but Saudi Arabia didn't have that much back then. Their wealth all came about after the war."

Jock brought his cup to the sink. "Allawi is tied to this in some way. A guy like him doesn't just hire out muscle. He's involved."

"I don't get this," I said. "Wyatt's list didn't have any Arabic names on it. The whole thing seemed to revolve around World War II types and the possibility that some of them got out of Europe after the war. Are we on a wild-goose chase? Maybe Wyatt stumbled onto something to do with Islamic terrorists and the list is meaningless."

"If so," said Jessica, "why would they be concerned that we were looking into people on the list? Why would Hassan at the archives be interested in my research?"

"I agree," said Jock. "Somehow, they're all tied together."

"Can we find out anything about Hassan?" I asked.

"I already have," said Jock. "I asked my agency to check him out. He's just a stringer of sorts. He's a member of a radical mosque in Cologne, but we don't have any information that he's involved in any terrorist activity. I think he's been asked to pass on the information if anybody comes looking for certain people in the archives. Maybe de Fresne's name tripped a wire, or maybe it was somebody else you checked on, even if there was no information. If you typed a name into the archive's computer, it might have been one that Hassan was monitoring. Somebody will be discussing this with Hassan this morning."

Jessica looked at her watch. "I need to make reservations back to Paris. I've got to be at work on Monday."

Jock stared at her, a look of consternation on his face. "I don't think that's a good idea. People have been trying to kill us. If you go home, you're probably going to be dead."

Jessica blanched. "That doesn't make sense."

"We don't know that," I said. "It might make sense to the people trying to kill us. We've gotten somebody's attention, and I don't think they're going to leave us alone now."

"But the embassy is expecting me back on Monday."

"It's Friday," I said. "Let's give it another day or two. Jock can square things with your bosses."

She was reluctant, but agreeable. "Okay. But this is getting tiresome."

My cell phone rang once. Another text message. I flipped the phone open and looked at the tiny screen. I was staring at a picture of Logan Hamilton tied to a chair. A man wearing a ski mask was pointing a gun at his head.

CHAPTER THIRTY-FIVE

I showed the picture to Jock and Jessica. No one spoke for a moment, shocked at what they saw. Jessica looked at me. "Do you know that person?"

"My best friend on Longboat Key. Logan Hamilton. What the hell is this all about?"

My phone beeped again. Another text message.

Mr. Royal, you and Dr. Connor will meet me at the marina on the Tampa end of the Gandy Bridge at 11:00 p.m. on Monday. Drive to the point and wait for me. If you fail to show, Hamilton dies.

I looked at Jock. "They didn't ask for you."

"They don't have any idea who I am. They probably think I'm just some hired hand. You and Jessica are the ones they want for some reason."

"I know that area," I said. "They could come in by boat and take us, or kill us, and be gone before anybody knew there was a problem. If there's a police presence, they just don't bring the boat in."

"We can't do anything about Logan from here," said Jock. "Let me make a couple of calls."

"Okay. I'm going to call Bill Lester. This could be a hoax of some sort. A digitally altered picture."

Jock left the room, and I placed a call to Lester's cell phone. I knew he slept with it by his bed. It was 2:00 a.m. in Florida.

A sleepy voice answered. "This better be good."

"Bill, I'm going to forward you a picture and a text message I just received. Look at it and call me back."

"Are you sober, Matt?"

"Never more so. Take a look at the picture." I hung up, and forwarded the picture and the message to Bill's phone.

Two minutes later, my cell rang. "What the hell is going on?" asked Bill.

"I don't know. Can you find out if Logan is missing?"

"I just called his condo. No answer. I've got a unit on the way over there now."

"Let me know what you find out." I closed the phone and told Jessica what the chief had said.

"Good morning." The voice was female and heavily accented. I looked up to see the Blattners coming into the kitchen.

"Good morning, Herr Blattner, Frau Blattner," I said. "I'll find our hostess and see if she can get some breakfast for you."

"I'll get her," said Jessica, and left the room.

"Herr Blattner," I said. "Have you ever heard the name Mohammed Allawi?"

"No, not that I remember. Who is he?"

"A Saudi banker who lives part-time in Frankfurt. He owns the house where the men chasing us went to ground last night."

"I'm sorry, but I don't think I've ever heard of the man. I can't imagine why he would try to kill me."

Jessica came back into the kitchen, followed by the hostess. She spoke to the Blattners in German, and went to the stove to fix them breakfast.

Jock came back into the room and motioned us to follow him. We went into the living room just as my cell rang. Lester. "Matt, Logan's not at home. His bed hasn't been slept in, and there's no sign of struggle. His front door was unlocked, but it always is."

"Try Marie Phillips. Logan could be there."

"Okay. I'll get back to you."

"Nothing," I said to Jock and Jessica.

Jock nodded. "I had my people take a look at your phone records."

Jessica interrupted. "That was quick. You can do that?"

"Yes," said Jock, "we can. Both the picture and the message were sent from a computer in the Selby Library in Sarasota."

"At two in the morning?" I asked.

"Yes. They're certain that's where it came from. Somebody must have broken into the library to use the computer. That would make the message pretty much untraceable."

I shrugged. "They gave us until Monday to get there. Why?"

"Maybe they hope to get you while you're still in Europe. Or they might be worried that you can't get a flight soon enough to get there before Monday."

Jessica put her hand on my arm. "Matt, I know this is about your friend, but I don't see how I can just take off for Florida. I've got a job."

"I don't think you've really got a choice. Jock can square things with the embassy, and you'll be a lot safer with me than you would be in Paris."

She turned to Jock. "What do you think?"

"Matt's right. If we go today, we'll have time to set something up. Maybe get ahead of the bad guys, find Logan, and figure out what this mess is all about."

"I'll see about some airline reservations," I said. "It's probably too late to get on a plane today."

Jock grinned. "All handled. You two are scheduled on a Delta flight out of Frankfurt Monday morning. It'll get you into Tampa at about five in the afternoon."

"I thought we were going before that," I said.

"We are. There'll be a government Gulfstream at Rhein-Main Air Force Base this afternoon. It's already booked out of here, and the customs people have vetted the flight manifest. The three of us aren't listed anywhere, but we'll be on that flight. With the time change, we'll land in Sarasota just after dark today. Anybody checking on you will expect you to be on Delta on Monday."

"Jock, you continually amaze me," I said.

"Yeah, well I amaze myself sometimes."

My cell rang. Bill Lester. "Matt, we found Marie. She's okay, but she was tied up, lying on the sofa in her living room. She said she opened the door for a visitor at about nine this evening, last evening I guess now, and three men came in with guns. They tied her up and took Logan with them."

"So it's not a hoax."

"No. I've got the sheriff's crime-scene investigators on their way over there now. Maybe they'll turn up something."

"Can you call them off?"

"Why?"

"We need to keep this very close, Bill. Logan's life depends on it."

"What the hell have you gotten yourself into?"

"I don't know, but it's serious. There are some bad guys chasing us around Germany, and now Logan's a hostage. I'll be home by Monday to meet them, like the message said."

"I know that marina. There's a long channel running up to where you're supposed to meet. It's the only way in and out. If they come in by boat, we can slip in after them and block their way out. There's only one way in by road too. I think they've built themselves a trap."

"These guys aren't idiots. I don't think they'd set themselves up that way. You can bet they know about the entrance and exit problems. They've got something else in mind."

"I'll get in touch with the Tampa police and see if they have any suggestions. They'll know that area better than we do."

"Bill, don't do anything until we talk again. Let's keep this close for now. If cops show up, they'll kill Logan. Jock Algren is with me, so we're not completely helpless on this end of things."

"Ah, good old Jock. Well, if he's in the mix, I feel a little better. Give him my regards, and y'all keep me in the loop."

"We'll do that."

"I'll keep this within my department for now. My guys won't blab, but I can't keep a lid on it forever."

"I understand. Thanks, Bill."

CHAPTER THIRTY-SIX

The horizon was ablaze with the lights of Tampa. As the plane banked over Egmont Key to line up on the runway at Sarasota-Bradenton, I could pick out Anna Maria Island and Longboat Key by the lights that separated the dark waters of the Gulf of Mexico from those of Sarasota Bay. We had flown nonstop from Frankfurt in the big executive jet. Jock explained that we had been designated as a military flight for the controllers, and the airport had been alerted that we would not require customs.

The wheels of the landing gear sang briefly as we touched down. We taxied to the ramp of a private, fixed-base operator and into a hangar. The pilots shut down the engines, and opened the door, letting the small stairway touch the floor. Jock, Jessica, and I were the only passengers.

A black Suburban sat on the tarmac just outside the hangar doors. The air was alive with the roar of a commercial jet on its takeoff roll. The smell of burned aviation fuel rode the warm breeze, the temperature in the mid-seventies even after dark. We were back in Florida, and I was glad to see the last of the snow.

Jock led the way to the vehicle, and we climbed in. The keys were in the ignition. "Where are we going?" I asked.

"I've arranged to put us up with a retired agent who lives in Lakewood Ranch. He has a big house, and since his wife died, he's lived there alone. He'll be glad for the company, and it'll keep us hidden. We've got to figure out how to get Logan out safely."

We drove out of the terminal area to University Parkway and then east until we came to the sprawling upscale neighborhood just east of I-75. Jock negotiated the streets, using the GPS navigation system built into the dash of the government SUV. We pulled into the driveway of a large house.

The garage door glided open. Jock pulled in and parked. The door slid closed.

A man came out of the door that led into the house. He was medium height, blue eyes, gray hair. He was wearing cargo shorts and a golf shirt with the logo of the River Wilderness County Club embroidered on the left breast. "You're Jock Algren?"

"Yes. Orville sends his regards."

"How is Orville?"

"Fat. And ornery as ever."

"I'm Tom Hickey," the man said, sticking out his hand.

Jock shook it, and introduced Jessica and me. "These are the ones in danger. I don't think I'm on the bad guys' radar, yet."

Hickey led us into the house, through the kitchen and into the living room. A sixty-inch flat-screen TV with surround-sound speakers mounted in the ceiling dominated the space. "Make yourselves comfortable. I've got beer in the fridge and I've ordered pizza. Should be here soon." He left us alone.

"Who's Orville?" I asked.

"I have no idea," said Jock. "It's just a recognition code we were given."

"You cloak-and-dagger boys think of everything."

"We try."

"I need to call Marie. I'd like to hear exactly what happened last night."

"Don't let on that you're here," Jock said.

I dialed her number on my cell phone. "Marie, I heard about Logan. Can you tell me what happened last night?"

"We were eating dinner on the balcony about nine o'clock when somebody knocked on the door. I opened it and three men in ski masks carrying guns burst in. They pushed me out onto the balcony and told Logan they would kill us both if he resisted."

"Did you notice any accent in their English?"

"Only one of them spoke to us. He seemed to be in charge. His English was accented, but not much. When they talked to each other they spoke in a foreign language."

"Did you recognize the language?"

"I think it was Arabic, but it could have been any Middle Eastern language. Even Hebrew. I don't think it was European, and from what I could see of them, I don't think they were Asian."

"Was anything said that would give you a hint as to what they were doing, or what their plans were?"

"No. The only thing said in English was what I just told you."

"Were they wearing gloves?"

"Yes."

"So the police aren't going to find any fingerprints."

"I'm pretty sure they didn't."

"Are you okay?"

"I'm fine, Matt. Just worried sick about Logan."

"We'll find him."

I hung up and dialed Bill Lester. "How're things stacking up, Bill?"

"You're up late." It was after midnight in Germany.

"I'm worried about Logan. What have you found out?"

"We don't have much, Matt."

"Did you find anything at Marie's?"

"Nothing. As clean a crime scene as we've ever found. We did get a lead on their car, though. Turned out to be a dead end."

"What happened?"

"They came through the security gate in a Lexus. Opened the gate from the car. They apparently stole one of the remote control devices that the residents use to open the gate. They waved at the guard as they went through, but he didn't get a look at their faces. When they were leaving, the guard recognized Logan in the back seat. He checked the license plate, and it didn't belong to anybody who lived there. He put it in a report for the day guard in case they came back."

"Who owns the car?"

"A guy in Venice. It was reported stolen yesterday morning. We found it in the parking lot of the Super Wal-Mart on Cortez Road."

"Any evidence in the car?"

"No, but a security camera at the store showed them dropping the car off. A van picked them up and they left. The tape clearly shows Logan with his hands tied behind him. The van had a Missouri plate on it, but it turns out that the plate had been stolen off a pickup truck in Sarasota late yesterday."

"What kind of van?"

"A Ford panel van. There're a million of them on the road."

"Dead end."

"Afraid so. When are you coming back?"

"We've made reservations on a flight on Monday. It'll get into Tampa late in the afternoon."

"Who's this other guy you're with, Dr. Connor?"

"She's not a guy. She's a very attractive young lady. She's a historian who works for the American Embassy in Paris. She's been helping me with some research. I guess whoever wants me dead figures she knows what I know."

"Matt, you know if you make that meeting, they'll kill you."

"I know. And if I don't, they'll kill Logan."

CHAPTER THIRTY-SEVEN

We all knew that Logan was dead whether I showed up or not. They wouldn't kill me and leave Logan alive. We had to find a way to get Logan before the time for the meeting. If he was still alive.

My phone rang. Marie.

"Matt, I just remembered something. When the man who seemed to be in charge was talking to the others in whatever language he was speaking, I heard him say something that sounded like 'Gilley Creek.'"

"That's odd. Any idea what he meant?"

"There's a Gilley Creek out in East Manatee County. Could that be it?"

"That doesn't make any sense. It's probably nothing, but if you remember anything else, let me know."

The pizza arrived. Hickey brought it into the kitchen and we sat around the table eating and drinking cold beer. It was nearing nine o'clock, almost three a.m. in Frankfurt. It'd been a long day. Jessica looked as if she was about to fall asleep.

"Why don't you go on to bed, Jess?" I asked. "We're not going to accomplish anything else tonight."

"I'm ready," she said, getting up from the table. Hickey showed her to her room, and returned to finish his beer.

"Tom," I said, "did you ever hear of a Gilley Creek in this area?"

"Sure. It's not far from here. It runs into Lake Manatee."

"What's there?"

"Nothing. It's part of a nature reserve. There're still some working citrus groves out there, but that's about it."

"Does anybody live in the area?"

"I don't think so. There're a couple of abandoned houses fronting the creek near one of the groves, but that's all."

"You ever been out there?"

"Sure. My buddy Tim Wiley owns the groves. I go out there with him sometime just to get out of the house."

"Do you know where the abandoned houses are?"

"I know the general area. You think those houses might be where they're hiding your friend?"

"I don't know, but Marie Phillips heard one of the kidnappers say something about Gilley Creek. He wasn't speaking English, but she heard him say those words."

Jock drained his beer. "Can you take us out there, Tom?"

"Sure, but I don't think we'll find much. And we sure can't do it in the dark."

"Can you find the abandoned houses?"

"I think so. We'll have to take some old farm roads back into the area, but I know them well enough to get us there and back."

"Jock," I said, "we can't be driving through there in that Suburban. Anybody with half a brain will figure out that it's a government vehicle."

Tom said, "I can borrow my friend's old Jeep Wagoneer. That thing is more than twenty years old, and he just uses it in the groves. Even if somebody saw us out there, they're probably used to seeing that thing driving around."

"We can't let anybody else know what we're doing," I said.

"I know where Tim keeps his keys. It won't be a problem. Tomorrow's Saturday, and he's never out there on the weekends. He'll be on a golf course somewhere."

I lay awake for a long time, listening for the sound of Jess opening my door. It never came. I drifted off into a fitful sleep and dreamed of other women who were long absent from my life.

CHAPTER THIRTY-EIGHT

At daybreak on Saturday morning, Tom Hickey, Jock, and I left Lakewood Ranch in Tom's two-year old Buick sedan. Jessica was sound asleep in her bed. I put coffee and water in the maker and left a note, telling her we'd be back in a few hours. She probably wouldn't like that, but we thought three men in a grove on a Saturday morning wouldn't raise any suspicions. Somebody might take notice of a pretty woman.

We left the Lakewood Ranch neighborhood through a back gate and drove about five miles north before turning east on a state highway. After a few miles we turned south and then east again onto a narrow dirt road running through groves of citrus trees. We turned onto an even smaller road, rutted with the weight of grove trucks used to haul citrus to the processing plants. In a few minutes we came to a dead end at a large well-maintained barn.

We got out of the car and Tom opened the barn door using a key hidden in a crevice under the barn's concrete foundation. He disappeared inside and came out behind the wheel of a green Jeep Wagoneer. The old gal was dented and pocked from years of driving the groves. Her paint was rusted off in more places than I could count, but her tires looked new, and the engine sounded strong.

"Hop in," said Tom.

We followed a trail for about a mile, and then drove directly through the grove, between the rows of trees. The Jeep was in four-wheel drive and took the sand without missing a beat. Soon we came to another road that ran along the edge of the grove. There were citrus trees to our right and pines, oaks, palms, and palmettos to our left.

Tom was concentrating on his driving, keeping the old Jeep at a conservative speed. "The creek is just beyond that stand of trees. These woods run right down to it. In a minute we'll come to a clearing where the creek bends out. There's an old house there, but there's not much left of it. If anybody's there, they wouldn't expect us to stop. I'll keep driving. You two see what you think about the place."

The house was in ruins. The tin roof had caved in and brought one wall down with it. Weeds had grown up in the clearing, encroaching on what remained of the house. The forest was reclaiming the land taken so many years ago by the farmers who'd homesteaded this part of Florida.

"Nothing," said Jock. "Nobody's been near that place in decades."

"There's another one about a mile farther," said Tom.

We crossed another farm road that seemed to be the boundary of the grove we were driving by. On the other side was another grove, stretching as far as we could see down the dirt track.

"We'll be there in a minute," Tom said. "It's farther back from the road, and there's a lot of foliage between the house and the road, so you won't be able to see much."

This house was in much better shape, but appeared abandoned as well. I could see the creek in front of the house, and the yard seemed relatively free of weeds. The woods between the road and the house were not as thick as those on either side, but my view was still restricted as we went by.

"I don't think anybody's there," I said.

Jock shook his head. "Not so fast, podner. Did you see that glint in the woods to the right of the house?"

"Glint?"

"Yeah, like the sun reflecting off metal."

"No, I missed it. What was it?"

"I'm not sure, but it could be a car. It was fairly big."

"Want me to turn around?" asked Tom. "Go take another look?"

"No," said Jock. "Let's keep going. If somebody's there, I don't want them to get antsy. We'll come back tonight."

CHAPTER THIRTY-NINE

Jessica was not happy. When we got back to Tom's house, she was sitting in the living room drinking coffee. The morning's newspaper was on her lap, an angry look on her face. "What the hell did you mean by running off and leaving me here?"

"You needed your rest," I said.

She ignored me. "Where have you been, and why didn't you get me up?"

"Jess," I said, "we went looking for a house out in the middle of nowhere. We thought three guys in an orange grove on a Saturday morning wouldn't be suspicious. A pretty woman might make someone take notice of us."

She wasn't placated, but I had gotten her interest. "What house?"

I told her what Marie had said and how we'd found the house. "We think there may be a car parked in the woods next to one of the houses. It's hidden pretty well, but Jock saw a reflection off something. We're going back tonight to see if anybody's there."

"I'm going with you this time."

"No you're not," I said. "Just Jock and me. We're going in armed. This could be a dangerous situation, and you're not trained for that."

She chewed her lip, thinking. "I guess you're right," she said, finally. "But don't go off again without telling me what you're doing."

Jock made a phone call and then left in the Suburban, telling us he'd be back in a couple of hours. When he returned he had several weapons in the car and camouflage clothes for him and me. I didn't ask where he got them.

CHAPTER FORTY

The old cracker house was dark, no lights anywhere. Its front porch ran the width of the structure on the side facing the creek. It sagged in the middle, but appeared sturdy enough. Concrete blocks served as front steps. A lone plastic chair took up space on the porch. I couldn't see any power lines running to the structure, so I assumed there was no electricity.

The house sat alone on a wooded lot fronting Gilley Creek. Civilization had hardly touched this part of old Florida. There were no other houses for miles, a perfect place to hide. Thick stands of pine trees, palms, and palmetto surrounded the clearing in which the house sat. It had probably once been a farm, home to pioneers who came to this area of Florida before the Civil War. The little dirt farm road was lost in the darkness.

We'd parked the Suburban in the middle of the grove and walked in. Anyone coming down the road wouldn't be able to see the vehicle, and we'd come in from the other side of the grove without lights, slow and easy.

Fog was rolling in off the slow-moving creek, wisps floating into the clearing. The humidity was higher than normal, and the fog was thickening. There was no sound, the animals quiet in the presence of humans. A dark green Nissan was parked nearby, camouflaged with branches, the source of the reflection Jock had seen that morning. We were hunkered down at the edge of the palmetto forest at the side of the house, our rifles ready, locked and loaded, safeties in the off position. We were carrying M-16s.

Jock had worked his way to the creek, giving him a view of the front of the house. I was about 150 feet away with a view of the back of the place.

We each had a small radio transmitter-receiver stashed in a pocket and tiny boom mikes attached to earpieces. We could talk to each other in whispers, unheard even a few feet away. Our side arms were Glock 17 semiautomatic nine millimeters. We wore camouflage clothing, and our faces and hands were blackened with grease paint. It was a little after midnight.

We sat quietly for fifteen minutes. There was no movement in the clearing, no guards in evidence. I heard Jock whisper in my earpiece. "Let's go."

We moved slowly into the clearing, snaking along on our stomachs, rifles held in the crook of our arms. As we got near the house, I saw a white light flicker in a front window. I couldn't decide what it was, but it stopped us both cold. Somebody was in the house. Jock whispered again. "It's a TV."

We moved closer and then stood and flattened ourselves against the side of the house, Jock near the front and I at the back corner. I crawled along the foundation until I got to a window. I eased myself up carefully, peering into the window with the flickering light. I saw a man watching a battery-powered black-and-white TV. He was engrossed in what appeared to be an infomercial, but no sound came from the set. Then I saw a small wire running from the TV to earphones clamped on the man's head. He was keeping things quiet. Were there others sleeping somewhere in the house? No way to know until we got inside.

I motioned to Jock to take the front, indicating that I would take the back. We moved away from each other, keeping to the side of the house, ducking under windows. There was no porch on the back of the house. The door opened directly onto two wooden steps that led to the yard. Jock disappeared around the corner, and I went to the back steps. I tested both of them. They would hold. The door opened inward. I'd have to get to the top of the stairs before we moved. I wanted to make sure the door wasn't locked. Jock's voice came over my radio. "Ready."

"Hold," I said. I eased up the steps and tried the doorknob. It turned. I pushed slightly, and the door opened.

"Go," I said, and stepped inside. I was in a kitchen. I couldn't see much in the dim light from the flickering television, but I could tell nobody was there. I heard a surprised voice, raised, speaking in a foreign tongue, then a thud. I moved toward the door into the interior of the house. Jock was standing over a man collapsed on the floor. His rifle was pointing at the two doors that led off the small living room where he stood. A man came bounding out of the door nearest me, a pistol in his hand. Jock shot him in the chest. Another man was right behind the first. He stopped dead, flung his hands into the air, dropped to his knees, and said in English, "Do not shoot."

I moved toward the man, rifle at the ready. I pulled a pair of handcuffs from my jacket pocket, told him to put his hands behind him, and cuffed him. I searched him quickly. I found a cell phone, but no weapons. I nodded to Jock. "He's clean."

"Jock was kneeling over the man he'd shot. "This one's dead."

"The other one?"

Jock went to him. "I hit him with the rifle butt. Must have broken his neck. He's gone."

I moved toward the closed door to the other room. Jock took up position, his rifle trained on the door. If anybody came bursting through that door, he'd be dead. I slowly turned the knob, and violently pushed the door open, knocking it back against the wall, stepping backward as I did. There was no movement inside the room. I pointed my rifle into the darkness and went through the door. Jock moved to cover me, shining a large flashlight into the darkened space. The room was empty, except for Logan. He was tied to a cot, his hands bound to the steel rails that held the springs and mattress in place, his legs tied to the footboard.

Logan blinked in the glare of the flashlight. "About time you guys got here. I gotta pee."

Relief surged through my body as my brain registered that Logan was alive. I went to him, used my knife to cut the ropes holding him to the bed. He got up on unsteady legs and moved out of the bedroom and toward the front door. He stopped in the living room and stood over the man I'd handcuffed. "This is the leader. He beat the crap out of me yesterday. Just having a little fun, I guess."

Logan unzipped his pants and urinated on the leader, saturating him from head to foot. The man yelped, and tried to move out of the stream, but Logan had been holding it for a long time. The torrent finally ended, and Logan zipped himself up. "Bastard," he said, and kicked the man in the side.

"Get up," I said.

The man rolled over and worked his knees under him. Then he stood, looking at me with a doleful expression. "I only beat your man because he told me I looked like a pig's asshole. That is a terrible insult to a Muslim."

I laughed. "Logan can get a little feisty at times."

"And he pissed on me. That is not a manly thing to do."

"Hey, pal," said Logan, "be glad I didn't have to take a dump."

CHAPTER FORTY-ONE

We were in the Suburban, driving toward Lakewood Ranch. The fog was thicker, and our headlights bounced back at us, creating an eerie illusion of being under water. The leader, whose name was Tariq, was trussed in the cargo area. Logan sat in the front passenger seat, I in the rear. We'd stopped at an all-night McDonald's for food for Logan.

Tariq was wearing clean clothes. I'd held him at gunpoint while he washed urine off his face and hands and changed into dry clothes. He'd told us his name, but refused to answer any other questions.

Logan was in good spirits, his ordeal over. He'd been worried about Marie, but I assured him she had not been harmed. I explained that the reason for his kidnapping was to get me back to Florida, where I could be killed. I told him about Jessica and explained why she had come back with us. "I'll give you all the details later," I said.

"Why didn't they just kill you in Europe?" Logan asked.

"They tried. Somebody took a shot at me in Frankfurt, and then this Arab guy tried to kill us in Fulda. After that we went to ground. They couldn't find us. I think they wanted to get Jessica and me back home before killing us. Maybe they were afraid that if they killed us in Germany, somebody would put together the research we'd done on the Nazis and our deaths. I don't think it occurred to them that I might bring the cops here into this thing. If Marie had called the police, you would have been just the victim of a random kidnapping. There'd be no connection between them and me."

"How do you figure that?"

"I think they were going to kill you and bury you so that nobody would ever find the body. If they did the same to Jessica and me, it would be almost impossible for anybody to make the connection to what we were doing in Europe. If we disappeared while in Europe, somebody might have put two and two together. But by getting us home, there'd be airline reservations to prove we had left Europe. "

"What are you going to do with Tariq?"

"Kill him, I suppose."

Tariq had been listening. "No," he said.

"Tariq," Jock said, "you're of no use to us. You won't answer questions and you whine a lot. It'll just be easier to kill you."

"No. I can answer questions. Lots of questions."

"Okay. When we get home, I'm going to need some information from you. I know a lot, but I don't know it all. If you lie to me, I'll probably know, and you'll be dead. Understood?"

"Yes."

We pulled into the garage in Lakewood Ranch. Hickey was in the kitchen making sandwiches. The wall clock showed 2:30 a.m. "I figured you guys would be hungry after an operation. Who're your friends?"

Jessica walked into the kitchen, relief painted on her face. She came to me and hugged me, then Jock. "I'm glad you guys are okay."

Jock pointed to Logan. "This is Logan Hamilton and he needs a bath. This other person is Tariq, the kidnapper."

"I thought so," said Hickey. "The handcuffs sort of gave him away. I'm done with the sandwiches. There's beer in the fridge. I'll be in my bedroom if you need me."

"Jess," I said, "you might want to go with Tom."

"Not a chance. I'm in this too."

"This could get a bit nasty. We might have to kill Tariq, or at least cut him up some."

I heard two sharp intakes of breath, Jess and Tariq.

"No, you won't have to do any of that," said Tariq, a tremor in his voice.

"I hope not," said Jessica, looking at Tariq, "but I've seen them do worse." She understood the game.

Jock unlocked Tariq's handcuffs and pointed to a chair. He placed a sandwich and a glass of water in front of the Arab. "You have one chance of leaving this place alive, Tariq. You have to tell us what we want to know. If you lie to us, I'll kill you."

"What will you do with me if I cooperate?"

"I'm not sure. I'll probably turn you over to the police. They'll prosecute you for kidnapping, but that's a lot better than the alternative."

"Okay. What do you want to know?"

"Who do you work for?"

"I do not know. I am a soldier of Allah's Revenge. I do what I am ordered to do."

"I'm familiar with your organization. Did you blow up Mr. Royal's car?"

"I had it done."

"Who did it?"

"I do not know his name. He was sent by our leader. I showed him the car that belonged to Mr. Royal, and he put the bomb in it."

"Where is the bomber now?"

"Again, I do not know. I think he works for an embassy in Washington."

"Which one?"

"I do not know."

"Who is your contact person?"

"What do you mean?"

"Who do you report to?"

"A man in Germany. His name is Farouk. I call him, and he gives me direction."

"What's the number?"

Tariq recited a number.

Jock looked at me. I looked at the stored numbers on the cell phone I'd taken from Tariq. The number was there, along with the name Farouk. I nodded.

"Do you have a specific time to call him?" Jock asked.

"Yes. I call him at eight each morning to let him know we are okay. I can call him anytime if I need something. He calls me sometimes as well."

"What happens if you don't make the eight o'clock call?"

"I do not know. I guess he will know we've been compromised, and he will do whatever he has to do."

"What were your orders concerning Mr. Royal and the woman?"

"I was to kill them and drop their bodies into the sea."

"What about Logan?"

"Him too."

"Bastard," muttered Logan.

Jock gave him a sharp look. Logan raised his hands in a gesture of surrender, and then made a zipping motion across his mouth.

Jock asked, "Why were you supposed to do these things?"

"I do not know. I do not question my orders."

"Would you recognize the bomber if you were shown a picture of him?"

"Of course."

"Have you ever met Farouk?"

"No. I have only talked to him on the phone."

"When did you come to this country?"

"I have been here for six years. I was a student at the University of South Florida."

"And now?"

"Now I live in Tampa. I am to hold myself ready in case I'm needed."

"Is this your first operation?"

"Yes."

"Who were the men with you tonight?"

"Their names were Anwar and Gamal. That may not be their real names."

"Have you known them long?"

"No. They were sent to help me."

"How did they get here?"

"They were smuggled into Tampa on a ship."

"What ship?"

"I do not know. They never said."

Jock looked at me. "We've got five hours before he has to make the call."

I shrugged. "He can tell Farouk that things are fine."

Jock laughed. "I think they'll be speaking Arabic. Even if one of us spoke the language, there could be a code word that would close things down."

"Okay. I'm tired. I'm not thinking too straight."

"I think it's better not to make the call at all. Farouk might think there's a problem with the phone, or something else that's delaying Tariq's call. It might create enough confusion to give us an extra hour or two."

"Any suggestions?" I asked.

"Yeah. Let's see if we can find out who owns that number in Germany."

An hour later we had an answer. Jock hung up his cell phone. "That number is a cell phone, a disposable one. Farouk bought it at a store in Frankfurt and paid in advance for its use. There's no way to trace it."

"Another dead end."

"Not necessarily. If Farouk is in Allawi's house in Frankfurt, maybe we can figure it out. One of our German-speaking agents is going to call the number at eight o'clock our time. We know Farouk will be expecting Tariq to call then, so he'll answer the phone. The agent will talk to him, apologize for the wrong number and hang up. We'll have a truck on the street in front of the house that has equipment to monitor any cell phone use in the area. If the phone's in the house, we'll know it."

CHAPTER FORTY-TWO

The morning crawled along. We were all on edge, waiting for something to happen. We'd made a start, put a few pieces of the puzzle together, but we were a long way from the whole picture. We'd tied Tariq to a bed in one of the bedrooms. He was comfortable, and Jess checked on him occasionally to see if he needed anything. Jock or I would take him for bathroom breaks, but otherwise he was quiet.

Tom Hickey had arranged for an agency clean-up team from Tampa to go to the Gilley Creek house and take care of things there. We didn't want the bodies or the Nissan to be found and an investigation started. The car would be towed to the agency's facility in Tampa and gone over by technicians. They might find something that would lead them to more terrorists.

A little after nine, Jock got a call from Germany. He hung up, grinning. "Farouk was at Allawi's house in Frankfurt. He waited an hour and then called a number in Riyadh. He talked to the man himself and told him he'd lost contact with Tariq. Allawi is heading to Frankfurt."

"Jock," I said, "we need to talk to Allawi. There's a connection there to Wyatt's death."

"What?"

"I don't know, yet, but think about it. We stumbled across some names of Nazis in the Bonn archives. Then Hassan apparently alerted somebody to what we're doing. Right after that, an Arab tells us to go home, and the next day the same guy shows up at the Blattners to kill us. He knows we're there because his bosses tapped Blattner's phone. The only reason they tapped his phone is because he had a tie to de Fresne, who put twenty million dollars in the Confederated Bank Suisse. The very bank that established a corresponding relationship with the Allawi Bank in Riyadh when it was a start-up, probably with no capital. Then the killer's buddies follow us from Fulda, and they go to Allawi's house. Now Tariq is trying to kill us in Florida, and he's tied to Allawi through Farouk. Allawi holds the key to this puzzle."

Jock stepped out of the room, his cell phone to his ear. He was back in five minutes. "Get packed. We're going to Frankfurt."

"How?" asked Jessica.

"The Gulfstream is in Tampa. It'll be at the Sarasota-Bradenton airport in an hour, fueled and ready to fly to Frankfurt. It's about a nine-hour trip. Allawi is coming from Riyadh, which is about a six-hour trip, but his plane doesn't have the range to make it all the way. He'll have to land and refuel. With any luck, we can get to Frankfurt before he does."

"What about Tariq?" I asked.

Jock looked at Tom Hickey. Tom said, "I'll take care of it. We can have some of our guys out here from Tampa in a couple of hours. They'll keep him on ice until you decide what to do with him."

Logan said, "I'm going with you. That bastard tried to kill me."

"You don't have your passport," I said.

Jock laughed. "Come along, Tiger. You won't need a passport the way we're going in. If you need one to get back in the country, we can arrange that with the consulate in Frankfurt."

Logan called Marie to tell her he was safe and not to worry; that he'd be back in a few days, but there was something he had to do. He told her he was with Jock and me and asked her not to mention anything about his release.

I called Bill Lester. "Bill, we've got Logan. He's okay."

I could hear the surprise in his voice. "Where are you?"

"Can't say. Sorry."

"Are you coming back to the key?"

"Not right away. And Bill, it's important not to let anybody know that Logan's been released."

"Damnit, Matt. I can't have a kidnapping on my island and just forget about it."

"Look, I understand. But this is bigger than a kidnapping. Jock is running things here, and we need to keep everything under wraps for now."

"Ah, goddamnned Algren and the goddamnned feds. Okay. Jock knows what he's doing, but you keep me in the loop. Understand?"

"I do, Bill, and I'll bring you up to date as soon as I can."

"Very soon, Matt."

"In a few days at the most."

By eleven thirty we were wheels up, climbing out over Sarasota Bay. I could see the islands, Longboat and Anna Maria, resting like two emeralds floating on the shimmering waters, separating the bay from the Gulf of Mexico. The wake of a motorboat cutting across the tip of Bean Point left a scar on the flat sea. I wanted to be on that boat, heading for the fishing grounds, a warm breeze in my face. Instead, I was on my way to a northern European winter, and a dicey mission that would result in somebody's death. I hoped it wouldn't be mine. Or my friends'.

We flew deeper into the night, the jet eating up the miles and the hours. We landed in Frankfurt at one thirty a.m., tired and out of sorts. Jet lag was taking its toll on all of us. We taxied to the military side of the airport and deplaned on the tarmac next to another black Suburban. The driver was waiting for us. The cold wind blowing across the open space of the airfield cut into me, causing a shiver. I liked the Florida weather better.

"Your agency must have gotten a deal on these cars," Logan said. "I guess you buy in bulk, you get a good price."

Jock laughed. "Yeah. I think somebody at the top wants us to be inconspicuous. People probably think we're the CIA or FBI."

"Right," said Logan.

We were bundled up in the heavy clothes we'd packed. We'd stopped at a store on the way to the airport in Sarasota and gotten Logan some winter clothes. I didn't think he'd survive in the shorts and tee shirt he'd been wearing since he was kidnapped.

"Where're we going?" I asked.

"To another safe house," Jock said. "In a suburb called Oberursel. We'll get some rest and then go get Allawi."

"How are we going to get to him?" Logan asked.

Jock chuckled. "We'll ask him nicely to join us."

"Just like that?" asked Jessica. She'd been quiet since we landed, lost in her own thoughts, chin buried in the heavy scarf she'd put around her neck.

"Our invitation will be persuasive," said Jock.

"You mean kidnap him," Jessica said.

Jock waved his hand in the air, a dismissive gesture. "Something like that."

Logan let out a snort of disgust. "Bastard's got it coming."

CHAPTER FORTY-THREE

Genoa. Ancient hometown of Christopher Columbus. The American was driving an open jeep, the sun glinting off the gold oak leaves attached to the epaulets of his Class A uniform. A private sat in the front passenger seat, his left arm hanging to the floorboard. A close inspection would have shown that the soldier's wrist was handcuffed to the seat's steel frame.

The great port was in shambles. The British Navy had shelled it into oblivion, but the town was pretty much unscathed. It was late May, and the sun was warm, a welcome respite from the cold of Frankfurt. The American had spent the past six weeks waiting for the final campaign of the American 5th Army to rout the Germans in the Po Valley of northern Italy. That was accomplished, and the Nazi Army had surrendered in the first week of May.

The American had gone to the military prison outside Nice that morning. He showed his credentials and a fake set of orders to the officer in charge, and left with de Fresne. The trip to Genoa was only about a hundred and fifty miles, but the roads were clogged with refugees returning home now that the war was finished. Ruined buildings dotted the landscape as the men neared Italy, a sign that the war had come this way. It took most of the day to reach Genoa.

There had been little talk since leaving the prison. As they drove out onto the main highway, de Fresne asked, "Where are we going, Major?"

"To Genoa."

"Not Rome?"

"No. Plans have changed.

"Why Genoa?"

"You'll go from there to Argentina."

"Argentina?"

"Yes. It's the gateway to the States."

"I don't understand."

"You don't have to. Now, shut the fuck up."

"Yes, sir."

They drove into the city in the late afternoon, the major squinting into the pale sun. The American navigated along a road that skirted the bay, giving them a view of the destruction of the port. The stark beauty of the bay freckled with sunken ships and destroyed piers did not move the American. He'd seen it before, that and worse, and he had become inured to the horrors of war.

They took a left onto a street running to the east and came to the Cathedral of San Lorenzo. The church had sustained some minor damage when a British naval shell pierced the roof and landed on the floor of the sanctuary without exploding. The American had heard that the bishop planned to leave it in the church as a reminder that in war evil can come to even the holy places.

They parked and the major unhooked de Fresne. "If you try to run, I'll shoot you."

"Don't worry, Major. I'm with you."

As they entered the building, a priest wearing a cassock intercepted them. "May I help you, Major?" he asked in heavily accented English.

"We're here to see Monsignor Petranovic."

"May I tell him why you're here?"

"Tell him that Bishop Hudal sent us."

A look of surprise briefly crossed the priest's face. He seemed confused, unsure of himself. "I do not mean to seem disrespectful, sir, but I don't believe the bishop would send an American Army officer to see the monsignor."

"Father, there is a lot of money involved here. I desperately need his help in getting a good man out of the clutches of the de Gaul government in France. Tell the monsignor that I'm from the OSS."

"Give me a few minutes, sir," the priest said, and turned and walked into the gloom of the cathedral.

De Fresne turned to the American. "What the hell was that all about?"

"There's a large group within the Catholic Church, headed by Hudal in Rome, that's devoted to getting Nazis out of Europe. Petranovic is Hudal's man in Genoa. He can supply you with papers from the Vatican Refugee Organization, and those will get you a displaced person passport from the International Committee of the Red Cross. That'll get you out of Genoa on a ship bound for Argentina. I have people in Buenos Aires who'll take over from there."

"How do you know about all this?"

"The OSS helps Hudal when it suits them."

"Do the priests get a cut of my money?"

"No. I'll see that they get paid well, but not from *our* money. From OSS funds."

"Are you just going to turn me over to the monsignor?"

"Probably. Keep in mind that I have people in the group who'd just as soon toss you overboard as look at you. One misstep on your part, and you're a dead man. You'll be met when the ship docks in Buenos Aires."

"Then what?"

"Then we'll get you to America."

CHAPTER FORTY-FOUR

The safe house was small, tucked behind a copse and a low stone wall. The trees were leafless, stark in their nakedness, standing guard against the night. The ground was blanketed with a light covering of snow that reflected the sparse light of a waning moon. The steeply pitched roof was bare, but small stalactites of ice hung from the eaves. The property sat on a dirt track that ran for half a mile off the main road leading to the Taunus Mountains in the near distance.

Jock parked the car in the dirt driveway that ran next to the house. The agency man in the Suburban had taken us to downtown Frankfurt, where another gray Mercedes was waiting. It was nearing three when we arrived, but light shown in the windows of the house, providing a sense of safety and warmth, an oasis of good cheer in a bleak and snowy world.

Jock had a key to the front door and let us in. The living room was small, with overstuffed furniture taking up most of the space. A fully equipped kitchen, three bedrooms, and a bath completed the accommodations. I heard the soft sound of a furnace somewhere in the house, and warm air flowed from vents in the baseboards.

Jock sat in a chair, exhaustion written on his face. "We've got to move on Allawi today. If we hit them in mid-morning, Allawi should be sleeping. He'll be as tired as we are after his flight. His men won't be expecting anything in broad daylight."

"We?" asked Jessica.

"Yeah," said Jock. "My agency gives me plenty of support, but it can't have its people involved directly in taking Allawi down. The Germans would raise nine kinds of hell if they thought we were operating in their country."

Jessica frowned. "What about you?"

"I'm retired, pretty much. If my involvement came to light, the agency would just take the position that I'm a retired agent helping out a friend."

"Are four of us enough to do this?" asked Jessica.

I spoke up. "First of all, there're only three of us. You're not going to be involved. Secondly, as soon as the sun's up, I'll call Burke Winn and see if he can give us a few soldiers from one of the antiterrorist units stationed around here. Those guys are used to operating out of sight of the authorities."

Jessica exploded. "Bullshit. I'm part of this. Those bastards tried to take me out, and I'm not going to sit around like a good little girl while you big hairy men do all the heavy lifting. I know how to handle a gun. My dad made sure of that. I'm going with you."

"Okay," I said, holding up my hands in surrender. "Okay. We'll work out a plan that includes you."

She smiled, all the bluster gone. "Okay."

Logan stood. "We need to get some sleep. We've got about four hours 'til sunup. We can't do anything until then."

At seven o'clock, I called Burke Winn. "Are you in Berlin?"

"No. I'm still stuck in Frankfurt. Where are you?"

"Frankfurt. I'll explain it later, but I need some help. How many soldiers can you give me for a couple of hours?"

"Two."

"Two? You're a general for God's sake."

"Yeah, but I don't command any troops. I'm the frigging attaché, remember?"

"Right. Are the two you've got any good?"

"Among the best."

"Not embassy weenies, I hope."

"Yep. Olenski and myself."

"Olenski? Burke, I don't need a typist."

"Ski is Ranger qualified. I brought him with me from the special ops command I had before I let them talk me into this dumb-ass job."

"Burke, this thing could blow up in our faces. I don't want your career to go down the tubes."

"Is this about Wyatt?"

"Yes."

"I'm in. Are you by yourself?"

"No. I've got three friends with me. One is a Vietnam infantry grunt who became a chopper pilot, and another works for the government — one of those agencies nobody knows about. The third is a female historian."

"Where can we meet?"

I gave him directions to the safe house. "No uniforms and no official vehicle."

"Geez, L.T. I wish I'd thought of that." He hung up.

Winn and Olenski arrived two hours later, driving an Acura SUV. They were dressed in jeans, down jackets, and hiking boots. They came inside and hung their coats on the rack next to the front door. Both were wearing side arms that looked like .45-caliber semiautomatics. I introduced them to Jessica, Jock, and Logan.

I explained who we were after and why. I gave them every detail I knew, told them everything that had happened since I'd visited the consulate the week before, and spelled out Jock's and Logan's involvement, as well as Jessica's.

"General," Jessica said, "why are you here?"

"I owe it to Wyatt."

"That's it?" she said, a wisp of incredulity tingeing her voice.

"Yes, ma'am."

She turned to Ski. "And you? Do you owe Wyatt too?"

"No, ma'am. I owe the general."

"And Jock and Logan are Matt's friends, and Matt owes Wyatt," she said. "What is with you guys?"

It was a question I'd heard before. Some people cannot understand the bonds that often join men together. I think it's a genetic need, some atavistic craving for a nexus that provides security. The human race is built on relationships. It used to be the tribe or the clan. It's still that way in many parts of the world. But in the more industrialized and modern West, we've lost that sense of tribal identity. We have our families, but as we grow up and leave home, we tend to get spread out, cut off from daily contact with our blood relatives. We start to form new associations, new loyalties. Go into a local bar or pub anywhere in the world, and you'll see that kind of bond. It doesn't run deep, but it's a connection. Or you have friends, like Logan and Jock, who become your brothers, closer than the blood relatives you seldom see. And sometimes, when there is great danger, you form the bonds that soldiers know, ones that last a lifetime, even when your contact with each other is rare. And when you need help, like I did on that snowy day in Germany, the clan gathers. Or when justice needs to be done for one of us, we band together to mete out the punishment due.

"It's complicated," I said. "It's kind of a tribal thing. We take care of each other."

Jess was silent for a beat. "*Un pour tous, tous pour un,*" she said quietly. "Like in *The Three Musketeers*."

Burke grinned. "Dumas understood. 'One for all, and all for one.'"

"It's a hell of a philosophy," she said.

"It's more than a philosophy," Jock said. "It's a way of life."

Jess stared at us for a moment, a hint of a smile tugging at her lips. "I think I'm about to die of a testosterone overdose," she said. "Have you guys come up with a plan?"

"I think so," I said, and laid it out for them.

CHAPTER FORTY-FIVE

At ten thirty, we were parked on Allawi's street, one block from his house. The six of us were crammed into Burke's car, Jessica sprawling over the small third seat in the rear.

We men had the same kind of small radios Jock and I had used at Gilley Creek. Jessica was dressed in a heavy jacket, ski pants, and hiking boots. She had strapped a small transmitter to her chest just below her breasts. We'd be able to hear her and whatever was said around her, but we wouldn't be able to talk to her.

Jessica was going into the house. We wanted to make sure Allawi was there before we started busting down doors. If he hadn't arrived yet, we'd be making a lot of noise for nothing. He'd be alerted, and we'd probably never see him again.

She pulled the coat's hood over her head and got out of the car. She walked toward the house as the rest of us watched. She went up the front steps to the small stoop, knocked on the door, and waited. In a moment the door opened, a swarthy man dressed casually stood at the threshold. Jessica spoke to him in German.

"I am sorry," the man said in heavily accented English. "I do not speak German."

"I'm here to see Mr. Allawi," Jessica said in English.

"Who are you?"

"A friend. I'm not to say anything else except to Mr. Allawi."

"Come in, then."

They disappeared into the house. We got out of the car and separated. Jock and I hung back as Burke and Ski walked up a side street toward the entrance to the alley that ran behind Allawi's residence.

The conversation in the house was coming over our radios.

"Wait here," said the man with the accent.

I watched the others until they disappeared into the alley. Jock and I walked toward the house on the opposite side of the street. As we approached the house, I heard Burke whisper into the radio mic, "We're directly behind the house."

"What can you see?" I asked.

"Nothing. The backyard is paved over and there're a couple of cars parked there. I only see one door into the house."

"Can you move up closer to the house? Will the cars shield you?"

"Yes. We're going to slip in one at a time. If anybody's watching, we'll know as soon as we start to move."

Jock and I were in front of the house, standing casually, talking. Two old friends out for a walk. I heard Jessica say, "Are you Mr. Allawi?"

"No. My name is Farouk. Mr. Allawi is not here. May I ask your business?" A different voice, the English flawless, no hint of an accent.

"I was told to speak only to Mr. Allawi."

"Who told you that?"

"My superior at the American Consulate."

"Do you mean the American Consulate here in Frankfurt or the embassy in Paris?"

"I don't know anyone in Paris."

"Ah, Dr. Connor, I do not think you are being completely truthful."

"Move! Now," I shouted into the radio.

Jock and I sprinted to the front door. He kicked at it with the heel of his boot; once, twice, and it flew open. I could hear loud voices from the back of the house. We went in, pistols held in front of us. Sounds of gunshots came from the kitchen area as we turned into the living room.

A man was standing behind Jessica, his arm around her neck, a pistol pointed at her temple. Another man stood a couple of feet away from Jessica and her captor, smiling. "Drop your weapons," he said

Jock and I stopped cold, standing, facing the scene, our weapons pointing at the two men.

Winn shouted from the rear of the house. "We're coming in."

"Stay where you are," I called.

I turned to the smiling man. "You're Farouk."

"I am he, Mr. Royal."

"If you will order your man to release Dr. Connor, I won't kill you," I said.

He laughed. "Come now, Mr. Royal. It sounds as if you have other men in the house. The only way Dr. Connor gets out of this alive is if you put your weapons down and allow us to leave with her."

"This is your last chance, Farouk."

He laughed again. "And yours, Mr. Royal."

Jock fired, his bullet taking Jessica's captor in the forehead. He dropped, pulling Jess with him, his gun falling to the side. He was dead before he hit the floor. Jess screamed and then rolled away from the dead man. She picked up the pistol and sat on the floor, pointing the gun at Farouk.

Logan, Burke, and Ski ran into the room, guns at the ready. They stopped, surveying the scene, taking it in, assessing the situation. Satisfied, they relaxed. Logan said, "Three dead guys in the kitchen. You all right, Jess?"

"Yeah."

Ski moved toward the stairway. "I'll check upstairs. See if Allawi is here."

"I'll go with you," said Burke. "Might be some more bad guys up there."

"Is there anybody else in the house, Farouk?" I asked.

"No."

"If I hear any kind of ruckus from up there, I'm going to shoot you. Understand?"

"Yes. There is no one else."

Ski and Winn move cautiously up the stairs, weapons ready.

"Where is Allawi?" I asked.

"I do not know," said Farouk.

"Farouk, I want you to listen to me very carefully. If you don't answer my questions, I'm going to kill you. But I'll do it by degrees. I'll start shooting at your ankle, and move up from there. That's going to be a very hard death."

"I swear to you, Mr. Royal, I do not know where he is. I talked to him yesterday, and he said he was coming to Frankfurt. Then he called me later and said that when he landed to refuel there was a mechanical problem with his airplane and he would be delayed."

"How long of a delay?"

"He did not say."

"Where did he refuel?"

"He did not say."

"How did you know who we were?"

"I have seen pictures of you and Dr. Connor."

"Did you send the man to Bonn and Fulda?"

"Yes. What happened to him?"

"He died. Why were you after us?"

"Mr. Allawi said that you were dangerous to our cause and that you had to be taken out of the picture."

"What cause?"

"I cannot say."

"In which ankle do you want the first bullet?"

"No. Okay. Allah's Revenge."

"How do you communicate with Allawi?"

"Cell phone."

I turned to Jock. "Can you get an Arabic speaker to the safe house?"

"Let me make a call." He left the room.

Burke and Ski came back down the stairs. "We've got to move, Matt," Winn said. "If somebody heard the gunfire, the cops could be here any minute."

"We're on our way," I said. "Let's go out the back door."

Jock came back into the room. "We'll have a translator at the house by the time we get there."

I turned to Farouk. "Let's go. If you try to run, I'll shoot you. Any noise from you, you're dead. We're going out the back door, down the alley, and around the corner."

Burke said, "I'll take Jessica out the front door. If anybody's looking, maybe they'll think we're visitors just leaving."

We left the house, Logan and Ski in front, then Farouk, and then Jock and me. When we got to Winn's car, I put handcuffs on Farouk. There was just enough room in the small cargo space behind the third seat to stuff him into.

Burke said, "Ski, you stick around here and let me know if anybody shows up at the house."

"Yes, sir," said Ski.

"Is that a good idea?" I asked. "We don't want him picked up by the cops."

"I'll be fine, L.T. I speak enough German to get along, and I'll just tell anybody who asks that I'm waiting for my girl. Besides, I've got a diplomatic passport. Nobody will bother me."

"Call me if anything happens," Burke said, and got into the driver's seat. Jock and I were in the middle seat, Jessica in the front passenger. Logan crawled into the backseat so that he could keep an eye on our passenger. We pulled away from the curb, heading for Oberursel.

"Jock," Jess said, "what if you'd missed."

"I didn't."

"I know, but a couple of inches one way and you'd have shot me, a couple the other way and you'd have missed, and the guy would have shot me."

"I wouldn't have taken the shot if I hadn't been absolutely sure, Jess. And, I knew if we put down our guns, we'd all be dead."

"Thank you," she said.

I said, "Farouk, can you hear me?"

"Yes."

"When we get to our house, you will call Allawi. There will be an Arabic speaker listening to every word. If you say anything to alert Allawi, I'll shoot you. If you use a code word that would alert him to danger, we'll know it eventually. And then I'll shoot you. Do you understand?"

"Yes."

Fifteen minutes after we left Allawi's house, Winn's phone rang. When he hung up, he said, "We may have a problem. Four men just drove into Allawi's driveway. They're inside now. Ski doesn't think they're cops."

"If they're Allawi's men," I said, "they're not going to call the cops."

"No," said Jock, "but they'll call Allawi."

"Farouk," I said, "do you have other men in Frankfurt?"

"No, but we were expecting some new ones in today. From Libya."

"Are they in contact with your boss?"

"No. I am the only one who knows how to contact him."

I turned back to Winn. "I don't know about this. Let's go with what we've got. Let Farouk make the call."

Burke was nodding his head in agreement when his phone rang again. When he hung up, he said, "The four guys were inside for only a couple of minutes and drove away. Ski will stick around in case they come back."

I was standing in the living room of the safe house, my nine-millimeter pointed at Farouk's head. He was facing me, seated in a chair five feet away. Jock, Logan, and Burke Winn were standing quietly on the other side of the room near the kitchen, their weapons holstered. Jessica was sitting in the chair across from our guest.

Farouk's cell phone was hooked up to a device that recorded both sides of a conversation. The Arabic speaker from Jock's agency sat over the machine, a pair of large earphones covering his ears. He was translating for us in real time.

Farouk: "Excellency. We have a problem in Frankfurt."

Allawi: "What?"

Farouk: "Matt Royal knows about your house. I saw him and another man on the street in front of it a few minutes ago."

Allawi: "Where are these men now?"

Farouk: "They are gone. Are you coming here, sir?"

Allawi: "I think not."

Farouk: "Then let me come to you.

Allawi: "Where are the other men?"

Farouk: "They are here. I can send them away."

Allawi: "How would Royal know anything about me?"

Farouk: "I do not know, sir."

Allawi: "Maybe he followed your men to the house when they lost him on the day he was in Fulda."

Farouk: "That is possible."

Allawi: "Arrange for the men to fly to Algiers. Get them out of the house immediately. If Royal or the police come to the house, you tell them that you have no idea why anyone would think I could be involved in anything illegal. Tell them that I am in Saudi Arabia, and am not expected back in Frankfurt for several weeks."

Farouk: "Are you in the homeland, sir?"

Allawi: "No. Once you have made the arrangements for the other men, call me. I will bring you to me."

The line went dead.

Jock moved to the phone hanging on the wall next to the kitchen door. "I'll call the airlines and make reservations for the dead guys. If Allawi's able to check that, he'll see their names on the list. Then we'll have Farouk call him back."

The front door of the little house burst open and flew back on its hinges, banging against the wall. A swarthy man wearing a parka and a black watch cap came through the opening, an AK-47 assault rifle pointing into the room.

CHAPTER FORTY-SIX

I reacted instinctively, turning toward the intruder and firing. The bullet caught him in the face, and he sprawled forward, his rifle discharging as he fell.

"Get down!" I yelled, and dove for Jessica. She had started to stand, was half out of her seat when I tackled her, taking both of us to the floor. Out of the corner of my eye, I saw the other men react, pull their guns, drop behind the furniture. Another man came through the door, his rifle spraying bullets.

Farouk went down. He hadn't had time to react from the first man's entrance. He was sitting in his chair watching the action with a detached air, as if he wasn't sure what was happening. A heavy slug from the second intruder's weapon caught Farouk in the chest, pushing him over backward, the look on his face turning to surprise and, in an instant, to the slackness of death.

Jock fired twice, catching the second man in the chest and head. He died as he fell to the floor. The window on my right exploded with the impact of high-velocity bullets. Incoming. Logan and Burke were firing back, what we used to call suppressing fire, keeping whoever was out there at bay. Jock had disappeared through the back door.

Jessica was okay, shaking a little, but not hurt. She pushed at me, trying to get me off her. "Be still," I said. "This isn't over." She quieted down and lay still. The Arabic speaker was under the table on which his equipment rested. He was balled up in a fetal position, his hand covering his head. He worked for Jock's agency, but he wasn't a field agent.

The sofa was between the front door and me. I eased my head up so that I could see over it. There was nothing but the two dead men. The smell of cordite was heavy in the room, the cold air assaulting us through the open door and broken window, stirring the smoke left by the weaponry. Burke and Logan moved cautiously toward the window. I heard a volley of shots from outside, the sounds of pistol fire, no AKs. I moved quickly to the front door, stood with my back to the wall and slid down onto my haunches. I slowly moved my head over to the opening at about knee height, hoping that whoever was out there wouldn't be looking that low for a target.

I saw an Audi parked on the road about two hundred yards from the house. Jock was walking toward two bodies lying on the ground, their blood marking the snow like black amoebas. I wondered why it wasn't red, but knew it had something to do with the cold, and with the angle from which I viewed the scene.

Jock saw me, and waved me out. "That's all of them. Anybody hurt in there?"

"Farouk's dead, but everybody else is fine."

The others joined us and helped us move the bodies inside. There were no close neighbors, but we didn't want anybody driving by to see two dead men on the front lawn.

Jock picked up Farouk's cell phone, punched in some numbers and stared at the tiny screen. "Farouk had a damned GPS system in his phone. Shit. I should have thought of that."

"That's how they found us," said Burke. "They must have seen the bodies, realized Farouk was gone, and locked into his GPS signal. Damn."

"He knew about the GPS," I said. "He took a chance his buddies would bail him out. I wonder if he said anything to alert Allawi."

"I think that's a safe bet," said Jock. "Allawi's in the wind. We may never find him."

Burke pulled out his cell phone and dialed a number. "Ski, can you get into the house without being seen?"

Silence for a beat. Then, "I want you to search the place. See if you come up with any documents, anything that will tell us where Allawi might be." Burke gave him a synopsis of what had happened at the safe house and hung up.

Burke turned to Jock. "Can you get these bodies handled?"

"Yes. We keep piling them up. Sooner or later, my director is going to get tired of this."

Burke said, "Let's go get Ski. He'll have the place picked clean by the time we get there." He looked at the Arabic speaker who'd gotten into a chair and was finally calming down. "We need you to go with us in case we have to read documents in Arabic."

"No sweat," said the Arabic speaker. "You guys are a lot of fun."

We took both cars, Jock's rental Mercedes and Burke's Acura. Logan and the Arabic speaker rode with the general. An hour later we pulled into parking places on Allawi's street. Two Frankfurt police cars were parked in front of the house, another in the driveway, blue strobes reflecting off the windows of the houses on either side of the street. Uniformed officers stood in a knot on the sidewalk, tucked into cold weather gear, slapping their hands together to keep warm. Little puffs of clouds escaped their noses as they exhaled into the cold air. A coroner's van made its way down the street and turned into the driveway.

There was no sign of Olenski.

CHAPTER FORTY-SEVEN

The wind off the Rio de la Plata was bitterly cold. The heavy topcoat worn by the American did little to blunt its force. He shivered and wrapped his arms around himself in a futile attempt to find a little warmth. He was wearing a three-piece wool suit under the coat, white shirt, regimental tie. His black lace-up shoes reflected the lights of the quay.

A tugboat was pushing an old ship, the M.V. *Don Zierke*, a tramp with a straight-edged bow, into the wharf behind the chain-link fence. The American's companion was of medium height and stocky. His large nose was red, the sign of a man fighting a cold. From time to time, he'd put a handkerchief to his face and blow his nose. He wore a long overcoat over black trousers. A purple zucchetto, the skullcap of a Roman Catholic bishop, perched on the back of his head of gray hair.

Just as the weather in Europe was moving toward a mild summer, the American had flown into Argentina in the middle of its winter. No matter. He'd only be here a few days. Then back to the States. The OSS money deposited in the account controlled by Monsignor Petranovic in Genoa had a long reach.

The American had arrived in Buenos Aires a week before. He'd sought an audience with the bishop, a man called Augustin Barrere, whose name he'd been given by Petranovic. The bishop was expecting him, and he was shown to a comfortable study in the rectory next to the church. There was a fire blazing in the hearth, casting a warm glow into the room.

Bookcases lined the walls, each filled with leather-bound volumes. Thick Oriental carpets covered a hardwood floor, the furniture leather and manly looking. The bishop offered a snifter of brandy.

The American took a sip, frowned, the alcohol burning his throat as it went down. He coughed, slightly. "It's been a long time since I've had a shot of good brandy."

"Enjoy. How can I be of help to you?" The priest's English was good, but accented by the Rioplatense Spanish spoken in the area.

"I'm not sure when the ship from Genoa is supposed to get here, but I need to meet my man and get him out of Argentina."

"The ship will dock in seven days, weather permitting. It is making good time from Italy, but it is an old and slow ship. How will you arrange to get your man into the U.S.?"

"I didn't say we were going to the U.S."

"Sorry. I just assumed that since you are an American officer, that's where you'll go."

The American's lips twitched, perhaps a smile, but one with a hint of steel. "I paid extra so that no one would remember that I'm a serving officer."

"No one knows other than two people in Genoa and me. Your secret is safe."

The American relaxed. "I've got my end handled, but I'll need your help in getting him out of Argentina."

"Do you have a passport for your man?"

"Yes."

"I will need to have it for a few days to get the proper clearance."

"Okay."

"What name is on the passport?"

"Andrew Bracken, but that's not the name he'll be using after we clear your country."

"Tell me where you are staying, and I will be in touch when I have more definite information."

The American handed over the passport and left the bishop sipping another snifter of good brandy. He spent the next few days sightseeing and tasting the amenities of a city not ravaged by war. His trip from Europe had been long and arduous, and he enjoyed the leisure time to overcome its effects.

The cold weather continued, and on the sixth day a messenger came from the bishop. The American was handed an envelope containing the passport and necessary exit documents in the name of Andrew Bracken. There was a note telling him to meet the bishop at the port the next night, and directions to the rendezvous.

On the appointed night, he found himself standing on a wharf on the Rio de la Plata waiting to rescue a man he loathed. Sleet was in the wind, the temperature dropping. He snuggled down into his coat, and wished the damn boat would get settled in its berth.

The ship came abreast of the wharf. Men on the bow and stern threw lines to longshoremen on the dock. The heaving lines were brought in and the heavy docking lines were slipped over bollards. The ship rested. A gangway was put over the side, and a man dressed in suit and tie went aboard. A customs agent.

The bishop and the American moved toward the gate where an Argentine soldier stood guard, his old Lee-Enfield rifle positioned at parade rest. He snapped to attention as the men approached, and said, "*Buenas noches, Excellencia.*"

The bishop nodded and spoke in Spanish, a language the American did not understand. The soldier relaxed and opened the gate. They moved toward the gangway, and stopped a few feet away.

A priest, dressed in a flowing black cassock, no overcoat, left the ship. The American moved toward him, and said, "Good evening, Monsieur de Fresne."

The priest tensed, looked closely at the American and relaxed. "Major," he said. "So good of you to meet me. I'm freezing."

"Come along. I've got a coat in the car."

They walked to the bishop and together went out the gate, the soldier again snapping to attention.

"What now?" asked de Fresne. "I've been on that fucking boat for three weeks. I need a bath and some good food."

"The bishop will drop us at a hotel," said the American. "We'll be here for a few days, and then we'll be going north."

"I hope it's warmer there than here."

The American grinned. "I think you'll like Florida."

CHAPTER FORTY-EIGHT

Burke and Logan were parked behind us, across the street from Allawi's house. The general was talking on his cell phone. He pulled out onto the street, lowered his window, and motioned for us to follow. He turned right at the corner and drove straight for about three blocks, slowed and pulled to the curb. We were in a shopping district, with low-rise buildings housing shops and small markets. A man, head down, carrying a briefcase, walked purposefully from the doorway of a shop that sold secondhand clothes. He was wearing a long overcoat, frayed at the elbows and cuffs. His head was covered with a knit hat riding low on his forehead and pulled over his ears. He walked to the curb where Burke's car sat, motor idling, the exhaust visible in the cold air. The back door of the Acura opened, and the man got in. Burke pulled back into traffic. Jock let two cars get between us and then pulled into the street.

"Was that Olenski?" Jessica asked.

"I think so," said Jock.

"I'm glad he got out before the cops got there," I said. "Maybe he found something."

We drove through the city streets, the snow coming harder, the windshield wipers straining. My cell phone rang. Burke.

"We've got Ski," he said. "I don't think we're being followed, but I want you guys to peel off and make sure you lose anybody that may be tailing you. Meet me at my apartment in thirty minutes." He gave me an address in a neighborhood near the consulate.

I told Jock what we were doing. He took the next turn and spent twenty minutes driving evasively, doubling back, turning into parking lots, going through one high-rise parking garage, and around traffic circles, exiting at high speed, cutting off other drivers.

We found the address Burke had given us. We parked and took the elevator to the top floor. Burke, Logan, Ski, and the Arabic speaker had just arrived. "Come in," said Burke. "This apartment is owned by the consulate. They house visiting diplomats here and in another apartment one floor below. This is my home away from home."

Ski threw the old overcoat and hat across the back of a sofa. "I heard you guys had a bad time of it. We should have thought about the GPS thing. A lot of cell phones have that now."

"What happened with you?" I asked.

"I got into the house and found Allawi's study. His desk had a stack of papers on it, but they were in Arabic. This briefcase was sitting on the floor behind the desk, so I opened it to put the papers in and found another stack of documents. These were in English.

"I was going through the desk drawers when I heard the sirens. Sounded like they were coming my way, so I went out the back door. There was a lady standing in the kitchen when I left. She might have been a cook or something. She was wearing an apron, and there was a bag of groceries that she'd dropped on the floor. She was crying and begging me not to shoot her. I think she must have come in to work and found the bodies. Called the cops."

Burke put the briefcase on the dining room table. "Let's see if there's anything here that'll help us."

He pulled a sheaf of documents with Arabic script and handed them to the translator. "See what you can make of this."

He looked at the papers written in English. "There's a lot here. Let's divide these up and see if we find anything."

Olenski went out to a neighborhood Italian restaurant and returned with several kinds of pizza. We sat around the table, perusing the papers and munching. Occasionally, someone would remark on a document. They all seemed to have to do with Allawi's banking empire; mostly business letters from branches around the world. Some were orders for oil drilling equipment, a few were in Spanish. Jock took those, but there was nothing of interest to us.

Jessica was nearing the bottom of her stack of documents when she raised her head. "This is interesting. It's a utility bill from Florida Power and Light."

"What's the name on the bill?" I asked

"Allawi."

"Does it have a service address listed?"

"Palm Beach, Florida."

CHAPTER FORTY-NINE

I looked at my watch. It was nearing six o'clock, almost noon on Longboat Key. "I'm going to call Debbie, see what she can turn up with her magic computer."

"I doubt that'll do us much good," said Jock. "Even if Allawi owns that house, he's probably got places all over world. We don't know where he's gotten off to."

"It's worth a try."

Debbie took what information I could give her and said she'd get back to me. She called in an hour. "That house is owned by Mohammed Allawi, whose mailing address is Frankfurt, Germany. Do you need any more information on it? Building plans? Costs?"

"Not right now, Deb. Thanks."

"What did you find out?" asked Logan.

"Allawi owns the house and has his tax bills sent to Frankfurt."

"If he's heading to Florida, he won't make it before tomorrow," Jock said.

"Is there any way we can check?" Logan asked.

"I've got an idea," I said, and picked up my phone. I called Chief Bill Lester on Longboat Key and told him I needed a favor.

"Where are you, Matt? And where the hell is Logan?"

"We're in Germany."

"Crap. Sorry I asked. I don't want to know any more about this."

"No, you probably don't. Do you know the police chief in Palm Beach?"

"Sure. We're both on the board of the Florida Police Chiefs Association. I see him at meetings all the time. Why?"

"Well, it has to do with that favor I need."

"I hope you're not thinking about screwing up somebody else's island."

"I just need some information. There's a guy named Mohammed Allawi who owns a house in Palm Beach. I need somebody to go by there on some subterfuge and see if Allawi is in residence."

"Is anything going to come back to bite me on this?"

"Absolutely not."

"Okay. I'll tell the chief over there that we're checking out a story that Allawi is involved in drugs or something and is supposed to be in Palm Beach. He can send an officer out to make sure Allawi is at home."

"Wait until tomorrow, Bill. I think he's on his way from Germany."

"What's this all about, Matt?"

"You really want to know?"

"Nope. Forget I asked."

"Call me tomorrow as soon as you find out something."

"Sure. What about Logan?"

"He's with me, and he's talked to Marie. I'd appreciate it if you'd handle this like a nonevent."

"Man, you and your buddies are going to cost me my job one day." He hung up.

We finished the pizza, and Olenski left for his quarters. The rest of us bedded down on the floor, giving Jessica the lone bedroom. We were past tired. The trip to Frankfurt, three hours of sleep, and the day of activity had taken its toll. I slept like the dead and didn't awake until past nine in the morning.

It was snowing again, the flakes piling up in drifts along the street. I heard a truck outside, straining, its tires spinning on the icy pavement. I got out of the bedroll Burke had given me in place of a bed. Jock and Logan were still sleeping on theirs. I heard noise from the kitchen, the general making coffee. I could smell it and was almost overcome with the intensity of my need for caffeine.

I went to the half bath off the small foyer, brushed my teeth and washed my face. I joined Burke in the kitchen, and he handed me a mug of steaming coffee. "That was fun yesterday," he said. "I haven't done anything like that in a long time."

"I appreciate your help."

"I want Wyatt's murderers, too, L.T. Where do you go from here?"

"If we can find Allawi, I'm going after him."

"I have to get back to Berlin today. I wish I could go with you."

"Get another couple of stars for Wyatt, old buddy. He'd be proud."

"Ski and I'll be leaving in a few minutes. He's on his way over with a car to take us to the airport. You can stay here until tomorrow morning. I've squared it with the consulate people, but somebody else is coming in tomorrow. From Turkey, I think."

"Thanks, Burke. I'll let you know what we're doing."

The others got up, drank their coffee, and ate pastries brought by Olenski. The general and his sergeant said good-bye, wished us luck, and left for the airport. The day dragged by, boredom and anxiety our companions. Jock made a couple of phone calls to see if he could get a jet in position in case we needed to leave for Florida.

I took Jessica aside, sat next to her on the sofa. "Jess, if we go, it's a one-way trip. We'll either get Allawi or we won't. Either way, we won't be coming back."

"What are you trying to tell me?"

"That you should go back to Paris, and pick up your life. I think the danger's passed. If not, it will in a few days. Stay in the embassy where you have security, and I'll call you in a couple of days and let you know what happens."

"Matt, I need to see this through."

"You've been a tremendous help. We wouldn't have gotten this far without you. But now, we're going to see more of what we saw yesterday. People are going to be trying to kill us. Logan and I were trained for this a long time ago. Jock, too."

She flared, her eyes narrowed, her face flushed. "I can handle myself."

"Not in this league, you can't. You'll get somebody killed. Every one of us will be watching out for you when we need to be on the top of our game." I said it more harshly than I meant to. I smiled, trying to soften the blow. "Jess, you're incredible. You're bright, you're beautiful, and you're tough, and I want to get to know you better when this is over. But that can't happen if you're dead."

Her face softened. "Okay. When this is over, you bring your sorry butt to Paris."

"Or, you could bring your pert little one to Longboat Key."

"Pert? Nobody ever called it that before."

"Probably," I said, "because nobody's ever studied it as closely as I have."

I put Jessica into a cab for the airport in the early afternoon. A security man from the embassy would meet her in Paris. She'd keep a low profile until I called her with the all clear. Jock's influence had ensured that the ambassador wouldn't ask too many questions.

As darkness was painting the windows, Bill Lester called. "Your man is in Palm Beach."

"You sure?"

"The chief himself talked to him. Saw his passport. It's Allawi."

"Thanks, Bill."

"Remember, this thing better not bite me in the butt."

I laughed. "Your secret is safe with me."

I told Jock and Logan what Lester had said. "I guess we're headed for Florida. How the hell do the airline people do this?"

Jock laughed. "They're younger. Let's roll. The Gulfstream's at Rhine-Main."

CHAPTER FIFTY

We came in by boat, beaching the twenty-footer in front of the Allawi mansion. It was two in the morning, a dark night with low clouds obscuring the moon. Jock, Logan, and I were dressed in black jumpsuits, camouflage paint smeared on our faces. We each had an M-16 and a holstered nine-millimeter pistol. Jock carried a dart gun in case there were dogs.

As we came in toward the beach, I dropped a stern anchor, a Danforth whose flukes would grab the bottom. I dragged the forward anchor onto shore and set it deep in the sand. There was little surf, and I thought the boat would ride comfortably.

We moved up the broad lawn toward the house. A stone patio flanked the back of the structure, with French doors leading into the family room. The swimming pool was to the side, so as not to interfere with the view of the ocean from inside the house. There were no lights showing, but we'd assumed that there would be motion-activated security lights closer to the house. We were prepared to rush the place as soon as there was any sign of alarm.

The houses along this part of the beach were placed far apart, generous lawns taking up the space in between. The fact that Florida was running out of water didn't cause any concern to this segment of the population. Acres of green grass were a sign of oblivious consumption, no thought given to the cost, which in itself was a sign of wealth. Let the farmers worry about water. These people had golf to play and balls to attend. They needed to glitter in their riches, and they did so with a thoughtless disregard for the rest of the world.

The night was quiet, the sound of a gentle surf teasing our ears. We crouched low as we approached the house. Lights flared in the darkness, bathing the lawn and us in white light. We ran toward the house, crouched, presenting as small a target as possible. We used our rifle butts to knock out the glass in the French doors, reaching in to open them. We rushed through the family room to the foyer and up the stairs.

A man was coming out of the first room on our right, wearing only pajama bottoms, a pistol in his hand. Not Allawi. Jock shot him in the leg. He went down, moaning, holding his thigh. Logan bent to search him. He was clean. Logan picked up the gun, handcuffed the man's right wrist to his left ankle, put his finger to his lips in a shushing motion, and went to check the other rooms on the floor. Jock and I moved to the end of the hall where double doors guarded the master bedroom. Jock turned the knob, and the door opened.

The room took up the whole end of the wing, with windows over-looking the ocean on one side and the road on the other. We rushed inside. Allawi was sitting on the side of the bed, confused, alarmed, and unarmed. He was a small man, five six or so and 130 pounds. He was wearing short-sleeved pajamas. His head was covered by black hair graying at the temples. His skin was a dark red orange, the color of a ripening persimmon. A middle-aged man cowered next to him, his hair mostly gone to baldness, drawing a blanket to his neck.

Allawi was agitated, fear written on his face. "Who are you?" His English was accented, the rounded vowels of his native tongue over-whelming the sharp edges of his speech.

"We've come to talk about Laurence Wyatt," I said.

"Who?"

I pointed my rifle at the other man in the bed. "I'm going to shoot your friend the next time you tell me a lie."

"No. Not Mustafa."

"Tell me about Wyatt."

"Okay. Let Mustafa go."

I waved the rifle toward the door. "Get out, Mustafa."

The man threw back the cover and darted from the bed. He was naked, his skin several shades lighter than Allawi's. He was thin, and I could see the bones of his spine as he ran from the room, almost running over Logan who was coming in.

"What the hell?" Logan shouted.

Jock laughed. "That's Allawi's playmate. He's harmless."

I turned back to Allawi. "I'll kill you where you sit unless you tell me why you had Wyatt killed."

"I didn't. It was the major who ordered it."

"Major?"

"Yes. Major McKinley."

"Who is this Major McKinley?"

"He's not a major anymore. He used to be, and so that's what we call him."

"Who is he?" I brandished the rifle, willing Allawi to hurry with his story.

"He is William McKinley. He lives near Boston."

"Why would he order Wyatt's death?"

"Because of the group."

"What the hell are you talking about?"

"McKinley was a major in World War II. In the OSS."

I was puzzled. "The Office of Strategic Services? The forerunner of the Central Intelligence Agency?"

"Yes."

"He'd be an old man by now."

"He is."

"So what does an aging former army officer have to do with Wyatt's death?"

"The major helped my father and another man get a lot of money out of Europe after the war."

"De Fresne?"

Allawi was surprised. His eyebrows shot up, his eyes widened. "Yes."

"The money from the Jews in Vichy France."

"Yes."

"How?"

"I'm not sure. My father was a man named Abdul el-Gailani. He fought with the Syrian underground during the war. Fought the British and the Free French. He was captured and was about to be executed when the major got him out of prison and sent him back to Saudi Arabia."

"Tell me about the money."

"My father's family had a relationship with a minor prince of the House of Saud. For a price, the prince helped him start a bank, got all the permissions required by our government. My father changed his name to Allawi and arranged to become a corresponding bank with the Confederated Bank Suisse. That wasn't hard, because CBS had twenty million dollars de Fresne had taken from the Jews."

"What happened to de Fresne?"

"The major got him out of Europe and set him up as an American. My father, de Fresne, and the major split the money three ways. De Fresne needed the major to stay alive and they both needed my father's bank to launder the money."

I heard sirens in the distance, coming closer. Jock and Logan reacted, moving to the windows that fronted on the street. "They're coming this way," Jock said. "I can see the blue lights."

"My silent alarm," said Allawi. "Do not shoot me. It will only go worse for you when the police arrive."

"Let's get out of here," I said. I thought about shooting the little bastard on the bed, but if we didn't make it out of the house before the cops got there, I didn't want to face a murder charge.

We raced down the stairs and out the French doors onto the rear lawn. I jumped into the boat and started the outboard while Jock and Logan brought in the anchors. I backed off the beach, got a little depth under me, and wheeled the bow to the east. We headed straight out to sea, the boat dark, gliding over the black water of the Atlantic Ocean.

We'd rented the boat from a place on Singer Island, just across the Palm Beach Inlet. We brought fishing gear and told the man that we'd be night fishing the south double ledges, a natural bottom formation that lies about three nautical miles south-southeast of the inlet. Nobody would be suspicious of three tired fishermen returning to port after a fruitless night on the water.

We threw our weapons and jumpsuits overboard and used seawater to wash the paint off our faces. If we were stopped by law enforcement on the way to the marina, we didn't want to be found with incriminating evidence. We emptied our live bait well, returning some relieved shrimp back to their homes. The Coast Guard would know that real fishermen wouldn't quit until they'd used all their bait.

Our return went without a hitch. We tied the boat to its assigned pier, got in the rental car, and drove north on Singer Island to our hotel. It was a little after three in the morning.

We were gathered in my room, drinking beer, trying to dampen the adrenalin rush we'd all been running on since we approached the beach more than an hour before.

"Who is this guy McKinley?" asked Logan.

"*Forbes Magazine* recently called him the richest man in America," said Jock. "They ran a piece on him. Before the war, he was a history professor, but when he was discharged he started a small manufacturing business in New England. Made uniforms on a contract with the army. He married into some money, and probably used that to build his business. He diversified over the years, and ended up in the missile business somehow. Now he's one of the largest defense contractors in the country."

Logan took a swallow of his beer. "I don't think he used his wife's money. More likely, he recycled the Jewish money. I bet if we dig deep enough, we'll find a link to Allawi's bank."

I said, "I'm disappointed that we didn't find out more about de Fresne. I only needed about two more minutes."

"We'll try again," Logan said. "Give him some time to feel safe, and we'll go after him again."

"Why don't we have a go at McKinley?" Jock asked.

That seemed like a good idea at the time. It didn't pan out as well as we'd hoped.

CHAPTER FIFTY-ONE

We slept late the next day, Thanksgiving Day, exhausted from the intense adrenalin-fueled activity of the night before. At mid-morning, we met for breakfast in the hotel restaurant overlooking the beach. It was a pleasant day, typical of Florida's autumn. The sun was already high, the temperature in the mid-seventies. People were on the beach, digging in the sand, diving into the surf, or just lying on beach chairs reading.

"I just put in a call to Debbie," I said. "I asked her to see what she could dig up on McKinley."

"How soon can she get it?" asked Jock.

"Late this afternoon. She was on her way to her aunt's house in Bradenton for Thanksgiving dinner."

Logan put down his coffee cup. "Should we go after him? He's a pretty big fish."

"I think he's the key. He set this up in the first place, so he's probably still in charge. He can also tell us where de Fresne is."

Jock said, "What are you thinking, Matt?"

"I wonder how McKinley knew about the money in the first place. How did he know that de Fresne had squirreled it away?"

"He probably got it through his intelligence network," Logan said.

"I don't think so. Too many people would have known about it."

"We know Blattner knew about it," said Jock. "He told us."

"Yes, but he didn't know what happened to de Fresne. I doubt anybody else did, either. As far as anybody knows, he was buried in the rubble of Frankfurt."

"Maybe Blattner knows something," Jock said. "He's probably still at the safe house."

Jock placed a call to Bad Vilbel, and using a code name to identify himself, asked to speak to Blattner. He handed me the phone.

"Good afternoon, Herr Blattner," I said. "I hope you don't mind if I ask a few more questions."

"Not at all, Mr. Royal."

"Were you debriefed by the Americans after France was liberated?"

"Oh, yes, but not until early nineteen forty-five."

"Do you remember who you talked to?"

"No. It was an OSS officer, but I don't remember his name. Lincoln, I think, or maybe Washington. The same name as one of your presidents. I remember that."

"Could it have been McKinley?"

There was a pause on the phone, an intake of breath. "That's it. Major McKinley. He seemed particularly interested in de Fresne's money. I told him that without de Fresne he'd never get it out of the Swiss banking system."

"Did you ever see McKinley again?"

"No. We talked for the better part of two days, but I guess he gave up on finding de Fresne and moved on."

"Did you tell him that you'd heard that de Fresne was in Frankfurt?"

"I don't remember specifically, but I probably did. It would have been a dead end for the Americans. By the time they got to Frankfurt in March, the city had been destroyed. I heard that the Gestapo headquarters took a direct hit."

I thanked him and hung up. I related Blattner's end of the conversation and said, "I think somehow McKinley found de Fresne and rescued him."

"How could McKinley have found the de Fresne needle in that haystack?" asked Logan.

"I don't know, but according to Allawi, McKinley got de Fresne and the money out of Europe at the end of the war. He also saved Allawi's father from the executioner and set him up in banking. And Allawi said it was McKinley who ordered the hit on Wyatt."

"That may have been a smokescreen to save his own ass," said Jock.

"Could be, but we've got to check it out."

"How're we going to set that up?" asked Logan. "You know a guy like McKinley has lots of security."

"I haven't figured that one out, yet," I said.

Late that afternoon, Debbie called and said she could fax me the material I'd requested. I gave her the hotel's fax number and went to the lobby to retrieve it as it came in. I didn't want the clerks to get a close look at the information.

McKinley lived north of Boston in a sparsely populated area dotted with homes of the very wealthy. Debbie had included an aerial photo of McKinley's place that she'd found on the Internet. It was huge, running to several acres and surrounded by a stone wall. Much of the estate was wooded, but there was a large expanse of lawn surrounding an enormous house. A long driveway meandered through the trees from a gatehouse to the main building.

"We'll have to get ourselves invited in," said Jock.

We were in my room, Debbie's fax spread over the bed. We'd spent the day doing nothing. We'd crossed the Atlantic three times in less than a week, and we were reeling from the jet lag. A day of dozing in the sun had brought each of us back to life.

"I agree," said Logan. "I don't think we can get in any other way."

"How do we get an invitation?" I asked.

Jock scratched his chin. "Let me work on that. The guy's companies do a lot of government work. That may be our key to getting an audience with him."

"We can fly to Boston tomorrow," Logan said.

Jock shook his head. "I don't think so. Airlines keep records of who flies where. If we kill McKinley, I don't want any evidence that we were anywhere near Boston."

"What do you suggest?" I asked.

"I can fly up there on one of my phony IDs, rent a car, and get us a hotel. You guys need to come up by car or train or something. Since we don't have a lot of time, I can't wait for my agency to get you set up with false identification."

"Do you think Allawi alerted McKinley about last night?" I asked.

"You can bet on it," said Jock.

"I think we should have another go at Allawi before we head north," I said.

"He's bound to have better security at the house now," said Logan.

"Maybe we can get a shot at him outside the house."

Jock shook his head. "I doubt it. He's got to be nervous, and I don't think he's going to be spending time at the grocery store. He'll stay locked up tight in his house."

"Let's think about it overnight," I said. "Surely we can come up with something."

But, as it turned out, that didn't happen.

CHAPTER FIFTY-TWO

The next morning, a small article on page 3B of the *Palm Beach Post* caught my eye. The headline read, "Palm Beach Billionaire Dies On Way Home." The story described the death of Saudi banker Mohammed Allawi. He'd left Palm Beach Airport in his private jet on a flight plan filed for the Azores for refueling and then on to Saudi Arabia. Allawi died of a heart attack enroute. The body was taken to Saudi Arabia for burial. The story mentioned that Allawi had a history of heart problems and had undergone bypass surgery in the past.

I was sitting in the hotel restaurant, when Jock and Logan joined me. I told them about the article.

"I don't think he's going to be of anymore use to us," Logan said.

"What now?" I asked.

"McKinley?" asked Jock.

"That's our only shot," I said. "Let's head for Boston."

Jock left on a flight for Boston that afternoon. Logan and I decided to fly to New York and take the train to Boston. Our flight left at mid-afternoon, a few minutes after Jock's.

We arrived at LaGuardia Airport and took a taxi into the city. We were too late to take a train that evening, so we checked into the Hotel Pennsylvania across the street from Penn Station.

We left the next morning on a six fifty-five a.m. train bound for Boston. When you travel by train you see the backside of America, the garbage dumps, decaying warehouses, junkyards, used car lots, rail yards, and abandoned buildings that are the flotsam and jetsam of an affluent society.

I've read of a vortex in the middle of the North Pacific that collects all the junk tossed into the oceans of the world. The prevailing currents bring in the garbage, and the flow of the vortex captures it, consigning it forever to a swirling mass of refuse. Scientists tell us that the plastic found there will last forever, a triumph of modern science. And in the end, this unintended consequence may destroy the planet's marine life.

The rail beds of the northeast pass by the land-bound versions of the Pacific Vortex, mounds of junk in its various forms, tossed out by a public surfeited by mindless consumption. Some day, our own garbage will inundate us all, and then we'll join the marine life in the grave of our own technology.

We arrived at the Boston South Station a little before eleven. Jock was there to meet us and led us to a parking garage where he'd left his rental car. We drove northeast on Atlantic Avenue and merged onto I-93 north. Traffic was heavy but moving steadily. It had snowed the day before, and small hummocks of dirty ice flanked the road. The remains of the salt sprayed on the highway splattered the undercarriage of the car, creating a small din that was not unpleasant.

We took the exit onto I-95 and continued northward. In a few miles we left the Interstate and drove onto a road leading toward Hamilton. We turned onto a secondary road, drove for three or four miles, and came to a driveway with a gatehouse blocking the entrance.

We drove a little farther down the narrow road and stopped. Logan got out. Jock and I were going in alone.

CHAPTER FIFTY-THREE

The house was huge, sprawling over several acres, more baronial castle than house. It fit the style of America's richest man: mock-Tudor with formal gardens lining a driveway almost a mile long. We'd stopped at the gatehouse, and the guard checked his list against our names. We were expected.

Jock and I drove up to the circular brick driveway that abutted the front of the house. Jock had called the day before, talked to the great man's secretary, and made the appointment. He'd told the aide that he was a government auditor and needed to talk to Mr. McKinley about the Confederated Bank Suisse. That was a pretty big hook, and it reeled in our fish. Or so we thought.

We were met at the door by man wearing a navy blazer, gray trousers, white shirt, and red tie, who introduced himself as Carl. He didn't offer a last name. He was tall, six feet two or more, and the jacket didn't hide the well-defined musculature of the weight lifter. Butler? Bodyguard? Maybe both.

The bruiser led us through a large foyer, its walls hung with paintings that looked to me to be originals by some of the old masters. We were shown to a large room in the back of the house, overlooking formal gardens. French doors opened to a patio that had lawn furniture stacked for the winter. Patches of snow covered the ground, and I could see a thin sheet of ice that had formed on the surface of a pond in the distance.

An elderly man stood to greet us. He was tall and spare, his face lined with age, gray hair parted sharply. His blue eyes reflected a keen intelligence. He was wearing a flannel shirt in a checkered pattern, chinos, and boat shoes.

"Come in, gentlemen," he said. "Can Carl here get you anything to drink? Coffee, soda, something stronger?"

We declined, and were asked to sit. The butler left, but I suspected that he remained nearby. The room was informal, a departure from the formality we'd seen in the rest of the house as we'd passed through. There was an overstuffed sofa and two armchairs placed around a coffee table to create a conversation area. McKinley took the sofa, waving Jock and me to the chairs. He must have noticed my inspection of the room.

"I'm not much on formalities," he said, chuckling. "My late wife liked the grandeur of an estate, but I preferred the simple things. We compromised. I got this room, and she got the rest of the house."

"It's a beautiful place," I said.

"I'm glad you like it, Mr. Royal."

Uh-oh. I suddenly felt like the mouse who'd just bitten into the cheese and realized too late that the trap was about to fall on his neck. I shrugged. "You didn't buy the government auditor crap, huh?"

"Mr. Royal, I have a lot of resources, and you are a persistent man. I knew you'd come sooner or later. My sources told me there was no audit, so I figured you were on your way. Who's your friend?"

Jock sat forward in his chair. "I'm Grant Ferguson."

"I haven't been able to get a handle on you, Mr. Ferguson. You must work for the government. CIA? FBI?"

Jock stared at McKinley, grinning, saying nothing.

McKinley stood, ill at ease with the malevolence implicit in Jock's demeanor. "It doesn't matter. Unfortunately, you won't leave this house alive. But, I must say, I admire your perseverance. What I don't know is why, Mr. Royal."

"You ordered my friend Laurence Wyatt killed."

"The group ordered it done. I act as the chairman, but it takes a unanimous vote to order someone's death."

"Why have him killed?"

"We thought it necessary. Why else are you here?"

"That's it."

"That's it? You've gone through all this because your friend was killed?"

"I owed him. The dead can't take their revenge, but sometimes the survivors can."

"Ah, so you're here to avenge your friend's death."

"Yes."

"Too bad it didn't work out."

"Tell me, Mr. McKinley," I said, "why did you have Wyatt killed?"

"Simple. He and that other guy in Gainesville were closing in on me. I couldn't let that happen. My son is going to be president of the United States. A scandal like that, even if not proven, would have wrecked his campaign."

"How did you know about Wyatt?"

"We have trip wires set out. If someone seems to be getting close, we're warned."

"Like Hassan at the archives in Bonn."

"Exactly. And we've got them in many places. If somebody stumbles onto our secret, we take certain, um, measures to ensure that there is no disclosure."

"By 'we,' you mean Allawi and de Fresne."

"Yes. Actually, de Fresne's son and my son. De Fresne is a despicable person, and I thought he'd have been dead years ago, but he keeps on breathing. He pretty much dropped out of our group. He hasn't taken part in our, um, deliberations in many years. So the three of us are running things, and after I die, my son will be in charge."

"If de Fresne is such a jerk, why didn't you just order his death like you did Wyatt's?"

"Trip wires. We've each set up arrangements so that if one of us dies under suspicious circumstances, the information is released to the press and the government. We set this up early on as a mutually assured destruction pact. There are incriminating documents that are irrefutable. We call them the MAD documents. If one of us is killed, all of us go down."

Jock spoke up. "Allawi is dead."

The old man smirked. "I know. I had him killed. The pact works down through the generations. I'm afraid Allawi was talking to you, so he had to go. Of course, his line has ended. No children, if you know what I mean." He winked.

"Because he's gay?" I asked.

"Because he's a goddamned queer. His father must be rolling over in his grave."

What about the trip wires?" I asked. "Wouldn't Allawi's murder create some big problems for you?"

McKinley shook his head. "Not if the death is from natural causes. Allawi died of a heart attack."

"How did you manage that?"

"Simple. He had a heart problem. I have people on his staff, and I'm sure he probably has people on mine. The meal prepared for him on his private jet for his flight to Riyadh was sprinkled with a drug that caused his heart to stop. It's virtually undetectable. Besides, Muslims are buried within twenty-four hours of their deaths, and autopsies are frowned upon. Everybody assumed he had a heart attack."

"Mustafa?"

"Yes. The playmate. He's dead by now."

"You saved me the trouble of killing Allawi," I said.

McKinley laughed. "Glad I could help."

Jock had sat quietly, listening, filing information in his prodigious brain. "Where is de Fresne?" he asked.

"So, you haven't figured that one out."

"Not yet," said Jock.

"You've heard about the cat who was killed by curiosity?" His voice had hardened, the genial host no more. The stone-cold killer had come out. "Since you'll be dead in a matter of minutes, I don't guess it'd hurt to satisfy that fatal curiosity." He laughed, a brittle cackle, cold, without humor.

McKinley looked directly at me. "You should know him. He lives on Casey Key, almost next door to your island."

"LaPlante?" I asked.

"Ah, you get the blue ribbon. We first got onto you when you began asking too many questions about him."

"So you blew up my car and killed a young man who had nothing to do with any of this. He had a wife and a small son."

"Accidents will happen." He chuckled.

"LaPlante is a Jew," I said.

"Yes, he is, but he never took it seriously until he met that rabbi's daughter. Then he went soft. He's always been the weak link in our little group. But we kept a tight rein on him, and, Lord knows, he made a lot of money. His son is a piece of shit, but he understands the program. We'll make him a secretary of some useless agency or other and keep him happy."

"Who is Robert Brasillach?"

"The queer French editor?"

"No. The one you sent to Banchori in Miami."

He laughed, a sour and joyless sound escaping his throat. "Just some Russian immigrant kid with a vivid imagination and an alcohol problem. He was a history major at the local community college. I had Carl spin him a tale about being from ODESSA, and needing help in transferring some money. Poor boy died recently. They never have found his body."

I was stalling for time. "Tell me, Mr. McKinley, how did a history professor become such an asshole?"

McKinley was pacing as he talked, never stopping, bleeding off nervous energy. He chuckled. "Have you ever been to war, Mr. Royal?"

"Yes. Vietnam."

"Then you can understand. Killing is a dreary business. It eats at you until all the goodness is consumed, and you're left with a block of ice where your soul used to be."

"Not always. Only the twisted ones end up like you. You're the ones who should've been on the other side. You're no better than the Nazi's you fought. At least, the Vietnamese I fought believed in a cause."

"But we all killed people."

"Yes we did. But we didn't have a choice. We were soldiers doing a dirty job so that the people we protected could live their lives. That's the way it's been all through history."

"Deep down, I'm a patriot." He was agitated now, red in the face, his voice loud, words tumbling out in a torrent of anger.

I smiled at him. "Deep down," I said, "you're a twisted little motherfucker."

McKinley stood stock still, glaring at me, his hands in the pockets of his chinos, mouth slightly open. I don't think anybody had called him a motherfucker to his face in a long time. He must have had something in his pocket that would call his butler, because the man moved into the room, a .45 pistol in his hand. "Bruce, show these gentlemen out." He grinned. "Good-bye Mr. Royal. Rot in Hell."

CHAPTER FIFTY-FOUR

A bullet flies too fast for the human eye to see. But on that day, standing in the study of America's richest man, I think I saw it; a 7.65-millimeter round fired from an M-16 rifle. The world slowed almost to a halt, grinding along in extreme slow motion. Time had no meaning. I watched the bullet as it came through one of the panes of a French door, shattering the glass. It moved steadily, without wobble, into Bruce's forehead. The back of his head exploded as the slug tore through his brain and out the other side. The crack of the rifle followed, the sound not able to keep pace with the speeding bullet.

McKinley turned from his butler, the sound of the rifle grabbing his attention. Another bullet broke another pane and plowed slowly into the temple of America's richest man. His brains, that gray matter that had been put to such pernicious use, flew onto the sofa where he'd sat when we first entered the room.

I snapped back into reality. I saw Logan standing on the lawn near the patio. He was pumping his arm in the infantry signal to "follow me." Jock was moving toward the French doors. I followed.

Logan said, "Hurry. I found a jeep in the garage with the keys in it."

"We can't leave the car," I said.

Logan shook his head. "There're security people on the grounds. If they heard the shots, they're on their way here. We've got to go."

"It's okay," said Jock. "We didn't leave any fingerprints in the car and it's rented in a name nobody will ever be able to trace."

We followed Logan to the garage and climbed into an open jeep, not unlike those that McKinley had probably used during the war. Logan took us cross-country to the very back of the estate. We came to the wall that surrounded the property. It was higher than I would have guessed, ten feet at least. There was a slender dirt track running along the wall, a road built for jeeps.

"I think this is their security road," said Logan. "They've got to have a way to patrol the wall."

He turned onto it and drove at a fast clip. Soon I could see a wider dirt road coming out of the trees at a right angle to our track. It seemed to stop at the edge of the wall. As we got closer, I could see a wrought iron gate built into the wall. A chain held it together and a large padlock secured the chain.

"Now what?" I asked.

Logan brought the jeep to a stop and pulled the key from the ignition. It was on a small ring with four others. He held the keys up like a trophy, and started out of his seat. "I think I know how to get us the hell out of here."

One of the keys fit the padlock on the gate. Logan opened it and drove through. I got out and relocked the gate. If McKinley's security people came this way, they might not notice that we'd left through the locked gate.

We found ourselves on another dirt track running through a thick forest. In a mile or so we came to a blacktop road, and Logan turned onto it.

"We've got to lose this jeep," said Jock.

"Let's drop it in Beverly," I said. "That's the closest town of any size. Jock can probably rent another car there."

"No," said Jock. "Head toward Salem. I think anybody looking for us would expect us to go to Beverly. It's the closest."

Logan headed south and turned west on Route 128. We found the Hertz agency on Canal Street in Salem. We drove past it and parked the jeep. We left the rifle under the backseat. The police would find it, but they'd have already figured out we took the jeep. The rifle wouldn't add anything to their investigation. It was untraceable, having been stolen fifteen years before from a National Guard Armory in eastern Montana.

Jock walked back the two blocks and rented a car, using yet another bogus driver's license. He told the clerk that he'd drop the car at Logan Airport. Logan and I walked in the opposite direction, wanting to put as much distance as possible between the jeep and us. We'd gone about ten blocks when Jock pulled to the curb in a four-door Chevrolet.

It had been a good plan, and it worked. Jock had gotten a rifle from his ubiquitous source and put it in the trunk of his rental. We had a layout of the McKinley house that Debbie had gotten when she hacked into the county building department's computer. An expert in Jock's agency office in Boston had overlain latitude and longitude quadrants on the diagram of the house. It was of such a large scale that the coordinates were in one thousandths of a minute, meaning that any object could be placed within about a six-foot radius. This was all fed into a handheld computer and given to Logan.

Jock and I both were equipped with transponders that would broadcast a signal every ten seconds. We'd taped them to the inside of our thighs, high up. Jock assured me that no male bodyguard would check closely enough to find them.

"What if it's a female guard?" I asked.

"Enjoy the moment."

"That's a comfort."

Logan's handheld would pick up the signals we transmitted and translate them into GPS cordinates that showed him exactly where we were in the house.

When we let him out of the car, Logan used a grappling hook to scale the wall and then walked overland to the house. I knew we had to give him time to get into position, or Jock and I would end up dead. It was a calculated risk, but one we all agreed was workable. And we were right.

Jock dropped Logan and me at the train station in Boston and drove to the airport. He'd get a flight to Sarasota that evening. We caught the 6:45 for New York, and arrived shortly before eleven in the evening. We took a taxi to LaGuardia Airport and checked into a hotel. Our flight left the next morning. We were headed home, and it felt good.

On the way to the terminal the next day, I picked up a couple of newspapers. They both ran front-page stories on the death of America's richest man, the father of the man who might be the next president. He and his butler had been murdered in the great man's study at his home north of Boston. They'd been shot with a high-powered rifle, apparently from the backyard.

There was a rental car in the driveway, and the gate guard said the people driving it had an appointment with McKinley. He thought the two men in the car were from the government. As it turned out, the renter's name was probably false, and the car had been wiped clean of fingerprints.

A jeep had been taken from the garage next to the house and had been found in Salem near a rental car agency. A man had rented a car there at a time that would have been near enough to the murder to make the police believe that the renter was involved. However, the name on the contract was another phony. The car had been found at Logan Airport, but there was no record of anybody with that name flying out of the airport that day. The car had been wiped clean of fingerprints.

The police were at a dead end; no suspects, no motive, and no idea who the visitors were. They were, according to the police spokeswoman, leaving no stone unturned, no lead uninvestigated. They would find the killer or killers and bring them to justice.

Senator George McKinley was in seclusion, mourning the death of his father. He'd brought in more private security personnel in case the shooting in Massachusetts had anything to do with his campaign. There were some calls for the Secret Service to get involved, but since the election was two years away, and McKinley had not officially declared his candidacy, that was not possible.

We'd covered our tracks well. I didn't think we had anything to worry about.

CHAPTER FIFTY-FIVE

"We've got a problem," Jock said.

We were sitting on my sunporch overlooking Sarasota Bay. The sun was low in the western sky, and its gold and burnt orange colors reflected off the clouds hanging over the mainland to our east. Logan was at Marie's. I was tired from the three-hour flight that morning from New York. I hadn't slept well the night before in the LaGuardia hotel, and I was looking forward to the first night in a long time in my own bed.

"Anything in particular?" I asked.

"We've got a United States senator who's a viable candidate for the presidency. His security is being beefed up in the wake of his old man's death, and we don't have the documents that would put him out of business."

"Jock, even if we were able to get the documents that make up the mutually assured destruction package, I don't think we'd be able to hang it on the senator. It might cause him a little embarrassment, but that's about all. Joe Kennedy was reputedly a bootlegger, but that didn't stop his son from winning the White House."

"This is more powerful stuff than bootlegging. Everybody drank a little whiskey during prohibition, but they didn't take money from Jews headed for the gas chambers."

"Technically, neither did McKinley. He took the money from the guy who extorted the Jews."

"Yes, but he should have killed that bastard de Fresne or at least turned him over to the French. He didn't do that, and the American people won't like it."

"But the senator wasn't even born then. I think he'll be forgiven, and we'll never prove that he was one of the ones who ordered Wyatt's death."

"We've got to kill him."

"Yes," I said, "we do."

"Does the senator have any children?"

"No."

"So if we get the LaPlantes and the senator, it ends."

"I guess. But the Jews are still out the money."

The next day, Jock and I drove south on Tamiami Trail and turned west onto Blackburn Point Road. We crossed the old-fashioned bridge that fastened Casey Key to the mainland, and drove south on Casey Key Road. Soon we came to an area where the island narrowed and large estates faced the Gulf, with property extending across the road and encompassing boathouses clinging to the bay.

Debbie had fired up her computer the night before and found the private number of the LaPlante house. I'd called it just before we left my condo. A young woman answered, and I asked if she were Mrs. LaPlante. She giggled and told me in Spanish accented English that she was the maid. I asked to speak to Mr. Dick LaPlante, and she informed me that he was at his office in Sarasota and would be there for the rest of the day. I hung up, and we started toward Casey Key.

We arrived at the LaPlante house at mid-morning. It was grossly excessive, taking up hundreds of feet of beachfront. There was an open park-like setting on the bay side of the road. A low wall that matched the one around the house separated the property from the street. A boathouse hung over the bay, and a pier next to it jutted fifty feet into the water. A Hatteras yacht was moored to the pier, stern to the road. The name on the transom was *Dick's Hussy*, a low attempt at humor that I suspected was original with Dick LaPlante.

I pulled my new Explorer to the gate, lowered the window and spoke into the speaker mounted on the brick column at the edge of the driveway. "I'm here to see Mr. LaPlante Senior."

A disembodied voice, sounding tinny in the small speaker, responded. "Do you have an appointment?"

"No, but tell him I come with a message from Major McKinley."

We sat for a few moments, and the gate began to open. The voice from the speaker said, "Come in and park in the circular driveway."

A dark-skinned woman wearing a gray maid's uniform and sensible shoes like those the nurses wear on hospital wards met us at the door. She showed us to a formal living room overlooking the beach. The place was wholly contrived, as if an interior decorator with little taste had put it together with no intention of comfort or warmth. I doubt that anybody ever used the room.

In a few minutes a woman wearing nurse's scrubs pushed an old man in a wheelchair into the room. He was wearing a bathrobe, with pajamas underneath, and he had a blanket draped over his lap. He held out his hand to shake, and I took it. It was like holding a desiccated leaf. The skin was dry and had the consistency of tissue paper. His grip was as light as a butterfly's touch. "I'm René LaPlante," he said.

I said, "I think we need to talk privately."

He turned to the nurse. "Leave us please. I'll be all right."

The nurse bent over and tucked the blanket more firmly around his legs. "Call if you need me." She turned and left the room.

The old man waved to some chairs. "Have a seat gentlemen. I don't think you told me your names."

I was quiet for a beat. "You didn't tell me yours, either, Monsieur de Fresne."

His eyes widened a little, but there was no other response to my comment. "If you've come to kill me, I'd consider it a blessing."

"I'm not here to kill you, sir," I said. "I'm here to learn."

"And what do you think I can teach you?"

"Does the name Laurence Wyatt mean anything to you?"

"No. Should it?"

"He was killed on Longboat Key last month on the orders of the group."

"I assume you're talking about McKinley's group."

"Yes."

"I haven't had anything to do with them for many years."

"I know. McKinley told us that."

De Fresne frowned. "McKinley's dead."

"Yes. And so is Allawi."

"Allawi too? I didn't know that."

"McKinley had him killed."

"What makes you think that?"

"McKinley told us."

"Did you kill McKinley?"

I ignored the question. "Why would you consider it a blessing if I killed you?"

"I'm dying. Cancer. It hurts like a son of a bitch. The damn doctors tell me I've only got a few days left. I wish it'd hurry. I'm tired of living."

"Tell me, Monsieur de Fresne, how did a Jew like yourself end up causing the deaths of so many?"

"I never thought of myself as a Jew. My mother was an American Jew and worked as a maid for a wealthy New York family that was living in Paris. She met my father, a French soldier, who was Catholic. Neither one of them practiced their religion, so the differences didn't matter.

"My father was killed in North Africa in the thirties and I was sent to live with relatives in the south of France. My mother died soon after, and I don't think anyone from my father's family had ever met her. My Jewishness just never came up."

"But, surely you had some empathy for the ones you sent to the gas chambers?"

"Why are we discussing this?"

"Because," I said, "I want to learn. I want to know how human beings can sink so low. I want to understand."

"You're trying to understand yourself, aren't you? You've killed men before. It's written on your face."

I tensed. "We're talking about you."

"I didn't kill anybody. They were all headed for the chambers. I simply put off the inevitable and took their money in the process. Better me than the Germans."

"How did you get out of France after the war?"

"I was already out of France. I went to Germany in 1944. I was in Frankfurt when the war ended. Major McKinley came and got me. He'd found out that I had the money."

"How'd he get you to the States?"

"He got me to Genoa, and a Catholic group took over from there. I was stuck in Italy for a couple of months, so I learned a lot about that group. Did you ever hear of the ratlines?"

"Yes."

"Well, this one was run by a German bishop named Hudal who was rector of a seminary in Rome for Austrian and German priests. He worked with some Croatian priests in Genoa who were helping members of the Croatian Nazi party get out. Some of the Vichy French officials were getting out that way too. They got me papers from the Red Cross and a visa. They dressed me as a priest and put me on a ship for Argentina. McKinley met me there and got me into the U.S."

"What about your war record in the Pacific?"

"Bullshit. That's all it was. McKinley fixed all that up. The OSS had a lot of tentacles. They could do most anything."

"You've made a lot of money over the years."

"I have, and I've given a lot of it away."

"I know about your support of the Jewish causes."

"Yes."

"When did you decide you were a Jew?"

"I fell in love with and married a rabbi's daughter. She was my whole life. Her family was the only one I'd ever really known. I told them about my mother's background."

"Your son doesn't seem to have the same sense of Jewish identity that you do."

"My son is probably crazy."

"Why do you say that?"

"He's never worked a day in his life. He hangs onto that McKinley boy like he was some sort of god. He's taken over my spot in the group, but I don't know what the hell they're doing anymore. Apparently they kill people when it suits them. And the major was probably going to buy the presidency for his son, George. My son expects to ride his coattails to Washington. This country is ruined if that happens."

"If you think your son is so useless, why did you give him control of all your assets?"

"I didn't. He thinks he's in control, but I'm still running things. He thinks everything is in his name, but that's a bunch of legal mumbo jumbo. My lawyer made sure that I maintain real control. He has all the original authentic documents. When I die, my son will get a generous allowance from a trust fund, but the rest of the assets go to the State of Israel."

Now it was my turn to be surprised. "Israel?"

"Yes. The money needs to go back to where it came from. Israel will use it to compensate the Nazi survivors."

I leaned into the man, looking him in the eye, trying to assess his state of mind. "Monsieur LaPlante, your son tried to kill me on Longboat Key. He had somebody put a bomb in my car. A young man with a wife and child was killed in the blast."

"I'm sorry to hear that. There has been too much killing."

"I want you to add a codicil to your will. I want you to give that young man's widow some money."

"How much?"

"Enough to support her so that she can raise her son."

"What was the boy's name?"

"Jimmy Griner."

"You give my lawyer the particulars, and I'll have him draw a codicil. Tell him to hurry. I don't have long."

"Thank you, sir. I also want the MAD documents."

Once again, his eyes widened a fraction. "You know about that."

"Yes. Will you give them to me?"

"What will happen to my son?"

"The documents will ruin George McKinley's chances to win the presidency. Your son will have some embarrassing moments, being the son of a war criminal and all, but he'll survive."

"What will you do with the papers?"

"Nothing, until you die. Then I'll get with your lawyer, and we'll make a joint announcement about how you got the money, and that you've left it all to Israel to support the survivors. I'll turn the documents over to the press and the FBI."

"You'll do nothing until I die?"

"I'm a lawyer, Monsieur de Fresne. My name is Matthew Royal. I'd like to meet with your lawyer and review all the business documents you mentioned, and your will. If everything is as you say it is, the documents will stay in my possession until after your death."

The deal was struck. De Fresne called for his nurse and she wheeled him out of the room. He'd asked the maid to bring us coffee while we waited. He was back in a few minutes with three large manila envelopes held together by a stout rubber band. He handed me a handwritten note to his lawyer giving him permission to share all information with me. "Will that do Mr. Royal?"

"Yes. Will you call him and tell him I'll be coming by?"

"I'll do that today."

He shook our hands as we started to leave. He held onto Jock's hand for a moment, a twinkle in his eye, and said, "I enjoyed our chat, son."

Jock laughed, said good-bye, and we walked out the door.

"You didn't say one word the whole time," I said. "Isn't that taking the laconic secret agent thing a little far?"

"You were doing great, Counselor. Besides, you talk enough for both of us."

CHAPTER FIFTY-SIX

Late that afternoon, I phoned and made an appointment with de Fresne's lawyer for the next morning. He'd been expecting my call. Logan and Marie joined Jock and me for drinks at Tiny's, and a late dinner of pizza and beer at the Haye Loft. Jock had two pieces of coconut cream pie for dessert.

I visited de Fresne's lawyer the next morning. Arthur Goldblum, Esquire, maintained a small suite of offices in a mid-rise building near the waterfront in downtown Sarasota. His ownership of the entire building was the only reason it had not been razed to make way for another overpriced high-rise condominium tower built to house the invading horde of refugees from our more northern climes.

It was an ancient building with its aches and pains plainly visible: peeling paint, worn linoleum flooring, poor lighting. To one accustomed to the new skyscrapers of a young city, the slow ascent of the elevator was maddening. It creaked and groaned and concerned me that it would give up the ghost before I reached my floor.

Goldblum's suite was small, consisting of a tiny reception area covered in green shag carpet of indeterminate age, a conference room with a scarred table taking up most of the space, and an office for the lawyer. A lady as old as the building, was seated at a secretary's desk against the wall of the outer office. She showed me to the conference room, offered coffee, and brought me something dark and strong in a chipped mug bearing a faded logo of the Tampa Bay Buccaneers. One taste and I knew that I would do without drink during our meeting.

The conference room smelled of ancient mildew and dust balls decaying in their corners. My chair had once been handsome, high-backed and covered in red leather. Now it was ripped and faded with age, one armrest loose. I was beginning to worry that de Fresne's lawyer would be as worn and shabby as the office.

I was not disappointed. A wizened little man, stooped to about forty degrees, with sparse gray hair combed carelessly across a bald pate entered the room. He was wearing rimless bifocals, his eyes watery behind the plastic lenses.

I'd never met Arthur Goldblum, but he was a legend in Florida legal circles. For more than fifty years, he had represented some of the most astute business and political leaders in the state. He'd also written several books on business law, one of which was used in law school classrooms across the country. The large firms regularly came to him with offers of big money to join them and bring his clients. He'd always turned them down. He saw himself as one of a near extinct breed, the lawyer who cared for his clients and did their bidding only as long as it fit his rigid code of ethics. He made a good living out of his own labor, eschewing the idea of using young lawyers as profit centers for their elders. I had a tremendous amount of respect for him, and was ashamed that the legal profession saw his kind as dinosaurs.

I wasn't prepared for this little man, a frail shadow of my image of him. He stuck out his hand. "Mr. Royal, I'm Arthur Goldblum." His voice was strong, his grip firm. "I'm told that you have a written waiver of confidentiality from Mr. LaPlante."

"I do, sir." I handed him the document.

He looked carefully at it and then sat at the table behind a stack of files. "You are free to look over all these files, or we can chat, and I'll tell you what you want to know. The files will have all the documentation to support what I say."

I smiled. "Let's just chat."

And we did. We talked for an hour. Goldblum answered all my questions, and from time to time during the conversation, would pull one document or another from one of the files. He'd explain what he'd done, and why. The conversation was a primer on business law, delivered by a brilliant practitioner. His body may have been failing, but his mind was as sharp as any I'd ever met.

At one point he offered more coffee. I refused. He apologized for the office, but told me that he would be retiring soon, and would give the building to a son who wanted to tear it down and build, what else, condos.

LaPlante's will was the last document I reviewed. It was as he'd told me. He'd set up a generous trust fund for his son, Richard, with the remainder, that is the part that was left at Dick's death, to go to the State of Israel. The rest of his estate, and it was very large, would be distributed to various funds controlled by the Israeli government to support survivors of the Nazi death camps.

"Satisfied?" asked Goldblum.

"Very much so. I appreciate your courtesy."

"Mr. LaPlante wants me to set up a trust for the family of a young man who died in a bomb blast. He said you would give me the names."

I told him the names of Jimmy's wife and son and gave him their address in Bradenton. "May I ask how that is to be done?"

"There'll be ten million dollars held in trust at SunTrust Bank for the benefit of the widow and child. They cannot invade the corpus except in dire emergencies. The interest will give them a good life. At the death of the mother, or the twenty-fifth birthday of the child, whichever comes later, the trust will be dissolved and the money will go to Israel. I'll take the documents out to him this afternoon."

I thanked the old lawyer for his time and courtesy, and left the office. I called Jock and Logan and asked them to meet me at The Old Salty Dog restaurant on City Island for lunch. It was a pleasant day, and a leisurely lunch overlooking New Pass would clear the smell of mildewed carpets from my memory.

The mild weather was holding, and a gentle breeze blew from the north as we took our seats on the outdoor patio of the restaurant. The blue green water of the pass reflected the sun in dazzling highlights, painting a picture in pastels. A rental boat chugged through the no-wake zone near the bridge, a family of four taking the sun. The children were small and wrapped in life jackets, the mother wore a bikini, and dad sported a long-billed fishing cap.

I watched them motor under the bridge, wondering idly about them.

Where was home? Were they as happy as they looked on that day? What chance had brought them to this place at this time when I was sitting with a view of the pass and a few moments to savor life on a beautiful day? They passed under the bridge, out of my sight and immediately out of mind.

The waitress took our drink orders and left menus. I ordered the salty dog, a deep fried concoction that is better than it sounds. Jock asked for the fried chicken sandwich, and Logan settled for a hamburger. I told them what I'd found in Goldblum's office and assured them that the documents were solid. De Fresne had told us the truth.

Our food came, and we talked about what to do about Dick LaPlante and George McKinley. "I'm tired of the killing," I said, "but I can't let those bastards get away with killing Wyatt."

"What're you going to do with the MAD documents?" Logan asked.

"Nothing for now. I promised de Fresne that I'd hold them until after his death."

"And then?"

"I'm not sure. Let's let that play out. I don't know that releasing them will sink McKinley's chances at the presidency. In fact, what the papers are calling 'his father's brutal murder' seems to be generating sympathy for him."

"I noticed that," said Logan. "And he's apparently beefed up his security in a big way."

"I've got to get back to Houston," Jock said. "There're some golf balls calling my name."

"You go ahead," I said. "We can't do anything until de Fresne is dead, so let's let it rest for now."

And that's what we decided to do. Jock left the next afternoon for Houston, and Logan and I prepared to settle back into the island lifestyle we loved. After dropping Jock at the airport, we drove back to the island, stopping at Tiny's for a drink in the middle of the afternoon. We left after a couple of beers. Logan was taking Marie to dinner and invited me. I declined, thinking they needed some time alone. I went back to my condo, nuked a frozen dinner, and watched the evening news as I ate.

I knew I would have to deal with LaPlante and McKinley, or I'd never rest easy. Wyatt's useless death needed to be avenged. More useless deaths? Maybe. On the other hand, McKinley could do a lot of damage to this country if he won the presidency. Maybe I could just take him out. LaPlante was nothing without McKinley, and he'd slowly sink into oblivion. He'd have enough money to live well, but not the obscene amount he had now. The money was going back to where it belonged, and Dick LaPlante couldn't do a damn thing about it. But Wyatt's ghost demanded full justice, and that included LaPlante.

I was still haunted by what I'd done to Chardone. The world was a better place without a rogue cop who was a murderer and a pedophile. But, I'd put myself in a position to kill a man when I didn't have to. If I'd let the law handle him, he'd still be alive. Maybe he'd be free to kill again, and good people would die. But that wasn't my call. Or was it? For good or bad, he was dead and wouldn't kill again. If I hadn't tracked him down with murderous intent, I wouldn't have had to shoot him in the head. I might as well have killed him in cold blood; shot him in the head while he begged for his life. That image was etched on my brain, and I couldn't erase it. It wasn't the killing that bothered me. It was the manner in which I'd done it.

I decided I'd try not to think about it for a while. I couldn't do anything until de Fresne died, and that'd be at least several days, maybe weeks. In the meantime, I'd go back to being a beach bum. It'd be like a vacation.

I couldn't have been more wrong.

CHAPTER FIFTY-SEVEN

They came for me in the night; a discreet knock on my front door and then a pounding. I'm a light sleeper, a leftover response from a long ago war. The first taps awakened me, and the pounding provided a sense of urgency. I looked at my watch. Two a.m. Who would be coming by this time of night? Either a drunk buddy looking for company or an emergency of some sort.

I slipped into a pair of shorts and a tee shirt, and padded to the front door. I turned the dead bolt and started to open the door when it was pushed violently back against me. I dodged out of the way, taking a strike on the arm, and the door slammed into the wall. *What the hell?* I thought.

A man wearing jeans, a dark tee shirt, and running shoes pushed his way inside. He was slender and muscled, about five foot ten. His face had a day's growth of beard, his eyes small, squinty, flint hard, and placed above a nose that had been flattened by a fist at some time in the distant past. He was grinning, showing a top row of yellowing teeth with gaps where the canines should have been. He had a nine-millimeter pistol in his right hand, pointed at my midsection.

"Sorry about showing up without an appointment," he said. "But Mr. LaPlante wants to see you."

"Come in," I said. "Can I get you some coffee?"

His grin dissolved, slowly fusing his face into a grimace. "Fuck you, smartass. Go have a seat." He waved the gun toward my living room. "And shut those drapes." He pushed the door, not closing it all the way, and followed me into the living room, gun unwavering.

I did as he said. I drew the drapes over the sliding glass doors that led to the sunporch, and took a seat on the sofa. The man pulled out a cell phone and placed a call. He said one word, "Okay."

"What do you want?" I asked.

"Sit tight. Mr. LaPlante will be here in a minute."

We sat quietly for a few minutes, I on the sofa, and the gunman in the recliner. The door opened and a dapper man came into the living room. He was about six feet tall and had the slender body I always associate with the patricians. His hair was dark with gray highlights at the temples, a long face, slender nose, and bright blue eyes. He was smiling as if greeting a fellow member at the country club ball. His teeth were white and even. He was wearing a navy blue suit, powder blue shirt, and a blue and yellow regimental tie. His wingtip shoes were polished to a high shine.

"So, we finally meet, Mr. Royal," the man said. "I'm Richard LaPlante."

"You should've called first, Dickie. I'd have prepared some hors d'oeuvres, chilled some wine."

"Ah, yes. I've heard that you're something of a smartass."

"And I've heard that you're something of an asshole."

The friendly smile disappeared, the blue eyes tightened, the voice dropped a register, the friendly tone suddenly gone. "You have some papers I want."

"I don't know what you're talking about."

"Come, Mr. Royal. My father died this afternoon, and I couldn't find the MAD documents. The nurse told me that good old Dad gave you a bunch of papers just yesterday."

"I'm sorry for your loss."

"Not much of a loss, actually. Now I've got the money, and won't have to put up with an old man's regrets."

"I wouldn't bet on that."

"On what?"

"Control of the money."

"I'm the only heir. It's all mine."

I let it go. I hoped to be around to watch his reaction when his father's will was read. "The papers are in a safe place. If anything happens to me, the press and the FBI get them."

"Then, Mr. Royal, you need to get them for me."

"I don't think so."

"Come along then. We'll go back to my house. Maybe I can persuade you."

The parking lot was dimly lit, with just the security lights of the building giving any illumination. We walked to a Mercedes, one of the big ones.

"I'll drive, Mr. Royal," said LaPlante. "You take the front passenger seat. My friend here will be in the backseat with his gun pointed at your head."

I knew this was not going to have a satisfactory outcome. If I got to LaPlante's house on Casey Key, I'd never leave alive. God knows what he had planned for me, what persuasive techniques he wanted to use to get the documents, but I knew they wouldn't be pleasant.

I'd stepped into a pair of boat shoes as I left my condo, and I was still wearing the tee shirt and shorts I'd put on to answer the door. The only thing in my pocket was the cell phone and a little cash that I'd left there when I went to bed. I had no weapon, and the gunman's attention was focused on me the whole time we'd been together. I hadn't seen an opening at all.

I stopped at the door to the car, stalling for time, trying to get my brain in gear, find a way out. "Let me ask you one question, LaPlante. Why did you have Wyatt killed?"

The gunman was beside the back door of the passenger side of the Mercedes, standing still, his gun pointed at me, my left side to him as I talked to LaPlante over the roof of the car. I could see the thug in my peripheral vision.

"That's a fair question, Mr. Royal. He'd apparently stumbled onto the money trail left by my dad and the major after the war. I don't know how he did that, but he was backtracking. There was the possibility that he'd figure it out."

"Why kill the professor in Gainesville?"

"He was a specialist in World War II. Wyatt recruited him into his research. We found out about them when they accessed the archives in Bonn."

"So you're just the gopher for the McKinleys. You go for things, like pizza and beer, or maybe hookers."

He was insulted. "Absolutely not. I'm the one who recruited the hit-man and oversaw the whole thing."

"That'll look good on your résumé when you go to the Senate for confirmation of your cabinet nomination."

He laughed. "You'd be surprised at what gets left off résumés. Let's go. Get in the car."

"One more question. Was that you at the restaurant with Rupert the night before he murdered Wyatt?"

He looked a little surprised. "How did you know that? Rupert never knew my name."

"No. He'd have given you up before I killed him."

"You killed him?"

"That's right. McKinley, too. You guys all signed your death warrants when you decided to kill my friend."

He laughed. "I think your time has run out, Mr. Royal. No more death warrants will be, um, executed. Except maybe yours. Get in the car." His happy face morphed into a scowl.

A siren whooped nearby, its wail dying out as soon as it began. The gunman started, was distracted for a second, turned toward the noise. I moved quickly, grabbing his right wrist with my left hand, pushing down with all the force I could muster. At the same time, I brought my right fist into his jaw, catching him just under his mandible. I heard his teeth click together at the same time I felt pangs, like electric shocks, shooting up my arm.

I had no time to think about the pain. I had to get the pistol. The gunman's head bobbed backward, the reaction to my fist impacting his face. I struck him again, oblivious to the pain in my hand. Two quick jabs, powerful and destructive. He went down, his head making a hard sound as it hit the asphalt. I was still holding his wrist and had begun twisting it as he fell. The pistol popped loose and skidded across the parking lot. I dove headfirst for it.

The gunman lay on the pavement, his head behind the right rear tire of the car. He was unconscious, no longer a threat. The gun ended up in the empty parking spot to the right of LaPlante's car. I picked it up and rolled onto the grassy border, coming to a position on one knee, pistol pointed at LaPlante.

He was in the driver's seat, and had gotten the engine started. He hit the accelerator and the car backed out of the space. I heard the sickening noise of the gunman's head collapsing under the rear wheel. I called to him. "It's over, LaPlante. Get out of the car."

He was two car lengths into the lot. He dropped the transmission into drive and poured on the gas, the rear tires making a little screeching sound as they fought for purchase on the sandy asphalt. He was coming right at me. I shot him in the face.

I jumped to my left, out of the way of the car, which bounced over the curb stop at the front of the parking place and slammed into a car parked facing it. I hit the pavement on my shoulder and rolled, absorbing the sharp sting of small rocks spraying onto my exposed skin. I'd have a sore shoulder and some road burn, but I was alive.

I got up, and cautiously approached LaPlante's car, now smashed grille first into my neighbor's Lexus. A Longboat police cruiser was coming into the lot at high speed. I dropped the gun and raised my hands. The young cop, Steve Carey, came on the run, his service pistol pointed at me. When he was close enough to recognize me, he holstered his weapon. He was the same officer who'd been first on the scene when my Explorer was bombed.

"Jeez, Matt. What happened? They try to take out your new car?"

"Not exactly. How'd you get here?"

"I stopped a speeder at the corner, and just as I was getting out of my car, I heard gunshots. What happened?"

I gave him a truncated version of the events. "The guy in the car was the one who blew up my Explorer."

We went around to the back of the car where the body of the gunman lay. I'd seen a lot of death in my time, but I'd never before seen a head squashed like a ripe melon. Blood and gray matter stained the asphalt, and the man's face was unrecognizable.

There'd been no movement from the Mercedes. Carey and I went to the driver's side and opened the door. The front airbag had deployed and was holding LaPlante in place against the backrest of the driver's seat. There was a hole drilled neatly into his forehead, and he was as dead as roadkill.

"Good shooting, Matt," said the young officer. "Who was he?"

"His name was Richard LaPlante."

"The society guy?" Incredulity had slipped into the cop's voice.

"Yep."

"I'll be damned."

Carey walked over to his cruiser and came back with a camera. "Chief's on his way, Matt. Said for you to stay here." He took a number of flash shots, and then went back to his car.

Two other cruisers came into the parking lot followed by the fire department's ambulance. Carey went over to talk to the paramedics, and they left. The uniformed officers took up station around the area and one began to roll out crime-scene tape. A man in civilian clothes came over to us. The chief.

"You all right?"

"Yeah."

"You're getting to be a big hit with your neighbors."

I looked toward the building. The rail along the walkway was lined with my friends, most in bathrobes. One of them called out, "What happened, Matt?"

"Nothing much. Guy tried to kill me."

"Well at least he didn't blow up your car." He turned and went back inside.

The chief looked at me. "The officer told me you shot Dick LaPlante."

"Yeah."

"Why?"

I told him about my meeting with the elder LaPlante and that he'd given me some papers that had a bearing on Wyatt's death. I didn't go into any detail about the MAD documents, but said that Dick LaPlante was involved. He'd come for the papers along with his gunman and they were probably going to kill me.

"We'll need detailed statements. You know the drill."

"Yeah. Do we have to do this now?'"

"Afraid so."

"You got a tape recorder?'"

"In the car."

"Why don't you come on up, and I'll put on some coffee and we can talk."

I spent the next several hours giving a statement and watching the crime-scene technicians go over the parking lot. The bodies were loaded into a coroner's van and taken to the Manatee County morgue. A wrecker hauled off the damaged cars. By the time the sun came up, there was no evidence of a gunfight.

The chief left for home at sunrise. I took a sleeping pill and went to bed. I knew that without the pill I'd dream dreams of dread, of bodies of bad men and good, and of soldiers I'd known who were no more. Those specters would gnaw at the edge of my sleeping brain, asking why I lived and they died. And I didn't know the answer.

CHAPTER FIFTY-EIGHT

I slept late the next day and rolled out of bed shortly after noon. I was rested, thanks to the pill, but still shaken by the events of the night before. It had been a close thing, and I hadn't been at all sure I was going to come out of it alive. But everything clicked. Sometimes, it's better to be lucky than good.

I made some coffee, ate a bowl of oatmeal, got the paper from the front door, and nestled into an easy chair on my sunporch. November had slipped away without my noticing. The paper told me that today was the first of December. A heavy snowstorm had blanketed the Midwest, and the northeast was awaiting its turn. Fires were burning in Southern California, stoked by the Santa Ana winds sweeping out of the high desert and down the mountain valleys. A suicide bomber had blown himself up in the middle of a Tel Aviv restaurant, killing forty. A Miami mother was carjacked after finishing her Christmas shopping at an upscale mall in Aventura. Her body was found hours later on the side of a road leading to the Everglades. A Saudi Arabian diplomat had been killed in a car crash in suburban Washington, and his embassy spokesman said that he left a wife and three children in Jiddah.

Longboat Key is separated from the mainland, and we islanders like to think we're somehow safer for it. The past few weeks had put the lie to that conceit. We were a part of the world at large, with all its foibles, disasters, and heartaches. We knew that a couple of bridges couldn't isolate us. Yet, we were shocked when that rough world intruded into our island serenity.

My neighbors would not like the violence that had been visited upon them. First, the bomb that took out my car, and now an attempt on my life and two dead bodies in the parking lot. Rita Thompson would surely think the destruction of her Lexus was at least as bad as the bodies.

I called Logan to tell him about the night's events. He was upset that he'd been sound asleep during all the activity. Mr. Dewar's elixir had put him to sleep and left him with a hangover, but he was used to that, he said.

I called Jock in Houston and told him about LaPlante and the gunman.

"Do you need me to come over?"

"No. Logan and I can handle things on this end."

"I'm glad you've got Logan," he said.

"It'd be tough without him. He tends to liven up the island."

"What are you going to do about McKinley?"

"I don't know. I'm tired of killing people."

"You haven't killed anybody who didn't deserve it. Lighten up on yourself."

"I can't let McKinley go. Besides, if LaPlante talked to him before he came here, McKinley knows I've got the MAD documents. He'll come for me."

"I hadn't thought of that. Maybe you'd better come out to Houston for a few days."

"Let me think on it, Jock. The only way I'm ever going to be safe is to get rid of McKinley. If I give the documents to the press, he won't have any reason to go after me. Maybe that's the solution."

"Don't do anything yet. Can you give me a day to figure something out?"

"Like what?"

"Like, for instance, your car bomber."

"What about him?"

"The AP ran a story this morning about the Saudi diplomat dying in a car wreck."

"Yeah. I saw it in the paper."

"That was your bomber."

"What?"

"Our buddy Tariq identified him from photographs. My agency confirmed that the diplomat was the bomber and then took him out."

"Not a car accident?"

"Not really."

"Are you suggesting that your guys take out McKinley?"

"They wouldn't touch an American citizen, much less a U.S. senator. But, I know some guys who might. With the proper documentation."

CHAPTER FIFTY-NINE

I stayed in the rest of the day dozing on the sofa. Logan called to say he was watching re-runs of *Cops* on his big-screen TV, and would be there all day if I needed anything. I ordered pizza to-go from Ciao's restaurant, and drove the mile down the island to pick it up. I went to bed early.

The next morning, just as the sun was peeking over the mainland, burnishing the bay with bright colors, Jock called. "A guy's coming to see you today. He'll say that Fran Masse sent him. Give him the original MAD documents, but keep a copy. He won't give you his name, and you don't have to engage him in a conversation. He'll be out of your hair in two minutes."

"Who is he?"

"Don't ask."

"Okay. If you're sure."

"I'm sure."

I fixed breakfast, had my coffee, read the newspaper, and took a shower. I retrieved the documents from my safe, and drove to the UPS store at the Centre Shops to make copies. I only had to drive a mile, but I was getting a little paranoid. I looked carefully at everybody I met in the parking lots, and stayed aware of the cars around me on the short drive. I had my .38 in my pants pocket.

I returned to my condo and settled in to wait for Jock's man. I hadn't talked to Jessica since my return from Europe, so I called her at the embassy. I was put right through.

"Matt, how're you doing?"

"Fine. It's in the low seventies and the sun is shining."

"Crap. It's cold and drizzly in Paris."

"Why don't you come to Florida for a few days?"

"I'd like that, but I'm getting a lot of flak at work. One of my buddies says there's some kind of pressure coming down on me from Washington."

"What kind of pressure?"

"Nitpicking. I don't know how better to describe it. A friend of mine at the State Department in Washington called to say they were getting pressure to fire me. Nobody seems to know just where the pressure is coming from, but it's high up."

"That doesn't sound good." I had an idea where the pressure was coming from, but I didn't want to discuss it over an open line to Europe.

"Oh well, I'll survive. I think. If not, I can always teach."

We chatted for a while, and I hung up when I heard a knock. I went to the front door. "Who is it?"

"Fran Masse sent me."

I opened the door to see a slight man dressed in a bright Hawaiian shirt, shorts, and running shoes. He had blond hair that fell over the tops of his ears, blue eyes. He wore wire-rimmed glasses, the kind that tint automatically when the sun hits them. They lightened visibly as he stood at the door. He extended his hand. We shook, and I invited him in. I offered coffee.

"No thanks. I've got to run. I'm told you have some documents for me."

He had a slight accent that I couldn't place. Middle European maybe, but he'd been in America for a long time. I handed him the manila envelope containing the original MAD documents. He thanked me and left.

I called Jock in Houston. "Your man just picked up the documents."

"Okay. Stay loose, but stay on your toes. I think you're all right for now, but we can't be too sure."

"What's up?"

"Can't tell you yet, podner. I'll talk to you tomorrow."

CHAPTER SIXTY

The days unfolded slowly, one morphing into the next. I moved about the island armed, following no set pattern, but not skulking either. I was constantly aware of my surroundings, always on guard, eyeing strangers with suspicion. It wasn't a pleasant way to live, but it gave me confidence that I'd at least keep on breathing.

Jock had called me on Friday, the day after the man picked up the documents, and told me that something was in the works. Senator George McKinley had been contacted directly and told that he could have the original MAD documents for a price, but that if Matt Royal was harmed in any manner, his secrets would be revealed to the press. There were ongoing negotiations concerning the price to be exacted for the papers and the manner of transfer.

"Jock," I'd said, "that'll cover my butt, but McKinley will be safe and maybe president."

"Hang tough, Matt," he said cryptically. "The situation is fluid." Whatever that meant.

On Tuesday morning, pictures of Senator George McKinley and a piece on his death dominated the front page of the *Sarasota Herald-Tribune*:

TERRORISTS KILL MCKINLEY

Senator George McKinley, widely considered the front-runner for his party's nomination for president, was killed last night in a bomb blast at his Rock Creek mansion in Washington, D.C. Details were sketchy at press time, but a Washington police spokesman confirmed that the senator is dead. A shadowy group that calls itself Allah's Revenge has claimed credit for the bombing, saying that McKinley epitomized all that is wrong with American society. In a written statement e-mailed to news outlets, the group said, "Allah has struck down another infidel, one whose outrageous appetite for extravagance robs the world of needed resources."

Senator McKinley's father was murdered a week ago in his mansion outside Boston. That crime remains unsolved, and police admit that they have run out of leads.

The article went on to recount George McKinley's rise to political prominence and discussed his family's great wealth. The reporter postulated that the deaths of the senator and his father were connected, but wondered why Allah's Revenge hadn't taken credit for William McKinley's death as well. Quotes from national leaders regretted the senator's death and vowed that the perpetrators of such a heinous crime would be brought to justice.

I could put my pistol away. There was a fitting irony that the terrorists, funded by money stolen from Jews headed for extermination, killed the son of the man who was responsible for their good fortune. If the elder McKinley hadn't gotten de Fresne out of Europe and recruited Allawi's father to be their banker, there would have been no money for the younger Allawi to lavish on his pet terrorists.

Wyatt could rest easy now.

I probably wouldn't.

CHAPTER SIXTY-ONE

The Christmas season lightens the heart and brings a sense of fellowship that permeates the small world that most of us inhabit. In Southwest Florida, the season is rife with contradictions: Crosby's "White Christmas" coming from the outdoor speakers while dining al fresco in seventy-five degree weather, posters of a jolly Santa climbing down a chimney in a land where there are few fireplaces, waitresses in shorts and tee shirts wearing reindeer antlers.

The season had also brought Jessica Connor to Longboat Key for a visit with Russ and Patti Coit at their home in the Village. She and I spent a lot of time together and found that we enjoyed establishing a relationship without the tension of a manhunt. I never did tell her the whole truth of the ending of the story.

"I read that Allawi died of a heart attack," she'd said over dinner one evening. "Did you ever find de Fresne?"

"Yes. Turns out he lived a couple of islands down the coast. He was an old man dying of cancer, and leaving his estate to the Israeli government to support Holocaust survivors. He died two days after I found him."

"I'm glad they're dead. In another few years there won't be any of the old Nazis left. I hope there's some after-life retribution. They deserve to burn in hell."

"How're things at the embassy?"

"A lot better, strangely enough. My friends in D.C. tell me that the pressure from above suddenly let up. I guess somebody just forgot about me."

"I guess," I said, but I thought I knew the reason the pressure had gone away. The cause of it was rotting in hell.

I didn't think it would be helpful to our relationship for her to know that I'd been responsible for the deaths of William McKinley and Dick LaPlante. During the week that Jess had been on the key, we had moved closer and closer to a real love affair, making up for the time we'd missed while chasing ogres. One evening when a full moon hung low over the bay, we made love on the deck of my boat, anchored in a small cove behind Jewfish Key.

There is an old wives' tale that holds that something good always comes from adversity. Perhaps there is truth in that aphorism, and the good flowing from the tragedy of Wyatt's death was named Jessica Connor. We'd see.

On the day before Christmas, Jock, Logan, Burke Winn, and I sat under the trees at Mar Vista restaurant, enjoying the warmth of the winter sun and the view of a placid bay. The general and his wife had come to Florida for Christmas with friends in Naples, and he'd driven up for lunch. Logan had picked Jock up at the airport, and driven straight to the restaurant. He and I would have Christmas dinner at Logan's, along with all the other displaced people that he invited every Christmas.

Logan said, "Jock, what ever happened to that bastard Tariq?"

"He's not going to be bothering anybody for about the next fifty years. He somehow ended up in an Algerian jail."

"How did you manage that?"

"Let's just say that my agency has some reciprocal agreements with some of the more moderate Arab governments."

"What about Hassan in Bonn?" I asked.

"He got fired from the archives, but he's living with his parents in Bonn and working in a library. My guys scared the shit out of him. He dropped out of the mosque and moved on with his life."

"So, Matt," said Burke, "Wyatt's revenge is complete."

I'd told Burke what happened after we left Germany, and how the thing played out. "Yes," I said. "Finally."

The general had a serious look on his face. "I read about McKinley's death, of course. I was surprised that Allah's Revenge thought it necessary to take him out. They must not have known about his ties to Allawi."

Jock grinned. "There's something you guys should know about McKinley."

"You been holding out, Jock?" asked Logan.

"Just until we got together. Turns out McKinley's death resulted in my agency getting a lot bigger budget from Congress. There's nothing like a dead politician to make the others a little more aware of the need to deal with the terrorists."

The general laughed. "I think the military benefited some from that dose of reality, too."

"And," said Jock, "it seems that the congressional committee that oversees my agency felt that it would be prudent to loosen up a little and send us after Allah's Revenge without restraint. A lot of those assholes are now in the arms of Allah and the virgins."

I nodded. "Jock, who was the man who came for the MAD documents?"

"I don't really know. Let's just say that the Israelis have a long memory and even longer arms."

"Are you saying that the Israelis had something to do with McKinley's death?"

Jock grinned. "No, I'm not saying that. But, think about it. If somebody put a bug in the ear of a friend who happened to be an Israeli intelligence agent, and if that friend happened to want documentary proof, and if somebody could provide that proof, then theoretically, it could endanger the life of a very bad guy. And if that guy's death happened to open the congressional purse and focus the congressional vision, and get rid of a very dangerous group of terrorists, then, well, hypothetically, you can see the advantage to it all."

I laughed. "I can see that. Jungle justice is a little complex sometimes, eh General?"

"That it is, L.T. That it is."